A WEALTH OF STORIES

Dan FitzGerald

authorHOUSE®

AuthorHouse™ LLC
1663 Liberty Drive
Bloomington, IN 47403
www.authorhouse.com
Phone: 1-800-839-8640

Published by AuthorHouse 08/19/2014

ISBN: 978-1-4969-2943-3 (sc)
ISBN: 978-1-4969-2942-6 (e)

is dedicated to

the memory of MaryClare FitzGerald Goss

1

Irish Truth and Consequences

Late Monday morning a group of New York travelers walked off a green and white Aer Lingus plane at Shannon Airport. They moved through the terminal until they saw a man holding a sign reading "Green Ireland Tour." The woman standing beside him looked like a junior college professor. She held a list in one hand and smiled at the cluster of tourists streaming to her.

The woman introduced herself as Molly O'Brien, who would be Tour Director for their 7-day stay in Ireland. She identified the man holding the sign as Dave, their bus driver. She counted 44 people, then pointed over her shoulder.

"Our bus to The Clare Inn is beyond that door," she said. "I'll call your name. Listen for your seat assignment." Knowing the sunny weather outside would get her tour off to a fine start, she began calling the names on her list. A dozen people walked through the door to the bus.

"Mr. and Mrs. Joseph Kelly," she said. A tall man of forty with a full head of dark hair stepped forward. A younger, auburn-haired woman took his hand and accompanied him to the Tour Director.

The man hid his astonishment. Unmarried and touring Ireland alone, Joseph Russo Kelly glanced at the unknown woman who held his hand in a vicelike grip. "Help me" she whispered. "Say nothing. I'll explain later."

"Seats 11 and 12," the Tour Director said. She checked off the Kelly's and returned her attention to the list.

"After you," Joe said to the woman holding his hand.

"Thank you." Releasing him, she climbed three steps into the bus. From the back her hair's wavy ringlets reached the shoulders of an ivory sweater. Slightly taller than average, she wore neat navy slacks which tightened when she moved up the steps, drawing brief attention to a mature figure.When Joe reached the aisle she was already seated at the window beside seat 11. He took the seat next to her.

"Thank you," she repeated. She turned her head towards the window, allowing him only a partial profile of regular features. Apparently, she had decided not to talk further. When the bus moved he looked over her shoulder and out the window.

A scenic drive ended with a turn into a blacktop lane which curved through a pair of white stone pillars. Molly's amplified voice announced their arrival at The Clare Inn, a sprawling building surrounded by rolling hills. She distributed room keys and assured the group their bags would be brought to their rooms.

"Once you've unpacked, a nap before our local tour and the banquet at Bunratty Castle tonight would be a good idea," she added. "If you're starved there's a dining room. It's up to you. You may be better off with a nap."

Ten minutes later, Joe led his unknown companion into a deep, high-ceilinged room. He walked past twin beds to the room's oversized white-framed window and looked through the lace curtains at a sloping green lawn.

Behind him, the door clicked shut. He turned. In addition to the beds the room held a desk, a pair of chairs and a TV console, all finished in dark mahogany. The unsmiling woman sat erect on the bed near the door. Joe slouched into a chair.

"I'm waiting," he said, before adding "Mrs. Kelly."

"My name is Stasia," she began. "I'm a friend of your secretary..."

"Anne?"

"...who told me you were going on a Green Ireland Bus Tour. She said you're stubborn but honorable."

"Me? Stubborn?"

"...so she said. I'm here because my sister manages a travel agency. She changed your reservation to Mr. and Mrs. Kelly and I paid my share of the expense. A few more keystrokes and you were guaranteed two beds at each hotel because of your wife's medical problem."

"Which is?"

"They think I have allergies."

"Do you?"

"No."

"But?"

"Because of a car accident I sometimes suffer serious headaches. I can't travel alone. I'm determined to be on this tour and I will be, whatever the price."

"So you decided to travel as Mrs.Kelly," Joe stated. "Isn't that nice? What in the world did Anne tell you, Stasia? Does she think I'm a saint? Well, I'm not. I've questions for you and I want answers. Who are you, anyway? What makes you think I'll agree with what you want, and what do you mean by 'any price'?"

"My full name is Anastasia Jane Ryan Cassano," she began. "I'm called Stasia. I plan to travel with you on this tour as Mrs. Kelly. I'll cause you no problems. You can use the bathroom first. I'll sleep in the second bed. If paying the price includes your taking my body, let's discuss it now. It won't be the first time someone's lined me up." She paused a full five seconds before adding "although I wish you wouldn't."

Her voice had softened. She looked down at her fingers. Joe noted the play of light from the window on her thick hair and wondered if she colored it. When he said nothing she continued talking.

"The Tour Director said they would leave our bags outside the door. They may be there now. I've a single bag. If you bring in the bags you can go through mine and satisfy yourself as to what's in it. You'll find a minimum of clothing, a camera and film, a travel umbrella and a few miscellaneous items. I'm out of aspirin and must get some in the lobby. I'll be back shortly."

Joe watched her rise and go out the door. He remembered a film with Anastasia as the daughter of the last Tsar of Russia, suggesting

Stasia Cassano's lifeline began with a Russian influence. He dismissed the odd memory. Instead, he thought about what he faced.

An attractive woman in her mid-thirties with an inviting body planned to travel with him for the next week as his wife, but in name only. He recalled the comment about using her body and it chilled him. If anything, he felt sorry for her. She had furnished no explanation for her need to be on the tour. Her deep-set eyes and serious expression offered him no clues.

If she was a friend of his secretary she knew more about him than he knew of her. She wasn't timid, either. She was willing to share a room with a man she'd never met.

A knock from the hall interrupted his review.

He looked out, and seeing two large bags near the door hauled them in. One was his. The other was new but inexpensive. Its tag read "Mrs.Joseph Kelly" and included his street address. He didn't open Stasia's bag, nor would he. He would respect her privacy though he knew the next move was up to him.

He shifted his thoughts to himself. Seven years ago Henry Mitchell recruited him into the giant New York accounting firm of Watkins and Stewart. For five years he and Mitchell worked closely together. Then, things started to go wrong. Mitchell brought in a younger man and gave him some of Joe's work. Last year a second man was hired. Suddenly and completely Joe was outside Mitchell's world without knowing why.

Joe didn't complain. Unwilling to quit, he simply worked harder.

A month ago, he mistakenly clicked an unknown file onto his computer. It was a project Mitchell's group was working on. Being curious, Joe reviewed the file. He soon realized Mitchell and his assistants were far outside the firm's normal business practices. Joe clicked related files. Two days later he stared at proof Mitchell and associates were diverting huge sums of money to obscure accounts and transferring the money elsewhere.

Although he owed nothing to the firm of Watkins and Stewart, Joe felt they were entitled to a warning. He also suspected Henry

Mitchell had downrated his job performance. It was time to rebuild his career elsewhere.

He acted quickly but not perfectly. He asked Anne to find him a good travel agent, a request which attracted Stasia Cassano's attention.

He'd hoped a vacation might invigorate him. He hadn't taken time off for two years and his Irish heritage gave the Green Ireland Tour special meaning. He'd done well in the market during his years as a workaholic and if he wished could stay on in Ireland for weeks or even months.

Friday afternoon in New York he typed his resignation and delivered it personally to the office of a senior partner, attaching to it a memo suggesting a review of Mitchell's projects.

Sunday he went to JFK Airport and boarded the Aer Lingus flight to Ireland.

Now, he sat in Ireland's Clare Inn with a problem he didn't need, a confusing and unpredictable involvement with a woman he'd seen for the first time a few hours earlier, a woman whose plan had caused him aggravation and might cause him trouble in a country where he knew no one and no one knew him.

The door handle jangled. Stasia walked in, glanced at her unopened bag and sat on the far bed. She ran a hand through the auburn ringlets.

"I've checked with the Tour Director," she said. "Most of the people on this tour are older than 50. Some are much older. I'm 35. I might be good company."

"I don't like your plan," Joe said.

"You only have two choices, you know. I make it easy for you or I don't."

"Which means?"

"The easy way, you accept my offer. We dress alone and meet in the lobby. During the day I don't ask personal questions and you don't, either. I call you Joe, you call me Stasia. We discuss the Tour and behave like a married couple who like each other. At night, we're in separate beds on good terms."

"I don't think so," Joe said.

"The hard way begins when I take off my clothes," she said, looking away. "Crudely stated, I'll provoke you until you act like an animal. You will, you know. You admit you're no saint.

However, you're guaranteed no pleasure. When you're finished we'll continue on the tour but you'll be miserable. You know it and I know it, and I just met you."

"I don't think so," Joe said, less than certain he was making the right decision.

"Have it your way," Stasia murmured. She stood up and faced him, her face devoid of expression. Her sweater was on the bed. Joe watched as her eyes glassed over. She thrust her arms upward, pulling off the T-shirt she'd worn under the sweater to reveal a full white bra. When she reached behind her to unhook the bra Joe jumped up.

"Stop."

"Yes?" Though her face had paled it remained expressionless. Her eyes seemed fastened to a spot over Joe's head. She stood absolutely still.

"I agree," Joe said. "I'll try what you call the easy way, but with one condition."

"Which is?"

"If we keep touching, all bets are off. A 7-day Tour is a long time."

Stasia stared at him.

He hadn't expected silence and didn't know how to handle it.

"It won't be a problem," she said, finally.

Taking a terry cloth robe from her bag she went into the bathroom. Two minutes later she climbed into bed and closed her eyes without a glance at Joe.

He stood at the window trying to erase from his mind the disturbing outline of Stasia's shapely body under the sheet beside him, aware he hadn't demanded to know what she wanted so badly, and suspecting she wouldn't tell him.

The time difference between New York and Ireland meant Anne would be at her desk at Watkins and Stewart. If he called he could ask her about Stasia Cassano. If he took the time to call he risked jet lag, which could affect his ability to think clearly. He weighed both sides of the question. Sleep? Or call? After deciding to call he hurried to a lobby phone.

"Anne, this is Joe Kelly. I'm in Ireland."

"Ireland, Mr. Kelly?"

"Yes. I've met Stasia Cassano, who says she's a friend of yours. She also says you told her I'm stubborn as well as honorable. Did you?"

"Yes"

"Why?"

"She wanted to know your faults. I didn't think it was her business, so I told her "none" and she said "Nonsense. Everyone has faults.""

"Oh."

"That's what she said. Anyway, I came up with 'stubborn' because it describes most of the men I know.I hope you don't mind."

"What else did you tell her about me, Anne?"

"I didn't know much to tell her about you, except you'e the best boss I've had and you're single. I know you lift weights and you take pictures on weekends. Be careful, Mr. Kelly. Stasia acts like a sister with me but she's good at getting her own way."

"I'll keep it in mind," he said, aware her comment was more accurate than she realized. It was no time to mention he'd agreed to Stasia's travel plan.

"Mr. Kelly," she said. "Mr.Mitchell was here looking for you the first thing today. He was really steamed. Three people from upstairs were also looking for you. Can you tell me what's going on?"

"I resigned."

"Oh, I'm so sorry, Mr. Kelly. I really mean that. I liked working with you. Good luck in Ireland and if anyone asks I'll have no idea where you might be."

"Thanks, Anne. I appreciate your help. And thanks for the good wishes, too. I may need more than my share of luck."

Joe returned to the room and climbed into the empty bed. At 4:00 he woke. The other bed was empty. The Tour's schedule called for assembly at five. He dressed for a cool May evening.

The moment he stepped into the carpeted lobby Stasia moved to his side. She wore navy slacks and the unbuttoned ivory sweater over a blouse of lime green, with a forest green scarf at her throat. A good brushing had tamed her hair and ceiling lamps highlighted it.

"In public we're friends," she reminded him. "You can manage if you try." She turned and talked to a sixtyish woman passing by, saying something Joe couldn't hear. Whatever it was, the woman seemed pleased and beckoned to her.

"Excuse me," Stasia said. She walked with the woman to where a grey-haired man waited.

"Joe Kelly, who are you trying to kid?" asked a woman's voice behind him.

He swallowed and turned.

"Hazel Morrison," he replied, numbly. The woman of fifty facing him worked for Watkins and Stewart. He'd sat with her on two committees.

"I finish my Irish vacation today," she said. "Hours ago I saw you stop at the desk and head for the phone. I checked, to learn you and the pretty redhead are registered as Mr. and Mrs. Kelly. I'm surprised at you, Mr. Kelly" she laughed. "I'm surprised you'e not in bed with her." She laughed again. "What have you to say for yourself?"

"Small world, isn't it."

"Joe, I never thought you had it in you. Boy, was I wrong. Why, you're blushing. I wouldn't have believed it. At first I thought you were shacking up, but I see she's wearing a wedding ring. Well, whatever devious courtship you conducted I expect a full report when you get back to New York. I don't know where you found her, but I certainly admire your taste."

No sooner had Hazel Morrison walked away than Stasia reappeared.

"You've been invited to meet Jean and Harry," she said, indicating the couple she'd been with. "We might as well start with them, since sooner or later we'll meet everyone on the Tour."

Joe stared at the gold band on her left hand. "Thank you for thinking of a ring," he said. "A woman I work with in New York is here. She leaves today. She checked the register and found us listed as the Kelly's and when she spoke to me I turned red. She was ready to pounce. Your ring saved me."

Stasia ignored his comment.

"Let's meet Jean and Harry," she said, "and see if you're as good as acting as Anne says you are at Accounting."

The forthright compliment surprised him. He wished he knew more about her. He shrugged. Hazel Morrison's comments echoed in his ears and, for the first time, he looked carefully at Stasia's face. Her pale skin was flawless. A straight nose divided long-lashed eyes. Her lips were too red to be real, and the perfect fullness of the lower lip attested to her skill with make-up. The overall effect drew attention to her lower lip, a shade lighter than the one above it.

He'd overlooked Stasia's attractiveness. Her aggressive proposal had taken him by surprise. Now, with some reluctance, he forced her appearance from his mind.

He accepted the need to be pleasant to the people on the Tour. Outwardly he would play his part. Inwardly, he would remain at arm's length. He would distract himself with the new digital camera he'd brought on the trip. It would justify wandering away from Stasia as often as he chose. He led her across the room and finessed the introductions. The older woman said "I see you've a digital camera, Joe. Please take our picture with it. Stasia, you stand between Harry and me."

Joe focused the camera and automatically said "smile." The older couple smiled. When Stasia smiled Joe watched in amazement. Years disappeared from her face. She projected the amiable friendliness of a little girl, an image so powerful the camera's viewfinder insisted she was born to be photographed. When he lifted his eyes the smile disappeared.

Now what? Joe thought. He ambled to the bus and followed Stasia to their seats. The bus drove off. Molly O'Brien picked up a mike and began describing the countryside. Joe ignored her. He thought of the woman sitting beside him who would undoubtedly challenge him for the rest of the tour. He wondered how it would end.

The night's highlight was a medieval banquet at Bunratty Castle, a restored stone fortress maintained as a tourist attraction. Costumed young waitresses with fine singing voices enhanced an atmosphere of fun and gaiety. Mead, a beverage popular in the middle ages and similar to cider though far stronger, enhanced an imaginative menu.

Joe sat beside Stasia. She acknowledged members of the Tour who passed by, and at intervals bestowed brief glances in Joe's direction to confirm their husband-and-wife seating. When Joe hauled out his camera for souvenir shots of the castle's interior Jean and Harry reappeared.

"Harry forgot his camera, Joe," Jean said. "Would you take our picture with one of the waitresses?"

Joe looked through the viewfinder to see Jean pull Stasia and a young waitress to her and Harry. "Tell us when to smile," she said.

"Smile"

Stasia's smile undid him again. He kept his face to the viewfinder until he regained his composure, and then joined the cheerful group filing out to the bus.

Joe realized his new problem before the bus reached the Clare Inn. He'd wanted nothing from Stasia except to leave him alone. Now he wanted her to smile at him.

She halted when they reached their room. "I think we'll do okay," she said. "Do I walk around while you take 15 minutes to get ready for bed, or the other way around?"

"I'll walk," Joe said.

When he returned she was asleep. Her clothes were on hangars and no toilet articles were in the bathroom. If she'd made a mess he would have been happier. He'd have felt in charge. Bothered by her neatness, he admitted a strong urge to battle her though she seemed to hold all the cards.

He remembered Anne had described him as stubborn and honorable.

"Anne was right about 'stubborn' he thought. "I intend to solve this problem my way, no matter what Stasia wants. If I can figure out why the tour is so important to her I'll have a better idea of what to do next."

He shook his head, aware it would not be easy. Minutes later, sleep claimed him.

In the morning before the bus took them to Limerick, Molly introduced the idea of seat-skipping. Each day everyone on the bus would move up two seats. Obviously fair to everyone, the procedure eliminated complaints. Molly also kept her fingers crossed. Two sunny days in a row were a welcome surprise.

A pleasant visit to the Hunt Museum was followed by a short walk to King John's Castle, a restored pile of gray medieval brick with a full collection of towers, ramparts and narrow twisting passages.

Joe enjoyed the Museum's paintings. Once inside King John's Castle he knew it wasn't for him. He took a few photographs, enjoying the chance to walk around and keep moving. He had no idea where Stasia might be. After joining an older couple at the Museum, she was somewhere inside the Castle.

"Hi, big guy," said a voice behind him. It belonged to a short, elderly white-haired woman who leaned on a black cane and smiled.

"Where did you park the redhead?" she asked.

"Beside the 'no parking' sign by the bus," was his quick rejoinder. "Or maybe I left her at the Museum. Don't worry. She's not easy to lose."

"I'm not worrying. Her loss is my gain. I'm Leslie, known to my former students as Lovely Leslie, and what I need is a man to lead me. You're elected, Joe."

"You know my name?"

"Be flattered. No one else will use it. They'll think of you as 'the guy with her' or 'the redhead's husband.'"

"What do I call you, Leslie or Lovely?" he asked, uncomfortable with her references to Stasia.

"Call me Leslie and be patient. Don't mind my chatter,and ignore good 'ol King Shorty here" she said, tapping the costumed wax image of the long-dead king who guarded the entrance. "Try not to step on his midget bride, either."

Joe relaxed, allowing himself a good laugh. He'd noticed the royal couple's shortness himself. Leslie meant to have fun and would be good company. She grasped his arm. "Lead us out, Joe," she said.

He took short steps. Leslie easily kept pace. She didn't seem to need his help. Perhaps, he thought, she would tire later in the day.

"We have time for a sandwich before the bus leaves," Leslie said. "I'm sure your redhead will have all kinds of offers. What say you and I try the food shop across from the bus?"

"Fine. I admit I'm hungry. Again," he said, and Leslie laughed.

They ordered individually, and took their trays to an empty table. No other faces in the shop belonged on their Tour.

Leslie finished her sandwich and sipped from a cup of black coffee. She tidied up, watching as Joe finished.

"We're not here by accident," she announced. "I've something to tell you."

"Which is?"

"My seat on the bus is behind yours. Every morning when we change seats I'll still be in the seat behind you."

"And?"

"I notice things. If you move towards your wife, she moves away. If she moves toward you, you turn away. Every time. If I notice it, others will, too. I don't know what's wrong but if I were you I'd fix it. Otherwise, Joe, despite your callow youth I've enjoyed my lunch with you."

"It's been a fun lunch for me, too, lovely Leslie," he said, "And thanks for the advice."

He started to stand. A glance at his companion told him she was about to say something. Thinking better of it, she said nothing.

"Yes?" Joe asked.

"Not now," she said. "We'd better get back before the others start gossiping about us." She accepted his arm. They emerged from the cool interior of the luncheonette into the daylight outside, and walked to the waiting bus.

Continuing the tour, Molly held everyone's attention with lively comments about colorful buildings, ruins or historic sites in each town they passed through. Excellent acoustics allowed passengers to relate what they heard with what they could see. Tall cranes, scaffolding and dozens of unfinished new houses dotted the countryside.

The sun hung lower in the sky when they reached Killarney. Dave maneuvered the big bus into a side courtyard of The Killarney Avenue Hotel, tour headquarters for the next three days. Once again, room assignments were handled smoothly.

Joe preceded Stasia to a nicely furnished room with two single beds.

He saw himself in the mirror. Although certain he belonged on the Tour he was not at all certain he was doing the right thing. He ran a large hand through his hair. He was edgy, looking out the second floor window at traffic when Stasia arrived behind him. Above navy slacks she wore a pale pink shirt and a crimson neck scarf.

"Well," she said. "We haven't talked much. Did you enjoy your day?"

"We need to change our arrangement."

"Why?"

"The woman who sits behind us on the bus told me we don't like each other. She said I avoid you and you turn from me at every opportunity. She's right. It's what we've been doing."

"It's what you wanted."

"I know, but it doesn't work. We have to pretend we like each other," Joe said. "And I'm not good at pretending."

Stasia paused. A thoughtful silence preceded her answer.

"I know I can," she admitted. "It's why I suggested it. But the key question is, can you? For 5 more days?"

"In all honesty, I don't know. You're an attractive woman and I'm no angel. I might handle this better if I knew more about why this tour is so important to you."

"Some things I'll tell you," she said. "For others you'll have to be patient." It was a semi-answer. They both knew it.

"I'm pleased you find me attractive," she continued. "However as far as the Tour goes you should know I'm on a tight budget. If you want us to do dinner and theatre in Tralee you'll have to pay for both of us. Otherwise I'll plead a headache. The same is true for the Abbey Theatre in Dublin."

"Forget money. I'll pay for the options. What else?"

Stasia looked Joe in the eye for the first time since they met. Her eyes were as blue as his own, which surprised him almost as much as the question which followed.

"Can you drive a standard transmission car on the Irish side of the road?"

"I think so. Why?"

"After 2 more days here our Tour turns north and I must get to Waterford. If you rent a car and drive us to Waterford you'll miss less than a day before you rejoin the tour. In other words, in three days I may be gone."

"Why 'may be gone'? Why not 'will be gone'?"

"I don't know what will happen to me in Waterford," she admitted. "It's the most frightening thing I've ever done, even more so than being on this tour with you."

"Thanks," Joe said, hurt more than he let on. He tried to keep his expression neutral. His voice gave him away.

"Oh," she said. "I'm so sorry. I didn't mean to insult you. You've behaved really well. I thought telling you our agreement may end in three days, well, it might help you enjoy the next two."

"I'll think about it. I'm still not sure. You could explain more of this nonsense to me, you know."

Stasia's blue eyes froze. They both felt the tension. Joe realized he'd crossed a line with the word 'nonsense.' He would learn no more.

"No," she said, predictably. "However, I'll try to act like your best friend and you might act like mine. It's more likely to work if we both try."

He was about to say "I don't know" when Stasia smiled warmly at him. He felt like he was facing a friendly girl of twelve, teasing him in grade school days. He was surprised how much it pleased him.

He swallowed his reply. He accepted the hand she offered, and when he closed his fingers he felt the gold band.

In a flash he saw himself in his new role. He would play-act the part of Stasia's husband and friend. He would walk with her, talk with her and be her constant companion. Although her powerful smile had pierced his defenses he would do the best he could.

"Excuse me, Stasia," he said. "I've some private business to tend to. I'll be back for dinner." He left the room without explanation. Two could play the mystery game.

He made a phone call from the lobby and followed with a short taxi ride to a car rental agency. After brief negotiations he sat behind the driver's wheel on the right front seat of a rented Audi.

"You're sure you can handle the shifting?" asked the rental agent.

"Shifting this car is easy for me because I'm left-handed," Joe said, "one of the few bonuses for being a left-hander. I need to familiarize myself with driving in Ireland. I'll be back in about an hour."

Joe drove the Audi until he felt competent. He made frequent turns, adjusting to the small cars around him and noting the virtual absence of trucks. He enjoyed every second of his impulsive move. He returned the car and thanked the pleasant young agent, who made no attempt to overcharge him. When the man gave him a map of the five surrounding counties Joe marked each of the roads which led to Waterford.

At dinner in the hotel Joe and Stasia joined a couple from Oklahoma City. The man introduced himself as Bill Byers and his wife as Grace, both veteran tourists. They'd been everywhere. They described their travels with charm and wit. The menu featured salmon, one of Joe's favorites. It was cooked perfectly. Stasia applauded each of Bill Byers' stories with genuine delight and won over Grace Byers, too. At dinner's end they were a happy group.

Stasia's contagious laugh ended Joe Kelly's hope of keeping his distance. He laughed along with Bill and Grace and when Stasia put a friendly hand on top of his he didn't dare move. He was sorry when the meal ended and Stasia went up to bed. He'd seldom enjoyed a dinner so much and his own contributions had been minimal. He knew himself and his urges well. At the end of dinner he'd wanted to bed Stasia. Instead, he went outside and walked for a long time in the quiet Killarney darkness. He needed protection from himself, and he knew he needed it soon.

In the morning Stasia woke and dressed first. She was gone when Joe opened his eyes. He met her in the carpeted dining room of the hotel and they made their selections from a splendid buffet. Beneath her sweater she wore a beige shirt accented by a gold and brown scarf, simple attire which looked fine. Moments later they were joined at their table by the Hallidays, an older couple from Australia enjoying a long-planned trip around the world.

When the foursome finished eating they sat back in comfortable high-backed chairs. Indirect lighting flattered the women. Garth Halliday glanced at his watch. Helen Halliday spoke to Stasia.

"I don't know how you do it, my dear. I'll need a half hour to repair my make-up after that wonderful meal. Your lipstick looks as fresh as if you just put it on."

Stasia laughed.

"Well, tell me your secret," Helen persisted. "How do you do it?"

"Helen," Stasia said, "I don't use make-up."

Garth Halliday chuckled.

Joe resisted the urge to stare at Stasia's mouth, and the two couples left the dining room. From the lobby they saw the predicted rain had arrived, already two days overdue. A steady drizzle, it proved so light no umbrellas were needed. When Joe and Stasia reached the bus door he noticed for the first time how her lower lip's delicate coloring gave a touch of vulnerability to her appearance.

The bus moved off with a double destination marked on the day's itinerary. A long ride towards Blarney Castle became more cheerful when the rain ceased and the sun reflected off the striking greens of the countryside.

At Blarney, a giant parking lot held tour busses from many other locations. Some folks headed directly into the three story brick building beside the lot which featured a complete array of products from Blarney Woolen Mills.

Joe and Stasia stayed with Molly O'Brien, walking a lengthy wooded trail to Blarney Castle itself. Travelers and vacationers of all ages and appearances, and in some instances in highly imaginative clothes, flocked to the line which led eventually upward to the famed Blarney Stone. A mandatory kiss required a backwards turn and the help of an aged attendant. Leaving the Blarney Stone,however, proved a surprise. Small and unsure rock stairs offered unsure footing which made most everyone uncomfortable until reaching the safety of solid ground. Joe took advantage of the sunlight, snapping dozens of pictures beside Blarney Castle. He knew those featuring Stasia's smile were certain to be winners.

They returned to the bus lot, then enjoyed a pub-style lunch in a nearby building with three senior tour couples. White hair and beards were inside and outside the pub, taking advantage of the final few weeks before schools closed around the world and family groups came to enjoy Ireland's treasures.

From Blarney Castle their route was south, to the southernmost coast of County cork. The blue waters of Bantry Bay proved a startling sight and cameras appeared everywhere. At the next stop, Glengariff they left the bus and boarded a private boat, The Harbor Queen II. Large enough to hold all members of the Tour, the boat seemed small. It headed through warm coastal waters for scenic Garinish Island. Ages-old mountains surrounded them, and the sun tickled white streaks on the blue water churned by the boat's propeller.

After boarding the Harbor Queen II for the return trip Joe and Stasia stood together. A mild breeze rippled her auburn hair. Beyond the boat dozens of lazy seals sunned themselves on a string of tiny islets.

"See the seals?" asked Dave, the driver. "They're here because of the warm water. Local fishermen hate them because seals eat the fish. Too many seals, not enough fish. Seals have been known to disappear suddenly, but more always come." The cheerful man led them ashore and onto the bus for the long ride back to Killarney.

The following day their visit to Ireland's southwestern tip began in a drizzle. The plan was to explore the Ring of Kerry, a procession of narrow mountain roads on which the bus hurried through ever higher turns. Yellow gorse accented dark green borders separating one meadow from the next on cleared mountainsides. On others, a preponderance of grey and white rocks announced a limited amount of fertile soil and hinted at hostile year-round weather.

When they boarded, Stasia, with a smile, had ceded Joe the seat beside the window. In the mountains he looked out and saw small pipes of less than knee height marching at the edges of the road. A triple strand of thin wire linked one to the next. Beyond the pipes the roads dropped down abruptly for hundreds of feet.

The thin low wires couldn't possibly prevent a tipped bus from sliding down the mountainside. No one had mentioned the possibility but recognizing it as real, Joe was alert to the importance of a capable driver who knew what he was doing. His admiration for Dave's smooth handling of their big transport was sudden and genuine. During a break in the drizzle the bus descended to the seaside town of Waterville, where a sign announced the inlet known as Ballinskelligs Bay. A happy girl and her sister rushed to satisfy the tourists who came into their small restaurant. Waiting outside with Stasia, Joe suddenly laughed. Her eyes lit with pleasure. She turned to him.

"What's so funny?"

"I could never live here. I couldn't spell the name of that inlet and no one I know could, either."

She squeezed his hand in hers.

"I think you're ready for a snack, my man," she said, stepping aside so an elderly woman with a black cane could pass.

"Good afternoon, Joe," said Lovely Leslie. She looked at Stasia's hand holding his. He recognized her expression as appropriate for a cat which had swallowed a canary. Moments later, the drizzle ended.

On the return trip to Killarney sheep or cows seemed in every pasture. Sheep wearing blue or red splotches of paint clustered all over the mountains, in a system which allowed easy identification of mixed flocks. A majority of cows displayed white and brown markings. Some stayed so long in one spot it was hard to be sure they breathed. Others moved a few slow steps, and even then as if to avoid punishment.

Once back, Joe led Stasia to their room. The night's program included a trip to Tralee. He would wear his usual uniform of khakis and open collar shirt, and add a light jacket in honor of the special occasion.Idly, and for no explainable reason, he wondered what she would wear.

"We have two hours before the outing tonight," she reminded him, "which is why Jean asked me to go shopping with her. We'll be back in plenty of time. If you'll dress first I'll change later."

Her absence gave Joe an opportunity to study his maps. If he rented a car in Killarney he and Stasia faced a hundred mile drive the next morning. Initially he would go southeast on route #22, then, once past Cork, continue east through the scenic coastal towns to Waterford on route #25.

On the maps the drive looked simple enough. Not knowing the roads could make it a challenge. He had no idea what Stasia would do in Waterford or how long it would take. She might step from the car and wave him good-bye, though this seemed unlikely. If she didn't need him along she wouldn't have suggested he drive her. He had no idea where they would be or if they would stay, or what to do about luggage. If they were to rejoin the Tour it would probably be somewhere north along route #7 or route #8, both of which led eventually to Dublin.

All in all, his only option was wait and see. He showered and dressed and went to the lobby, where he met Garth Halliday. The Australian insisted they have a drink in the bar and Joe welcomed the distraction.

He looked up from his barstool to see Jean and Stasia approaching, with Harry not far behind. Jean wore a powder blue dress, high white heels and a full complement of gold jewelry. Her silver hair surrounded a smiling face dominated by a pair of rhinestone-studded glasses. She smiled at Stasia, talking as they walked.

The auburn-haired woman who held Joe's attention no longer wore navy blue slacks and simple shirt under an outsize sweater. She wore fawn-colored slacks above tan walking shoes and sleeveless ecru blouse, simple in itself yet devastating, because both blouse and slacks displayed a figure so perfect as to cry out for compliments. Her red lips contrasted strongly with the pale skin of her face, calling attention from figure to face and back again. Every one of the two dozen men in the bar watched as she walked by.

"Oh, hello Joe," Stasia said. She was obviously pleased with her changed appearance. "Jean and I went shopping. How do I look?"

"You look wonderful," he said, a huge understatement. He followed her to the bus, trying not to stare and staring nonetheless. Only the darkness inside when Dave started the motor allowed him a respite from the beauty beside him. He rode to Tralee in silence, striving with all his might to get his emotions under control.

Dinner at the Galleon Restaurant meant each table contained full place settings of good crystal, fine silver and immaculate white table linens. Efficient waiters immediately surrounded the tables, taking orders for a choice of entrees and bringing wine to enhance the meal.

The wine undid him.

Each time Stasia turned her head she found Joe looking at her. At times he smiled and other times nodded. When he thought she might not notice he stared. Through it all she seemed unaware of his confusion and he was grateful. The fine dinner proved universally satisfying.

When dinner ended the guests walked straight across a busy street and onto the grounds of the prestigious Siamsa Tire National Folk Theatre. The night's presentation opened with coordinated dancing similar to Riverdance and drew sustained applause. The theme shifted. Young women wearing filmy white gowns danced barefoot on stage, their ethereal expressions suggesting meaning beyond the comprehension of mere mortals. For some in the audience it was theatre at its best. For Joe Kelly it was a nap opportunity and he took full advantage. When the lights went up he had thrown off some of the wine's effects. He escorted the lovely woman beside him into the cool night air, accepted her hand while they strolled and fought the demons rising within him.

On the return ride to Killarney he stared out the window, reading the signs visible at night. He saw a big sign reading Bally Seedy

Garden Center and thought the name appropriate until seconds later when he saw the Bally Seedy Gas Station and recalled 'bally' meant 'town.' A little further on, a huge white shield with crossed red bars in the shape of an X guarded the impressive entrance to the Earl of Desmond Hotel. It reminded Joe he didn't know the Kelly coat of arms. He decided to look it up before leaving Ireland.

When they reached the hotel Joe led Stasia from the bus, then reached behind him to help her down the stairs. He wanted to touch her any way he could. He wanted it a lot more than he knew would be wise. Once inside the lobby he hesitated before making a reluctant choice.

"You go upstairs first, Stasia. I'd like another drink before bed," he said, feeling like a hypocrite. The last thing he needed with her nearby was anything more to drink.

"I'd like a drink, too, Joe. Can I join you?"

"Fine."

They sat on side-by-side barstools. Several people from the Tour waved and two couples joined them for a nightcap.

Let's have another drink, Joe," Stasia said. "Both our glasses are empty."

"Have what you like but I'd better go slow. If I drink too much I feel sorry for myself, and then I'm trouble." He wondered why he was telling her this. The bartender responded to Stasia's waving glass. Two more drinks appeared.

Joe looked at her face. She looked even more beautiful than in the same bar hours earlier. He looked without apology at her tailored slacks and lovely white blouse, and catching himself, turned back to look at his drink. He could think of nothing to say. He sat and wondered what to do next.

Minutes later Stasia put her hand on his arm. He wished she would keep it there.

"Good night, Joe. I had a lovely night. I'm going now."

He sat forlornly in the bar for ten minutes. On impulse he called for the check and walked to the elevator. When he reached their room he opened the door without knocking and walked right in.

Stasia had been sitting on her bed. When Joe arrived she stood up. She wore a filmy white nightdress which barely reached her knees, a garment so thin he could easily see through it. Mesmerized by the reddish triangle below her waist, he shifted his eyes to her face. She watched him without expression.

"Stasia, I know I'm here early. I want a favor. I have to ask."

"Which is?"

"I want to hold you, kiss you good night. Would you mind?"

She said nothing. She walked to where he stood. She leaned against him until he put his arms around her. He could feel her heartbeat. He inhaled the gentle floral scent he recognized from earlier in the night.

He held her while they kissed. The softness of her lips penetrated his consciousness. He hoped she would respond but wasn't certain. He held her for extra seconds before backing away.

"Thank you, Stasia," he said. He turned and left the room, not hearing the quietly whispered "thank you, Joe," behind him.

He sat on a high stool in the bar and drank until the bar closed. In the morning his head felt as if it had been smashed with a heavy hammer. Nonetheless, he knew it was time to take charge. The Tour would head north at 9:00. Their plans must be complete before the bus left, which meant he needed information from Stasia.

They enjoyed an early breakfast before moving to a table in the corner of the hotel lobby.

"I've rented a car here," Joe said. "I'll be driving us to Waterford but I really must know where we're going and for how long if we're to make any sensible arrangements. Like luggage, for instance. Do we take it or don't we?"

She seemed tense when she replied.

"We're heading for the rectory of St.Mary's Catholic Church in BallyGunner, Waterford, and I'll give you the exact address. I called yesterday. Father Doolan expects me between 3:00 and 4:00 in the afternoon. I could be at St.Mary's for an hour, two hours or longer. I don't know."

"Luggage?"

"I don't know."

"Where will you be staying?"

"I don't know. In an emergency Father Doolan may be able to find me a place."

"Not much of a plan. Sounds to me like a lot of loose ends."

"Very loose."

Joe's next question was a shot in the dark. Her answer was unexpected.

"Have you ever been in Waterford before?"

"Yes."

"Would you tell me about it?"

"No."

"There's more to this than I'm aware of?"

"There's a lot you don't know, a lot I can't tell you."

She twisted the fingers of one hand with the other. "No matter what happens today," she continued, "I appreciate your sharing your room with me and driving me to Waterford. One more thing."

"Yes?"

"Your kiss last night meant a lot to me. Thank you so much. I'm still pleased by it."

His body rejoiced at her words. He wanted to jump the table and kiss her again but time was short and they needed decisions.

"All right," he said. "Let me help, if you don't mind. We'll leave our bags with the Tour. Maybe we can catch them in a day or so. I'll tell Molly. Let's travel light. Small items go in your shoulder bag or my camera bag. If we're lucky we'll find you a place to stay without bothering Father Doolan. Now, you get packed and I'll find Molly. If we hurry we'll be on our way in 15 minutes."

An hour later they were well clear of Killarney, headed south on route #22 in a clean, shiny Audi. Joe gave the small car high marks for power and handling and was surprised at its comfort. Outside, the day was sunny but windy. On several occasions gusts of wind required a firm hand on the wheel. Traffic was light. Joe watched the speed limit signs and the Audi ate up the miles to Cork.

Skirting the city of Cork and the harbor of Cobh where so many Irish had embarked for America, they moved onto route #25 for the trip up the coast. Stasia seldom spoke. Once again she wore her ivory Aran sweater over a forest green shirt Joe could see when she faced him.

At Youghal they stopped for food. They ate light at a small shop and Joe enjoyed taking pictures of Stasia with Youghal Bay in the background, a pattern repeated at Dungarvan. She insisted he show her how to take his picture at Dungarvan with the digital camera. She succeeded and bestowed on him the smile he'd hoped for since Killarney.

The Audi maneuvered off route #25 and onto #675.Its dashboard clock confirmed they would arrive in BallyGunner hours before Stasia's appointment with Father Doolan, so after passing through Knock and Annestown and nearing Waterford they agreed on a visit to Tramore. A visit to a friendly pub helped dispel their travel fatigue.

Waterside at Tramore was the next stop. Joe locked the Audi and they walked on a raised concrete walk overlooking the brown sands of Tramore beach. Lots of sea birds scooted around. High winds in early afternoon meant whitecaps on the blue water, with not a boat in sight. Looking to sea, the harbor's shape was enclosed by mountains three miles apart which defined its entrance.

Stasia took his hand. Joe wasn't sure if it was because of the wind or she'd forgotten there was no need to act friendly,or because she wanted to hold it. He wasn't about to ask.

"New around here?"

The white-bearded man who asked the question wore a leather cap and a buttoned sweater and held an obedient dog on a long brown leash.

"Yes," Joe answered. "Why?"

"You seem to enjoy walking. I do myself and so does Parnell." He indicated the patient dog. "I'm Tim Keane. The best walk around is the one over there," he said, pointing high and off to their right. "It's called the Doneraile Walk, and if you have the chance it's worth a try."

"We're starting to run out of time," Joe said, "but thanks anyway. Before you go, Tim -- do you know the way to BallyGunner?"

"Sure. My brother lives in Ballygunner. I'll draw you a map if you'll hold Parnell for me."

"That's sure nice of you."

Tim Keane gave them directions to BallyGunner and then handed over a small map. Joe and Stasia both thanked him. On returning to the Audi its clock read 2:55. Tim Keane had included directions to St.Mary's church and assured them they would find it easily.

Joe prepared to start the little car when Stasia spoke.

"Joe, at this point I...I don't know what to do about me, so I don't know what to do about you. I'm going to suggest you leave me at St.Mary's and come back in an hour. I'll tell you whatever I can. It's all I can say right now, Joe."

"I understand, Stasia," he said. He could see she was tense. He wondered if whatever awaited her at St.Mary's frightened her, and suspected it might.

St. Mary's, a tall gray stone church, stood on raised ground between two churchyard cemeteries. The rectory was off to one side, and when Stasia emerged from the Audi the door of the rectory opened. A tall, cassocked priest stood in its doorway, obviously waiting for someone.

Stasia got out of the car, took two steps and then turned suddenly back. She opened the car door.

"Here, Joe. Please hold this for me," she said. She threw something on the seat and shut the door. He looked down to see her gold ring. He looked up and saw her walk to the priest at the rectory door.

An hour later, Joe returned.

He knocked at the rectory door and the tall priest opened it. He wore a black cassock. Joe guessed his age as 60.

"I'm sure you're Joe Kelly," the priest said "I'm Father Doolan." He extended a hand in welcome. "We've been expecting you. Please come in."

Joe followed him into a small, sparsely furnished parlor. Stasia sat in a wooden chair beside an old desk piled high with books, magazines, correspondence, a tin of tobacco and several small curios. Father Doolan moved behind it and sat down. He exchanged glances with Stasia before he spoke.

"Joe, Stasia and I have been deeply involved with unusual family histories in the past hour. All of them affect Stasia in one way or other, which is why she's here. Some of them may affect you, which is why I'm talking to you."

"Me??

"She tells me you're an honorable man, Joe, and I believe her. She wants to invite you into our discussion, an invitation you have the right to decline. More importantly, she wants to change some of the things she's told you. Let me say she wants you to know the truth and she's prepared to accept the consequences."

Joe looked into the eyes of the auburn-haired woman he'd know for such a short time. She met his look without flinching. She was obviously tense. The fingers of one hand began wringing those of the other.

"Are you willing to answer all my questions?" he asked.

"Yes, Joe, and accept the consequences."

"Whatever they may be?"

She hesitated. Her fingers kept busy, but her chin pointed higher.

"Whatever they may be."

"Will you try this on, then?" Joe asked. From his pocket he removed the box holding the diamond ring he'd bought in downtown Waterford, a ring the same size as the gold band she'd tossed into the Audi.

"Yes," she whispered, accepting the box. Tears flowed from her eyes. She put the diamond ring on her third finger, covering the mark where she'd worn the gold band.

"Will you marry me, Stasia, Joe asked.

"Yes" she said, "If you'll have me."

Joe turned to Father Doolan.

"I'm prepared to absorb the whole family history, Father. All I'd like to know is, in your opinion is there any good reason for me not to marry Stasia, or her not to marry me?"

"None, whatsoever, Joe. Now I'm leaving you for the next half hour. Please kiss your fiancee. Let her tell you a few truths you don't know. When I come back the three of us will walk around the church to the cemetery on the other side, where the rest of her history is written. Literally," he finished.

Father Doolan slipped from behind the desk and went out of the room.

Joe walked to Stasia, and when she rose he held out his arms for her She raced to him. They kissed ardently, then embraced for several minutes. Stasia wiped tears from her eyes. She took Joe by the hand and led him to the chair he'd abandoned.

"Listen," she said. "Let me do the talking."

"My name is not Stasia Cassano. My name is Anastasia Jane Ryan. I was born in Waterford to Anastasia Jane Ryan and her husband, Patrick Ryan, Waterford's Fire Chief. When I was 2 months old a wall fell on my father at a fire and killed him. The accident destroyed my mother's mind. Her sister, Sheila, took me to America with her. She married a man named Cassanoand they adopted me."

"Here in Waterford the sisters of the Good Shepherd accepted Anastasia Jane Ryan as a nun. She lived out her days as a gentle member of the Good Shepherd community.

"The Cassano's had no other children. They never told me I was adopted. My adoptive mother conducted a long campaign for me to become a Good shepherd nun. When she succeeded, she rejoiced. Six months ago she died. My adoptive father, Anthony Cassano, had never agreed with the decision to keep me unaware of my real parents. In the meantime I'd become dissatisfied with a nun's life. It isn't for me. I had already left the order when he told me the truth. That was two months ago, and my mother was alive but very sick. I called Waterford. The Mother Superior here told me if I spoke with my mother on the phone she'd have no idea who was talking to her. Yet I wanted to see her before she died, so badly I was willing to go to any lengths to get here. She died 10 days ago when my plan was already in motion."

"Your secretary, Anne, was once a nun. I told her I needed an honorable man to get me to Ireland. She agreed you are honorable but wanted no part of my plan. She told me about your trip.

"I don't have a sister who works in a travel agency. Another former nun does. I convinced her to change your tour reservation. I told her I could defend myself.

"I wasn't in a car accident. I don't have headaches. I'm 34 years old, not 35.

"I didn't wear a gold ring to cover our story of being man and wife. It was the ring given my mother when she became a Good Shepherd nun. Father Doolan sent it to me. I was wearing it because I forgot to take it off."

Joe interrupted the litany.

"I've heard enough. I still want you to marry me. More than anything in the world."

"I accept. I want to be married to you more than anything in the world."

Father Doolan returned. "It's time to go to the grave," he said. He led the way around the church. On its far side a long row of similar tombstones honored nuns of the Good Shepherd order. Joe was surprised to see at least 5 variations of Anastasia, Statia and Stasia in the maiden names of deceased nuns.

Father Doolan led them further through the rows of monuments. Joe saw another six honoring deceased Anastasias or Stasias. His thought the name was of Russian origin disappeared.

Far in the back row, Father Doolan stopped. Small twin monuments identified Timothy Ryan, fire chief, and his wife, Anastasia Ryan. Inscribed on her stone were the words "Nun of the Good Shepherd" and below it "Mother of Anastasia Jane Ryan."

Stasia came to Joe and held him tightly. She looked down at the monuments at her feet.

"I never knew her, Joe, or him either. I'm glad I know who they were, and who I am."

On the walk back to the rectory Joe approached Father Doolan.

"Could you marry us, Father?" he asked. "I know banns are traditional, but are they always a barrier? Especially when we're both so far from our own country?"

"Joe, it's a strange question you ask me. After you proposed to Stasia I took it upon myself to call the bishop's office. I asked the same question."

"And?"

"If you're willing and Stasia's willing you'll be man and wife in, say, 15 minutes."

Later, Joe opened the door of the Audi.

"Would you please get in now, Mrs. Kelly?" he asked.

"I'd be more than pleased, Mr. Kelly," she said. "I'd be delighted. Where are we off to now, if you don't mind my asking?"

"We are off to the bridal suite of the Waterford Jury Hotel. We will enjoy all the hospitality it has to offer. In the morning we drive to the town of Cashel, where I will turn in our Audi and we will rejoin our Green Ireland Tour."

"The following morning a puzzled Joe Kelly sat behind the wheel a few miles south of Cashel, the Irish community where St. Patrick once preached. He looked at Stasia beside him and disclosed the reason for his puzzled look.

"It seemed to me my dear Stasia all the signs suggest strongly you never slept with anyone before me. I am your first and only lover."

"It's possible, Joseph."

"Then why did you talk about 'paying any price' the first night we roomed together?"

"Anne said you were an honorable man. Remember? An honorable man wouldn't attack me."

"What if Anne was wrong?"

"What if I told you Father Doolan told me it would be wrong if I killed myself if you went away without me?"

"Ae you telling me the truth, Stasia?"

"Husband dear, I believe the bus beside us is marked Green Ireland Tour. The woman standing beside it looks quite like a woman we know, a Tour director named Molly O'Brien. We should be rejoining her group, shouldn't we?"

In the morning the Kelly's climbed aboard the Green Ireland Tour bus. Molly pointed out their new seats. Joe settled himself comfortably when he felt a tap on his shoulder.

"Welcome back," said Lovely Leslie. "I do like the new ring Mrs. Kelly is wearing. It looks so much nicer on her."

"It certainly does," Joe replied. "All the girls are wearing them on honeymoon tours."

2

Emily Elizabeth

In the graduation picture taken thirty years ago Emily Gilmartin sits facing the camera in the third seat from the right, front row. She wears a white robe which reaches to her shoes and a flat white cap with a tassel which dangles beside her left ear. Wavy brown hair cascades from the sides of her hat to her shoulders. She is thirteen years old, one of twenty girls in a class of forty one. The picture was taken in a garden beside the school, allowing the noonday sun to paint shadows under Emily's deepset eyes. Like most in the group her face is blank and offers no clue as to what she is thinking.

Four cassocked clergymen sit in the middle of her row and stare at the photographer. A long second row consists solely of boys wearing dark gowns. Four taller boys stand on unseen chairs in the middle of the third row with girls on either side of them. Every graduate holds a thinly rolled diploma.

I'm on the right end, middle row. I was told not to smile and I didn't. My name is Frank Hagen.

My class endured the odd habit of our home room teacher of using full given names when she called on us. Her whim meant I was never "Franklin' or 'Frank" or even 'Mr. Hagen' but always 'Franklin LeRoy.' In the same manner Emily Gilmartin was always 'Emily Elizabeth.'

She was a quiet girl. She answered questions in low tones without elaboration. When she spoke she looked down at her desk as if seeking to escape public recognition.

I was aware of her because she was the lone barrier to my capture of all the graduation medals. Her grades were good but mine were better, with one exception. Her math grade was perfect. Unless she made an error or got sick she would get the match medal and I would get the others.

We never talked. Her mother drove her to school and picked her up. Boys ate lunch in one group and girls in another. Sometimes I wondered if she derived pleasure from frustrating me. Although I would look at her when she walked by she never looked at me. I was an inch or so taller. Her cousin Charlotte Clare was in our class. It seemed to me they talked only with each other.

Emily Elizabeth won the math medal. When I heard it I fumed. I could do nothing about it, and when they called her name at the graduation ceremony I looked down at the floor. I had some growing up to do.

After graduation we went our separate ways. I neither saw nor heard of Emily Gilmartin for more than a dozen years, during which I completed my studies and became a lawyer. Hard work in school resulted in my being hired by one of New York's prestigious firms.

I was guaranteed a substantial future. I also worked 80-hour weeks for several years, meaning no social life until I bumped into Jim Kane, a former classmate, while walking in midtown.

"Come to my party Saturday, he said. "Among others, Charlotte Conroy and Emily Gilmartin will be there. Remember them, Charlotte Clare and Emily Elizabeth? Emily just came back from California.

At the party Emily fascinated me. The quiet girl who frustrated me so much in school had grown up to be a stunning woman who laughed easily and walked with grace, which drew attention to her lovely figure and beautiful face.

I learned she had gone to California a year after graduation to visit her Aunt Adelaide, a native New Yorker moved west by her husband's job. Shortly after Emily's arrival Aunt Adelaide's husband died.

Emily's divorced parents had been fighting about their daughter's custody. They willingly granted Aunt Adelaide's request for Emily to stay on. In time, the arrangement became permanent. Much later Emily earned a degree in business and worked for a private financial firm. Her return east honored Aunt Adelaide's desire to spend her final years in New York. Emily came with her, she explained, and was fortunately able to transfer to her firm's small New York office.

Ours was not a long courtship. Our wedding involved few people.

A few weeks before the ceremony I was invited to an impressive Manhattan apartment where I met Aunt Adelaide. The old lady's eyes were alert and friendly and her greeting to me at our first meeting was cordial and unexpectedly humorous.

"I've heard a lot about you, Franklin LeRoy" she said, while inwardly I winced. "All of it is good. You take good care of my niece and I'm sure she'll take good care of you."

"Fear not, woman," I replied, trying to recover my aplomb. "If anyone appreciates Emily, it is moi."

"I hope so," she said. Her smile was warm.

After our wedding Emily called me 'Franklin Leroy' whenever she wanted my attention. It always worked. I retaliated with 'Emily Elizabeth' which caused her to laugh pleasantly, sometimes almost too pleasantly.

My legal future depended in great measure on R. Alexander Wiley, a senior partner who would be a major shaper of the firm's decision as to whether I would make partner, or when. Of late he had been requesting my involvement on matters of increasing importance. I did my best. Whatever his opinion, he kept it to himself.

Among the firm's lawyers Wiley was known as "Big Al," a tribute to his size, status and fondness for doing things on a heroic scale.

"Big Al" was more than physically big. He was a rainmaker who landed and held many of the firm's large clients. A successful yachtsman and race car driver, he was known to play poker for high stakes. Married twice before he was forty, his third marriage to a social worker amazed all who knew them.

Childless himself, he doted on his new wife and took enormous satisfaction in her work as operations director of The Children's Aid Society. Her days were as long as ours. Rumor had it she retired Big Al from poker the day after their wedding.

Six months after our marriage we received an invitation to dinner at the Sutton Place apartment of Mr. and Mrs. R. Alexander Wiley. It required less than genius to grasp the invitation's significance. The Wiley's were going to inspect my new wife. I understood this and resented it. I told Emily. She laughed.

"You needn't worry about me, Franklin LeRoy. I don't care whether they approve of me or not, and neither should you. I'm happy with you and my work and Aunt Adelaide is happy in New York. I need nothing more, least of all approval by a New York law firm. "You make a good living and I do, too," she reminded me.

Her comment intrigued me. I have an excellent memory and an ear for details. I was certain Emily and I talked but once about money. Before our wedding she announced she would take care of her own expenses and we would discuss money at some future time, a discussion which had yet to take place. I was curious. I was also working long hours. It was simply another detail.

We arrived at Sutton Place precisely at the time requested. Emily looked magnificent. We were taken in tow by Mrs. Rose Wiley, a charming, unaffected hostess with a wealth of children's stories and her affable husband, who almost ignored me as he followed Emily's every word and every move of his wife. The food was predictably excellent. I enjoyed the dinner.

As for Emily, she owned a private mannerism I had detected on other occasions. When specially happy or pleased she tilted her head slightly when she smiled, unconsciously enhancing the power of her smile.

Emily turned her head each time she smiled at R. Alexander Wiley. The man was thrilled and I was surprised as well as pleased. Remembering Emily's comments about the dinner invitation I assumed she was presenting her best side on my behalf, and doing a far better job of it than I might have hoped.

Not until we finished our coffee and were about to rise from the table did I realize I had been left out of the evening's conversation. Not a word was said about my job or the firm. Neither Rose Wiley nor her husband seemed to notice.

"Good night, Rose," Emily said, and I echoed.

"Good night, Alex," Emily said as I echoed.

"Good night, Elizabeth," said Big Al, "and give my best to Adelaide."

My ear for details buzzed twice. Once was too much. I didn't know where the 'Elizabeth' came from, but when he added Adelaide he rang my bell.

"You've met before?" I asked.

"Of course,: he admitted. "I see by your expression I've let a cat out of the bag but eventually it would come out anyway. Elizabeth?"

"Tell him," Emily said.

"Tell me, too," said Rose Wiley. "I'm all ears.

"The toughest high-stakes poker player on the entire west coast was Elizabeth's Aunt Adelaide. At one time I estimated she relieved me of upwards of a million dollars in a ten-year period, and her annual poker income ran to seven numbers. No one, and I mean no one, could beat her."

"And?" I asked.

"In recent years Aunt Adelaide sometimes suffered severe asthma attacks after games were scheduled, so she sent her niece as her replacement. Adelaide trained the niece. No one could tell the difference in their poker skills. It was a little easier losing to Elizabeth because she's so good to look at, but don't you ever play poker with Elizabeth."

"Elizabeth?" Is that the name she used?"

"Why, yes. Elizabeth Emily. I never did know her real name until tonight but it's been a joy meeting her again. I'm retired from poker now, as you may have heard." He smiled at Rose. "But you, young man, have been endorsed by royalty."

Once outside, Emily turned her head sidewise to me and smiled sweetly.

"I was going to tell you soon, Franklin Leroy. I just hadn't figured out how."

On Monday, the firm published the list of new partners. My name was on it. Frank L. Hagen, also known as Franklin LeRoy Hagen and proud of it.

3

"Bub" Harris, Football Coach

He is a big man with a year-round tan. His short gray hair is crewcut, a style seldom seen in corporate environments though common on golf courses and marinas. He's in his middle fifties, wide shouldered with alert blue eyes. Four months of the year he lives in Florida with his wife, Beth Ann. From June to January they live in Manhasset, Long Island, in a modest brick ranch which has been their home for 15 years. His name is Lester Harris, but he's known as "Bub." By occupation a professional football coach, he specializes in quarterbacks. He's also a scout.

Harris began his athletic career as a running back in a small southwestern college. He moved into the pros, gaining a reputation as a smart, heady player. A knee injury ended his career. As a coach he began in an Oklahoma high school. He progressed to the colleges, larger in size and prominence. He moved from Oklahoma to Ohio to Pennsylvania to New Jersey before arriving as quarterback coach for the New York Jets.

"Bub" Harris speaks in a soft voice which carries great weight with players and other coaches. When management needs a player evaluation or considers a trade with another team, Bub's reports receive careful attention.

Bub and his wife established their Long Island home when the Jets played at Shea Stadium. The team's move to New Jersey kept them within commuting distance. Arrival of a new management and a new coach caused a number of staff changes but Bub was invited to stay on. Wise in the ways of the football business, he helps train new coaches as well as new players.

On this early November weekend, the Jets have an open date. Practice on Friday at the Meadowlands ended early. Bub and a new defensive coach, Al Ososki, have driven back to Manhasset. Al's wife, Sue, will meet Bub and Beth Ann at Manhasset for the rare off-weekend. Beth Ann's home cooking ranks with Bub's football knowledge. The invitation is a prized one. Ososki's specialty is defensive backfield, and he looks forward to the chance to talk shop, one on one, with Bub Harris. He knows his wife will respond to Beth Ann, too, a friendly break for a young coach's wife whose own relatives are all back in Pittsburgh.

Saturday night, Jets general manager Ernie Wright stops by. The three men relax. The conversation enters on the Jets need for a kicker. Only one qualified kicker is available, and the player's agent, Sam Hotchkiss, is causing problems.

"You know Hotchkiss, Bub," Wright says. "The man's a weasel with no shame. He knows what his kicker is worth but he's pushing for an extra $100,000 because he thinks he's got us by the thumbs. I've checked on most every kicker I know, but so far no luck."

"How much longer can you wait, Ernie?" Bub asks.

"Probably until Wednesday, Bub. After that, the weasel's got me. I just hate to give him the satisfaction."

Late on Saturday, Bub issues Ososki an invitation.

"Like to spend a busman's holiday with me in the morning, Al?"

"Meaning?"

"Watch some six-man football. About a twenty minute drive, to Douglaston. Up early, though. We'll have to leave here by eight."

"Sure" says Ososki, puzzled. Like most in his workaholic profession he can't watch too much football. But six players to a side? Touch football? The suggestion is unusual but so is Bub.

Early Sunday Bub maneuvers the gray Buick down Northern Boulevard. They cross from Nassau's good concrete pavement into the shell-holed blacktop of Queens. Five minutes later Bub turns north onto Douglaston Parkway. They pass a string of tall brick apartment houses and cross a Long Island Rail Road overpass. They drive slowly through a community of large, expensive and gracious homes.

Bub turns, and a few blocks later they reach a vast, grassy park surrounded by trees which shield it from the community. Inside the park is a lined football field. Beyond the field's far edge, the waveless water of Little Neck Bay signals low tide.

Dozens of cars park haphazardly on the sandy slopes of a curbless service road. A hundred people mill around the sidelines. In the field's middle, two dozen sweatsuited players loosen up. Their ages range from twenty to middle thirties. They stretch or sprint or toss footballs around.

Ososki surveys the scene as Bub parks the car. He's surprised to see so many watchers turn out on a crisp morning in November.

"Good," says Bub. "The Forts are playing."

"The Forts?"

"The Fortunatos," Bub answers. "It's why all the people are here. You're in for a treat."

"The Fortunatos?"

"Two brothers. The ones that got away. Coaches died to recruit them, especially Danny Fortunato. He simply said "No, he didn't want to play on their football team. He would pay his own way to college and he did. He's finishing up at St. John's Law School. His brother Tommy is a traveling accountant. The Forts only play when Tommy's in town."

"Six-man touch football, Bub?"

"Right, Al. With blocking. Pretend you're scouting these guys. Enjoy it.

"Sure, Bub," Ososki says. He walks behind Bub. He shakes his head but says nothing.

The two teams line up.

Ososki takes in the scene. One team includes two big, dark-haired players. He assumes these are the Fortunatos. He counts the players on the other team. Seven.

"Six-man football, Bub?" he asks as a holder readies the football for the opening kick.

"When you play the Forts you get seven," Bub explains. He turns around and a big, dark-haired kicker wearing a gray sweatsuit kicks off. The ball soars skyward and comes to earth in the far corner of the end zone.

Ososki's interest increases.

The team with the ball makes a few first downs and then kicks. When their opponents line up, the defense shows six men at the line of scrimmage. The seventh stands in the middle of the field, twenty five yards back.

"Strange defense," Ososki thinks.

The ball is snapped. A receiver sprints downfield on either side, accompanied by a defender. The lone defender in the middle of the field keeps backpedaling. A blocker, tall and dark-headed, protects the passer. Ososki judges the passer, also dark-headed, has waited too long. The receivers are forty yards downfield before he throws the ball.

The ball goes skyward. It travels seventy yards in the air. It falls into the hands of a receiver who has run under it. Touchdown. There is clapping in the crowd on the sidelines, and groans from the supporters of the defense.

Ososki had watched the passer. The throw seemed effortless. Ososki knew better. He turned to Bub.

Bub said "Danny Fort, Al. Warming up."

The game proceeds. The Forts score twice more before the half. Ososki rivets his attention on Danny Fort. Fort has passed for three touchdowns.

He's also kicked. The shortest was 70 yards, one was a few yards longer and the third close to 80 yards. A whistle signaled the end of the half.

"What college did they go to Bub?" Ososki asks. He's mentally outlined a report on the Forts. Potential high-level draft choices. Both players stand close to six three, well-muscled and solid. Both have good hands and fast feet. Danny Fort's passing is spectacular, his kicking awesome.

"They went to St. John's Al, but they didn't play football."

"You're kidding, Bub," Ososki says.

"I told you they got away. They play for fun."

"They paid for college?"

"Mr. Fortunato owned a construction company. The boys started with jackhammers when they were twelve years old. That's for the muscles. They decided early in high school they would not play big-time football."

"Simple as that?"

"Not quite. The father took sick. They had to stay close by, and run the company while they went to school. Nothing easy about it, Al. They both graduated with honors."

"What about now, Bub?"

"They love football. As a game. People who know football love to watch them. I do myself. Look around."

Word had traveled about the Forts. Another fifty cars had increased the congestion around the field.

The second half was a repeat of the first. The Forts played their game, and the rest of the players on both sides did their best. When the game ended, Ososki turned to Bub.

"Amazing, Bub. Now what?"

"For lunch, both teams head for The Golden Oak, Al. It's a neighborhood place. I'd like to stop, too, for a word with the Forts."

"You know them?"

"I know them."

At The Golden Oak, Ososki was again surprised by his fellow coach. After a brief greeting to Danny Fortunato, Bub asked the big young man if he had a favorite charity.

"Yes, Coach," Fortunato answered. "Douglaston Volunteer Ambulance Corps. They're in a tough spot. Why?"

"Just wondering," Bub answered absently.

When the two older men returned to Bub's house in Manhasset, Ososki marveled at Bub's willingness to watch touch football on an off day.

"No problem, Al," the older man said. "Danny Fortunato is one of my favorite people. I love to watch football for fun rather than money. Which reminds me, Al. I have to give Ernie a call. Then we can settle down."

Around noon on Monday at the Jets home field in the Jersey Meadowlands complex, Al Ososki saw the unsigned kicker Pete Dose emerge from the locker room and walk toward him. He knew Dose, as he knew most everyone in the league.

"I'll need a few footballs, Dose said. "I'm being worked out. My agent's back there with Ernie Wright. After the workout. you'll probably sign me."

Bub Harris walked toward Ososki. Behind him were a pair of tall men wearing football cleats and sweatsuits. Ososki recognized the Fortunato brothers.

"Al, Tommy and Danny are going to do some kicking with Mr. Dose. See if you can round up some footballs. If Dose asks what we're doing, we're working out other guys, too," he added.

Ososki looked at Bub's tanned face. The older man's expression was unreadable but Ososki saw a glint in the steely blue eyes. He remembered the previous morning. He remembered Bub's reputation. He decided to watch carefully.

Ernie Wright adjusted the seat in the ground level box. Pete Dose's agent Sam Hotchkiss sat beside him. The agent simply refused to keep quiet.

"I know I've got you Wright," he said in his usual nasal tone. "There are no other kickers available. I've checked the same as you. Add $100,000 to your offer and my guy signs. Simple." He stopped briefly and laughed. The laugh, like everything about Sam, including his reputation, aggravated Ernie Wright.

"Who are those other two guys over by Pete?" Hotchkiss asked.

"You think you know everything? I've got other guys to work out," Wright said. He hoped Bub Harris had something up his sleeve.

He'd have to sign Dose if things went wrong, and $100,000 extra to the weasel beside him would ruin Wright's season.

"Ha" snorted Sam Hotchkiss.

Pete Dose completed his series of stretching exercises. He walked over to where Ososki waited, near the field's 10 yard line. A pile of footballs nested on the artificial carpet. Down the field, a few players had been recruited to catch the balls and return them.

Dose began a series of kicks. His motion was fluid and practiced. The kicks hung in the bright sky, initially at 65 yards and gradually a bit longer.

He seemed unaware of the other two men, until the first kick beside him. Tommy Fortunato's first try matched Dose's for height, and the 65 yard distance was respectable. Danny Fortunato matched his brother on the first attempt.

"Not bad," Sam Hotchkiss said to Ernie Wright in the box. "But wait until Pete opens up. Then your other guys can go home. I hope you brought the contract with you." His sneer predicted the outcome.

On the field, Pete Dose was surprised. The kicks of the other men matched his own in height. Worse, their distance was steadily increasing. He boomed his next effort skyward, and 75 yards downfield, a Jet player scooped it into his arms and raced to the sideline.

The player returned to position. Tommy Fortunato's next three kicks matched Pete Dose's longest. Two of Danny Fortunato's were even longer, and one came down 80 yards away.

Pete Dose turned for a better look at the two dark-haired men beside him. He recognized neither. Both seemed relaxed, as if enjoying a good time. He did recognize Bub Harris, though, who was feeding them balls. Dose glanced over at the box where he knew Sam Hotchkiss sat with Ernie Wright. He hoped things were going smoothly.

"You're right, Sam," Ernie said to the man beside him. I've got a contract with me. In fact, I've got two of them. Would you like to guess what the numbers are on them, Sam?" He was pleased to note the bead of sweat forming on the upper lip of Sam Hotchkiss. He was even more pleased at Sam's silence.

On the field, a few additional Jets players had gathered. They knew the team's need for a kicker. They knew Pete Dose and his capabilities. They wondered where Bub Harris found two other kickers as good as Pete Dose.

"The one on the left kicks better than Pete," one player said. "He's hit three for 80 yards. Big, too, isn't he?"

The kicking duel continued for another 15 minutes. Danny Fortunato was clearly the winner. Tom Fortunato's efforts had equalled Pete Dose in every respect.

"Thanks, Pete," Bub Harris said to Pete Dose. "You can get dressed now. We'll be staying." He took the two Fortunato brothers to the far side of the field.

Ernie Wright turned in his seat. He looked at Sam Hotchkiss squirming beside him. It was a sight he hadn't dreamed he would see.

"Well, Sam, I repeat my offer for Pete one more time. The going rate, without the extra 100 grand. Tell me now, or forget it. Bub's waiting for me. Nice workout, wasn't it?" He could hardly keep from grinning.

"We'll take it," Sam said. He knew what he'd just witnessed. Pete Dose joined them. In a matter of minutes the paperwork was completed. Both left the stadium quickly.

In the locker room downstairs, Bub Harris chatted with the two Fortunato brothers.

"Thanks guys. I appreciate you working out with me today. Danny, I'm glad you told me yesterday you and Tom had a week off, and with not much scheduled you'd have fun kicking."

"No problem, Bub. We enjoyed every minute of it."

"Not as much as I did," Bub replied. And my boss, too, if my guess is right. What was the name of that charity you mentioned, Danny?"

"The Douglaston Volunteer Ambulance Corps, Bub. Why?"

"Don't be surprised if the Jets make a donation." Bub saw Al Ososki come into the room in time to hear the end of the conversation. "Say hello to Al, again, guys, I'm sure he enjoyed your workout, too.

The $10,000 check made out to The Douglaston Volunteer Ambulance Corps was signed by Ernie Wright. It was sent to the home of the Fortunato's with a brief note.

"Kindly forward," the note read. "The N.Y. Jets are uniquely pleased to make this contribution in your name, at the suggestion of Bub Harris and with my full personal endorsement. We both wish you highly successful careers. Ernie Wright's signature appeared above his typewritten name. Below, he'd added a handwritten comment: If you decide on a career change in the next few years, please give me a call. Ernie."

4

The Smell of Incense

In the area where Shea Stadium in a future day would echo to cheers for the New York Mets, Kevin Sullivan had once been an altar boy.

Not by choice. His mother thought Kevin would make a perfect Pope, but she knew he would have to start as a priest. Altar boy experience would give Kevin an edge on the competition as well as an early start towards Popehood, so when he reached fifth grade she signed him up as an altar boy.

Four years later Mrs. Sullivan conceded her plan hadn't worked. In the interim Kevin helped at hundreds of masses, weddings, funerals and baptisms. Sometimes he hummed Gregorian chant. He often assisted at High Mass. In this rite Kevin held up a triple chain on which was suspended a gold cup called a thurible. In the thurible was a two inch hard cube of black incense. The priest lit the incense and they watched blue smoke rise. Kevin liked the smell of burning incense.

Mrs. Sullivan's plan failed because when other boys discovered girls, Kevin discovered girls. His interest in priesthood or Popehood vanished. Mrs. Sullivan, always flexible, shifted her hopes.

She felt if Kevin went to a good college and earned high grades he might someday lead General Electric or General Motors. She would suffer his absence if he had to live in Schenectady or Detroit, though she decided she wouldn't move with him. She encouraged the new option at every opportunity.

Kevin's decision to aim for good grades traced totally to his pursuit of Helen Curran, a tall redhead with interesting legs. Helen favored intelligent boys.

Thirty years later Kevin Sullivan and Helen were parents of two boys and one girl and lived in Alexandria, Virginia, where Kevin commuted to Washington, D.C. and his job with the FBI. A graduate of Georgetown, Kevin enjoyed writing stories in his spare time. His eye for detail helped both his job and his hobby. In the meantime, two Vatican Councils effected major changes in the American Catholic Church.

Traditionally, Mass was celebrated at an altar, often of marble. The priest who said Mass faced the altar with his back to the congregation.

After the councils most marble altars disappeared, replaced by simple tables. Priests now faced the congregation. At the same time, many people formerly in the congregation also disappeared, alerted by the councils to freedom previously unattainable.

Kevin Sullivan's attendance at a meeting in Manhattan in early September was scheduled for 10:00 on Monday. He came to New York and checked into a room at the Hilton. On Saturday he bought a small brooch for Helen and then enjoyed dinner with his mother in her comfortable apartment in Stuyvesant Town.

Early Sunday Kevin realized he could enjoy the warmth and sun of a Manhattan morning because his meeting preparation was complete. He now attended church only on special occasions.

Kevin planned development of a short story which featured a heroine named Monica. He rode the First Avenue bus to 80th Street and strolled casually a few blocks East, where 80th Street ended in an overlook. Below him cars sped in both directions on East River Drive. Across moving traffic he saw a shirtless jogger pump his way uptown. Beyond the jogger the blue waters of the East River sparkled in the sunlight.

Kevin smiled. He wondered if his heroine, hot-blooded Monica, might respond to the jogger's bare-chested appeal.

Kevin walked to 79th Street, turned East and was nearly to First Avenue when he glanced to his right and saw a red brick Catholic Church. Its black bulletin board identified the church as St. Monica's, a coincidence which drew another smile. Alongside the door on a marble stone he read "Incepta MDCCCCV." Founded 1905. On impulse, Kevin Sullivan went inside.

He found a seat on the end of a dark mahogany pew three rows from the back. Above him, light filtered through red and blue stained glass windows which towered over a congregation with many grey heads, a congregation far older than in the days of his youth.

A High Mass was in progress. Behind him an organ led a choir which handled "Kyrie-ay, Kyrie-ay-lay-uh-son" without strain. He settled comfortably on the hard, dark seat.

At the head of the church an old priest with his back to the congregation faced a Carrara marble altar. St. Monica's Church had resisted one change. The priest wore an elegant green robe whose back displayed a maroon center panel with a shining gold cup. Three women wearing black cassocks under lace surplices assisted the priest, another change from Kevin's altar boy days when all assistants were male.

The organ music stopped. The priest and his assistants gathered at the altar. One woman raised the top of a gold thurible and the priest hunched over. Kevin recognized the procedure. The priest lit the incense and at once a spiral of blue smoke rose from the thurible.

The priest gathered the gold chains of the thurible, walked a few rows up the middle aisle and saluted the congregation by waving the smoking censor toward them.

Though St. Monica's boasts a high ceiling it is a small church. Kevin anticipated the smell of the incense before the priest walked toward him. A smile which began at the corner of his mouth disappeared as a pungent aroma reached his waiting nose.

He inhaled. He turned to the frail, elderly, black-coated woman beside him, for he'd recognized the new and stronger aroma. After an impulsive look at her lined face he fled St. Monica's as quickly as he had entered.

The woman's preparation for Mass had included covering herself with a liniment so strong it overwhelmed the aroma of incense.

Ben Gay....

.... a link to Kevin's past, as intense as when his mother had smeared gobs of the stuff on his skinny chest at the slightest sign of a cold. Today, with traditional congregations much older, Ben Gay probably held more meaning than incense.

Ben Gay?

In the bright white light of Sunday morning Kevin Sullivan wondered if his lusty heroine Monica might use Ben Gay, or if she had even heard of it. He pondered the question as he looked out the window of the downtown bus.

—m—

5

The Deal

My father came to New York from Italy as a boy. He apprenticed in a barber shop downtown, saved his money and opened his own place, a narrow 2-chair set up with his friend Amerigo Spada on West 28th Street, on the edge of the garment district.

I grew up in Queens, an only child. I attended parochial schools and New York University, and began at NYU Law School where I stayed for two years until my funds ran out and I couldn't afford more tuition.

My Uncle Lou came for a visit one night soon after, at my father's request. We sat in our small kitchen. My mother disappeared without being asked.

"Tell him," my father said to me. At work he was a man of few words who listened well and gave a good haircut while letting his friend Spada do the talking. At home he didn't talk much unless he had something to say. It paid to listen.

I explained my predicament to Uncle Lou, my father's brother who is short and barrel chested and balding like my father. I didn't know what he worked at. He was always well dressed. I saw him infrequently at family parties, weddings and funerals.

Uncle Lou sat at our table holding a long cigar. He waited until I finished. Then he looked at my father before speaking to me.

"I'll help you, Thomas," he said. "I'll pay tuition and expenses for your last year at school. It's not free. When you finish, you owe me one year's work."

I knew enough to be quiet. I looked at my father.

"One year, clean work?" my father asked.

Uncle Lou tapped his cigar on a glass ashtray and paused. He looked at me and then at his brother.

"One year, clean work," Uncle Lou repeated.

My father nodded at me.

"It's a deal," I said. "Thank you, Uncle Lou."

I graduated from NYU Law School and at my father's suggestion rented a small office up the block from his barber shop. He helped me get started, often sending people to see me. On one occasion a new client arrived with shaving cream still on his face.

A year later I looked up one morning. Uncle Lou arrived. He wore a neat, dark business suit. With him was a man nearer my age than his, also well dressed. The other man held a black leather briefcase with a shiny brass clip.

Uncle Lou didn't waste words.

"Our year begins today," he said. "Meet Carmine Falvo. He'll tell you what I want done."

"Yes," I said.

"My regards to your father," Uncle Lou said. He went out the door, leaving me with Carmine Falvo.

Carmine settled his expensive blue suit in the chair beside my desk. A tall man with wavy dark hair and broad shoulders, his smile exposed perfect white teeth, like mine. He told me his age, which surprised me, because he looked ten years younger. I've always been taken for younger, too.

"What do you want to do?" Carmine asked me.

"What?"

"In business. What do you want? It's important we know what you want."

I noticed the "we."

"Odd you should ask. I'd like to be in show business," I said, "but I can't sing or dance. I have a good voice, and I'm thinking of the radio/announcers course at NYU."

"You want to be an announcer?"

"I'm not sure. Maybe station management or something like that. I can always be a lawyer," I reminded him, "though I don't find it too exciting."

"Good enough. Now you'll learn what you'll be doing for us. My instructions are keep it clean. No funny business from us or you."

I knew what he meant. I was grateful my father had drawn the line. Carmine continued.

Uncle Lou's organization owned interests in a number of businesses. They had been invited to participate in a series of real estate purchases in Providence, Rhode Island.

"We need someone to go to Providence and check out these situations for us," Carmine explained. "Investigate the titles to the properties. Find out who the owners are and for how long and anything else which might apply if we decide to invest. This isn't a short-term project and the discussions have just begun. We figure a year before we have to make a commitment."

"Full-time?"

"No. You'll need your practice here because Lou tells me we'll be paying you half rate. Put everything in writing. Someone will pick up your work at the end of each month. If you can spend two weeks a month in Providence you'e okay. We'll cover expenses but keep it reasonable. And confidential," Carmine added.

I had his word and he had mine. No fooling around, is what Carmine meant. Keep your mouth shut. He didn't have to tell me.

It was easy working out a schedule to handle Uncle Lou's project. Once admitted to the Rhode Island bar I spent two weeks a month in a motel in Providence, which turned out to be a large, bustling, clean, interesting and complicated city.

By mid-year I was expert in Rhode Island real estate law. My trips through the maze of interlocking real estate directorates opened my eyes to all kinds of transactions, legal and illegal. A half dozen prominent families whose lineage in Providence traced back over a hundred years seemed to be into everything. Some scams were so blatant they surprised me, and after a year in New York's courts I didn't surprise easily.

For relaxation I listened to the radio. My work involved a lot of driving and the car radio introduced me to more than a dozen stations with a marvelous variety of formats. I wondered how so many stations could stay in business.

At year's end I completed my reports. Carmine's courier picked up the final package the same day I considered an offer to join Citibank's mortgage department. It would provide me a steady income and I could take the announcer's course at NYU. I made the change, which included a good salary, a meaningless 'real estate associate' title and no great loss when I closed up my law practice.

The courier brought a $5,000 money order from Uncle Lou a few days later. The accompanying note read "You did fine work. Appreciated. A good deal. My thanks and best wishes to the family. Lou." I tucked the note away for future reference. I concentrated on my future career as an announcer.

At graduation, announcing jobs proved scarce. I remembered the many stations in Providence and sent a simple resume to each. The resume included my attendance at NYU as a history major and my job at Citibank. No sense in being rejected as overqualified.

An AM-FM station in Providence offered me an announcer's job, which I accepted. Uncle Lou's bonus meant I could cover my expenses on a low salary while I established myself. The job lasted three months. The station went out of business.

The Providence Journal's want ads offered a combination announcer/station manager job at WFAL. I applied and met the general manager, Geoffrey Wilson. Wilson's hearty welcome, his overendorsement of my limited background and my hiring all took place quickly.

I began working as an announcer while attempting to absorb the details needed at a well-managed station. My assignments increased.

My work week, initially 40 hours, increased to the point after three months I worked more than 65 hours weekly.

Then, disaster. My monthly paycheck did not arrive. I tried to contact Wilson but he was unavailable. "On vacation" his secretary told me. I worked the following two weeks, adding his duties to mine. I was nearly exhausted when, at the end of the month, Wilson finally returned. Early on a Friday morning I found him at his desk.

"I've been looking for you," I said.

"You've been fired," was Wilson's immediate response. His tone was a sneer, accented when he rose to his full height, almost a foot taller than my own. "Now, get the hell out of here, you wop bastard."

"You owe me two months pay," I reminded him.

"Try and get it," he said. "You'll need a lawyer, greaseball, and there isn't a lawyer in town who would dare cross my father."

"Your father?"

"Preston P. Wilson."

"Your father doesn't concern me," I said. "I want the two months' pay you owe me, and I'm asking you for it. Again."

"So that's why this job was open," I said, as I prepared to leave Geoffrey Wilson's office. "You've done this to others?"

"All of them," he said. "There's a sucker born every minute."

"I'm sure there is, I said. I remained much calmer than the circumstances might require. I remembered Preston Wilson was in my research for Uncle Lou, and I knew where I could find what I needed.

I checked out of my motel and returned to New YOrk, where I reviewed all my Providence files. A good lawyer keeps a copy of everything. Carefully, I avoided Providence for two months, during which I met a dark-haired, brown-haired beauty named Anna who helped fill my idle hours.

I asked my father to have Uncle Lou or Carmine call me before I returned to Providence, and the call reached me three nights later, early in the evening. Carmine.

"You have a question, Thomas, about Providence?"

"Yes. Do you or Uncle Lou have a problem with my personal lawsuit against Preston P. Wilson which will cost him over a million dollars?"

"I'll call you back, Thomas."

The phone rang at nine. Carmine didn't waste time.

"Any problems you might cause Preston P. wilson and his associates will please us greatly, Thomas."

"Thank you."

When I reached the reception desk at the law firm handling the affairs of Preston P. Wilson, a frosty secretary examined me with cold eyes before accepting the business card I handed her.

"You're an announcer, sonny?" she asked.

"You may tell the senior partner, J.J. Richardson, it is in his best interests and those of Preston P. Wilson he see me immediately" I said, to the tune of $2,000,000. Each hour or fraction he wastes is going to cost Mr.Wilson an extra $5,000. I've added another $5,000 so they can send you to charm school. Shall I wait or come back tomorrow?"

I can be unpleasant to deal with.

The sudden appearance of J.J. Richardson suggested the receptionist had conveyed my complete message. He fit the stereotype of a dry, expensive, prosperous lawyer. A thin man in his fifties, he wore gray pinstripe pants, a striped tie, a white shirt and suspenders. He didn't seem pleased.

"How nice of you to see me," I began. "Is there some place we might talk privately?"

I sat facing him across his enormous, expensive desk. He peered at me as if I were a specimen which had crawled out of his wife's flower pot. I took a packet of papers from my large legal briefcase and put them on a corner of his desk.

"You'll find here a series of affidavits for a class action lawsuit on behalf of myself and 8 former announcers at station WFAL, which is owned by the Wilson interests, as you know," I said. "The suit is for $15,000,000. We are willing to settle for $1,000,000 today, plus ownership of WFAL, plus $5,000 for you to send your receptionist to a school which will teach her politeness," I said," and finally, the permanent removal of Geoffrey Wilson from WFAL, from Providence, and if possible, from Rhode Island."

"You are a crazy person," said J.J. Richardson, in a thin reedy voice appropriate to the severe decor in his leather-filled office.

I met his stare with my own, and continued talking without breaking off eye contact.

"If you choose not to settle it will be my painful duty to call to the attention of the courts the interlocking Wilson directorates involved in Longblue Properties, Station Properties, R & C Incorporated, White Meadows Nursing Home, the Elmwoods Tower now under construction downtown and eleven documented instances of stock manipulation engaged in by Preston P. Wilson, his associates and his legal counsel in the past 11 years."

I paused. I learned the value of the dramatic pause from my father.

"That's for openers," I said. "If you're wondering, I have copies and photostats of every applicable document. I have a substantial collection of falsified signatures on official documents, affidavits signed by people known to be deceased, and secret ownership of at least a dozen corporations involved in ghetto real estate, pornography and insider trading in large local corporations."

J..J. Richardson stared at me. In his cool and comfortable air-conditioned office two beads of perspiration appeared at the top of his narrow forehead and trickled down his temple.

"You'll need an attorney and nobody in Providence would dare take us on," he bluffed. Senior partners know all the lines.

"I'm an attorney. Admitted to the Rhode Island bar, and only too happy to prove my competence," I said.

"That idiot Geoffrey hired an attorney?"

"He forgot to ask," I conceded. "He also forgot to send my paycheck along in the 60 days Rhode Island allows after two requests. Have you checked the statutes lately?"

"When do you want what you want?"

"Today," I reminded him. I smiled. I knew it would annoy him. I also reminded him the documents in question were matters of public record. They could disappear only if eleven separate public buildings suffered simultaneous fires, which seemed unlikely.

Now, two years later, Anna and I enjoy our Providence lifestyle. It's really a nice city and we plan to raise our children here.

In case you're wondering, a few months after I became owner of station WFAL a check arrived in the mail from Uncle Lou. The face amount of the check was $5,000 and the card enclosed with it read "Recent confusion at Wilson Property Management in Providence meant big profits for us. Thanks for your help. Lou."

I returned the check in the next day's mail. With it I sent my own brief note.

"Thank you for the card and the enclosure, which I'm returning with gratitude because I don't deserve it. A deal's a deal and you paid me the first time. With appreciation. Thomas."

—m—

6

Kathryn's Lottery List

I bore easily. It's one of my faults. I'm a good person and smarter than most. I'm organized and I plan ahead.

Gold letters on the big frosted window of my Long Island office identify my present occupation.

"Investigations."

Underneath and off to one side I've added "K.Keller." The office is one big room in an old storefront. Its door opens onto the sidewalk. You can't see in the window or through the door's glass. I have a back door, more room than I need and a basement for storage. The rent is low, which is nice. I park my vintage Volkswagen cabriolet with its ruined grey canvas top and scarred orange body in the alley behind the building. When I disconnected the car's speedometer it showed 190,000 miles. I come and go as I please.

I like to decorate and I'm good at it. As soon as I signed my lease I used my hammer and tools and a load of wood. I built two bookcases. I built a desk and a table. I painted the walls white, then using a sponge added a repeat pattern of peach swirls. Not for everyone. I love it.

I still have one big problem, which is the rotten floor around the desk. There's a big hole right in front of my desk, partly covered by a thin sheet of plywood. It's hidden by a fake oriental rug I found at a garage sale and bought because the colors harmonize with my walls. The rug's really too big for my desk and and two chairs and more

58

of it sticks out between me and the door than I'd like but it hides the hole until I finish the floor.

On the wall behind my desk is my college diploma. If you read it carefully you'll see it says "cum laude." With honors. Not the smartest in the class, but smart enough. It represents nine years of night school at five different colleges.

Now I'm in law school. Two years behind me, one year to go. "Investigations" means I do research for a number of lawyers too busy or successful to do it themselves. I get the work by haunting the courtrooms. I watch and listen.

"You did a nice job." I tell an attorney if I'm impressed. "I do investigations work." I hand over one of my cards. I've been at it three years now. It pays the rent and keeps me even with the guys at the garage when they fix my Volkswagen, which is all the time.

School just ended for the summer. I'm waiting on my grades. My guess is nothing lower than a B, maybe an A. I don't dwell on the past. I always look ahead.

My future includes winning the lottery. Someone has to win. It will be me. Each morning I buy one lottery ticket. If it doesn't win, I'm that much closer. For five years I've kept a list of what I'll do when I win the lottery.

When I drive around Long Island I think of my lottery list. I change it in my mind, adding new ideas and removing others. Sometimes I visit my girlfriend in Maine. I'm godmother to her five-year-old daughter. I think of my lottery list all during the long drives. Every Monday I make all my changes. Then I throw out the old list. I keep the new one on my desk where I can see it.

Today is Tuesday. It's sunny and I have enough work to occupy most of my morning. In the afternoon I'm off to the beach for some sun. Later, I'll stop by the Las Margaritas Bar in Oceanside. I love Pina Coladas. I'm also friendly with Richie, a cop in Garden City who tends the bar on his days off. Richie's okay but he has a tattoo on his arm which says "Rosie." Richie likes me. I'm a blonde and he likes blondes. I like tattoos if they say "Kathryn" but not "Rosie." Richie's a body builder and he likes exercise. I consider all exercise a form of mental retardation. Richie and I aren't destined for togetherness.

By 9:00 I've bought my lottery ticket, coffee, a roll and a newspaper and hurried to the office where I've begun sorting out my latest assignment, a credit check on four used car dealers by an insurance company. Some of the statements contradict each other. Once I figure out who's fooling who I'll check the lottery and head for the beach.

I hear a tinkling sound and look up.

The bells over my door announce the arrival of an unscheduled guest, a nicely groomed brunette in her middle forties. I rush to the door and lead her to my desk. She sits down beside me.

"You're Kathryn Keller?" she asks. It's obvious something is bothering her. Something is bothering me. I forgot to lock the entrance last night when I went out the back. I'm lucky the room isn't empty.

"Yes. Who are you?"

"Vivian. Vivian Arnette, and I've got a serious problem. I've just been to the courthouse and I've got to hide somewhere.

Anywhere." She looks over her shoulder as if someone might be following her. She's distracting me and I don't like it.

"Wait a minute," I say. I walk over and lock the front door.

"Thank you," she says.

"Why me?" I ask as I return to my desk. I push my lottery file and newspaper to one side.

"A paralegal at the courthouse suggested I come see you. Her name is Amy Bedell."

She hands me a card.

I recognize Amy Bedell's name before I look at the card. She works with a group who collect child support for divorced mothers and advise battered women of their legal rights. Amy Bedell has referred two lawyers to me. I owe her. I look at the card.

"Vivian's husband is NUTS," Amy had written. "Help her.!!!"

Subtle.

"What's the problem?" I ask.

"My husband owns a large company. When he started beating me I learned he's a cocaine addict. I can't handle the beatings or the cocaine. It's not pretty. I filed for divorce. He's threatened to kill me. I have money but I don't know where to hide and I'm sure he's after me. All I need is a few days, but at the courthouse only Amy Bedell did anything. Will you help me?"

I don't have much choice.

"Follow me," I say. I lead Vivian Arnette out the back door and soon we're in my car. I take her to Las Margaritas, which is just opening. We go inside, where I have Vivian take two twenties and hand them to the bartender in exchange for letting her stay until Richie arrives.

"Rotten problem," I say to myself on the return drive, quickly distracted by a change on my lottery list. I remember an ad for Switzerland. Definitely worth a visit.

The Volkswagen coughed when I turned off the key. I went in the back of the office and locked the door. The air inside was stuffy. I went to the entrance, opened the door and looked outside. A major mistake.

"Where is she?" asked the tall, grey-haired man who faced me. His tone was unfriendly and under other circumstances I would ignore him. It is difficult to ignore a hand holding a heavy silver gun pointed at your breastbone.

"Who?" I asked.

"I saw her go in here an hour ago. Walk inside and don't do anything stupid. I'm going to kill her and me, and maybe you, too.

I walk inside and he follows me. I'm not about to do anything stupid. My one contact with guns occurred when I allowed myself to buy one. It's in a bottom desk drawer. I don't remember how it loads.

"She's not here," he announces."

I'm shaking. I wonder if I'll die soon. I can't look at the man's gun. I sit at the desk and remember I forgot to check the lottery.

"Where did she go?" he demands.

"Out," I admit.

He's standing beside my desk. He lets his right hand, the one holding the gun, drop to his side. He stares at me. His eyes are wide, his hair uncombed. He wears a white shirt with no tie, and the top two buttons are buttoned wrong.

To my surprise, I've stopped shaking. I wonder if my mind is working. I touch the underside of the desk, which starts a recorder.

"You're going to kill her?" I ask.

"Yes. Just as I told you. And then myself. If you don't tell me where she is I'll kill you, and then I'll find her anyway. I don't know your name, and I don't care. Too bad."

He stares at me.

I don't like this man. I stare back at him. He knows who has the gun.

I open my mouth as if to speak and he watches me. I stand up slowly, hands on the desktop. I look him in the eye. I remember something my mother told me.

"Use your head, Kathryn," she said, so many times. "Use your head."

I do not use my head. Instead I turn it to my left while I talk.

"Here's the address where your wife is," I say. I hear a noise. He moves. I turn my head. I see him fall through the hole in the office floor, grabbing in vain at the paper on my desk. It is an eleven foot drop. The doors in the basement are steel. They are both locked. There are no windows. Unless he is Superman he's trapped.

I do not wait to find out. I'm out the back door and around the corner and dial 911, and in five minutes three police cars arrive, sirens screaming.

The next hour is busy. The police eventually get to the basement and find the man has carried out his threat. He's killed himself. There's a lot of blood and a lot of questions and I tell them where they can find Mrs. Arnette. They let me go for coffee, and I notice my hands are shaking again. The coffee helps.

I return to my office. Another officer has retrieved the papers from the basement. Many of them are spattered with blood. He has thoughtfully put a piece of clear plastic on my desk before putting the papers on it. He wears a short-sleeved shirt and I notice he has no tattoos on his arms. He's not Richie.

"I have to talk with you," he says, "but first, do you want these?"

"No," I say. I'm sure I will get many more papers from the insurance company and the whole pile is messy.

"Do you have a basket?" he asks.

"Right there."

He wraps the bundle and shoves it in my wastebasket. I apologize for the delay but messes bother me. I take the basket outside and put it on the curb for collection.

He asks me lots of questions. I tell him what I know and give him the tape from my tape recorder. Finally, he leaves.

I reach for the newspaper. I check the lottery and my contact lenses fog. I've won at last!

I reach for my lottery list. It's gone.

I run to the entrance, open the door and see a huge white Nassau County garbage truck pull away from the curb. In front of me is my empty wastebasket.

"Wait" I scream. "Wait, wait, wait. You have my lottery list."

The truck picks up steam and I begin running, fast at first and then faster. Richie is right and I am wrong. Running is torture. Ahead, the truck stops for a traffic signal. I'm ten yards behind it when the light changes. The truck's driver accelerates in a cloud of blue smoke. He can't hear me, and he can't see me racing to catch him.

I turn into the nearest store. It sells lamps and lampshades. I need a place to sit down.

"Can I help you, miss?" asks a salesgirl. "Your face looks awfully red."

"Yes," I say. "Tell me about Switzerland."

"What?" she says.

"Oh, don't mind me," I say. She wonders what I mean. When I get my breath back I'll explain. I smile. She smiles back.

I change my mind. I get up and leave. I don't have time for explanations. If I hurry I can get a ticket for tomorrow's lottery. Someone has to win. It might as well be me. I can begin my new lottery list on the way over.

7

The Chess Players

Jim Chelsea needed a place to go. It had to be near mountains. He knew that. The first fourteen years of his life took place in Albany, New York. Near the Adirondacks.

So, Albany it would be.

He wrote his Aunt Emily, who still lived there, the only family member left. On his papers she was listed as "next of kin."

She wrote back. He was welcome to stay at her house until he was settled. Nice of her. He hadn't written since leaving in 1990. He was then 14 years old. Leaving hadn't been his idea.

Every year she sent him a card or a note. Wished him well. Expressed an interest.

In Washington, the Director himself took him to lunch. It was a nice touch and he appreciated it.

"Jim, you survived heavy action in the dangerous mountains in Afghanistan. You got three men out. You've been starved, beaten, shot. You've done enough for us. You'll be edgy, jumpy for months. React in strange ways. It's time to get out, for your sake."

"Thanks. I agree. I'll appreciate whatever help you can give me."

He'd begun his return to the real world by eating better, pleased his weight was up to 145. The doctors said time and rest would add the missing 50 pounds.

He'd chosen Albany but the agency made the phone calls. An associate professor's slot at RPI would be his in the Spring term.

The Fall term would begin in another month but he wasn't ready. He liked to prepare.

He paid off the Washington apartment and all his bills. At 6:00 a.m. he rose, quietly removed his gear and parked the gray Honda. He drove off a few blocks before he doubled back and parked, watching everything. It didn't hurt to be careful. He waited fifteen minutes, saw nothing unusual, and left.

In Philadelphia, he sold the Honda and replaced it with a new black BMW, a genuine go-fast machine. He didn't need hundred mile an hour speed but he wanted it. Just in case.

He cruised along the N.Y. Thruway north of Suffern, slouched down in the driver's seat. He didn't look his six foot height as he shifted his gaze to the speedometer. He kept the needle at a steady 65. No need to hurry. Break the car in slowly.

The August light was bright and cheerful. He felt the sun warming him through the windshield while he watched the signs as well as the scenery. He cruised past the first Albany exit, slowed and used the second. On target.

He maneuvered over to Western Avenue, then headed back into the city. He knew exactly where he was going, a route he'd followed many times in his youth. At Manning Boulevard he turned south, dipped up and down on the hilly road. A left turn onto New Scotland Avenue completed the navigation.

He turned into his aunt's driveway, parked and walked to the door. He read the name over the bell. Emily Douglas.

It was a typical Albany house. White, double decked with sun porch on a small plot, a neat lawn touching the sidewalk, and grass out back. He went up the three steps at the front and rang the bell.

When the door opened he saw his Aunt Emily, a large woman in her middle fifties, widowed after a short marriage. His father's sister.

She smiled at him. He was surprised, because he knew she was looking at a tall man whose clothes hung too loosely on him. His tan had faded and his eyes were dark hollows. His hands and wrists protruded. He hadn't bothered to buy new clothes. The old ones remained too large. Only his shoes fit.

Her welcome was warm and courteous. Warned of his arrival, everything was ready. She showed him to an upstairs bedroom, opened the closets and waved at the bath.

"When you're ready, visit the kitchen," she said. "We'll eat."

He had forgotten lunch. He helped himself to the generous supply of food and listened while she talked.

"I taught Math at Albany High for many years," she began. "Too many. When that meant thirty, I retired. Money is no problem. I've been active in politics here. It's amazing how much work there is if you look for it. It's what I do now. Mostly."

She shifted subjects.

"If you don't mind, call me Aunt Emily. Do I call you Jim?"

"Fine with me," he replied.

"I like you, Jim," she said. "I always did. I'm glad you're here."

It seemed to her he was devoting his entire attention to the food. In reality, he carefully surveyed her.

Her hair was dark and slightly gray. Her features were regular, not unlike his own, hardly surprising for his father's sister.

Her voice was even and well modulated, with perfect pronunciation. Listening carefully, he detected the words that gave away the strength of her vocabulary.

He knew already she was an unusual, cultured woman. The house featured oriental rugs on the floors. Excellent furniture. Chess pieces sat on a board inside, placed for action rather than show.

He would be careful, nonetheless.

"I'm pleased to be here," he said. "My company made some middle management changes, and suddenly I'm looking for a new job. I'd been sick awhile, too. Now it's recovery time."

"Money"? she asked, quietly.

"More than enough." It was the truth. "Can I share expenses with you while I'm here?"

"How long do you expect?" she asked. Her smile continued. He realized she was studying him.

"About a week or two. Then an apartment."

"Two weeks are on me. If you play chess." She laughed.

"I play."

In the morning, he rose early. Dressed carefully to conceal the healing scars on his arms and the bullet wound in his right leg. His back was stiff and even a casual touch on the right side was painful. The leather seat in the BMW had helped. The doctors said he would come around. He hoped so. He didn't believe in babying himself.

A note on the kitchen table read "help yourself." No sign of Aunt Emily.

He left quietly and began organizing. He visited RPI, displayed his Georgetown degrees. Experience in math and computers backed him with the dean, but no need. The man knew.

He returned to Albany, picked up a copy of the Times-Union and began checking apartments. At first, a survey of the area would be enough.

The day warmed. He drove the Northway as far as Glens Falls. It was a section he knew as a youngster. He drove further north on a country road, pulled off and parked. He walked into the woods and stopped.

From a crouch, suddenly, he spun. Metal gleamed momentarily. Ten yards away, two steel knives pinned a falling leaf to a tree. The knives saved his life in Afghanistan. He still carried them. He owed instructor Rob Stuart, big time.

He was back at the house on New Scotland Avenue before 6:00. Aunt Emily was waiting.

"Dinner at 6:15 okay with you?"

"Fine."

"We'll have company. Then the chess."

He should have known. Matchmaking. He'd been a poor marriage risk. The work was too dangerous.

A woman arrived precisely at 6:00. Nancy De Forest. Blonde, tall, a talker. She noticed a scar on his cheek.

"It's almost tooth-shaped, Jim," she laughed. "Someone bite you?"

"A girl. When I was 11. She lived up the block. Hard to forget when you see her work every time you shave." The truth.

"Chess time, Jim," Aunt Emily said. Nancy De Forest had gone. The board was moved to a table between two comfortable chairs. Aunt Emily poured some wine for herself. For him, a soft drink. No booze yet.

"Here it comes," he told himself. "The questions."

There were none. Instead, she put on some music, tuned it low. Dylan. A surprise. She located knitting needles and a partly completed shawl. Sat down. Picked up two pawns and gave him the choice. Black. She began.

He played tough, expert chess.

He would humor her. Analyze her game quickly. Perhaps spot her a queen.

Her opening was classic Ruy Lopez. She developed it perfectly. Subtly. Imaginatively. He saw a trap coming and looked across the board. She was nodding her head to the music, but she watched him. Momentarily her eyes sparkled. She glanced back at the knitting.

He fought for two hours. She gave him nothing. He returned no favors. She shifted the music. Beatles. Springsteen.

At 10:00 she rose from her chair.

"Jim, I have an early morning tomorrow. Perhaps we can play again two nights from now?" Her voice was even, her expression pleasant. He knew he had underestimated Aunt Emily. Always be careful.

"I'll clean up,' he said.

"Thank you, Jim," she replied. "You don't need anything up your sleeve when we play."

He watched her move towards the stairs. Had she seen the knives? She stopped and faced him.

"Jim, may I ask how you explain the white streak down the center of your hair? Your father had no gray at all until he was forty."

"A chemical imbalance is what the company doctor told me," he answered quickly. "Something to do with improper diet. That sort of thing."

"Thanks," Aunt Emily said.

He hoped the answer satisfied her. His hair was short, still growing back. It had been thick, brown, curly. The white streak was unexpected. He wished the pigment would return.

He located an apartment in the Menands area. A Tudor building. Three stories high. Private entrance, including garage. He rented the first floor. It was near St. Agnes Cemetery, which held both his parents.

Dinner was at 6:15. This time, another woman guest. Brunette, quiet, thirtyish. The food was excellent. Aunt Emily's skills continued to impress him. Cheryl Bruce did not. When she left, the chessboard was activated.

He drew white. For his opening move he decided on a sophisticated approach designed to deceive Aunt Emily. In five moves she recognized his strategy and foiled it.

She made her move. He looked up.

"Aunt Emily, what's the word on the local college math talent?"

"Students or teachers?"

"Teachers."

""Two giants, and only two. Dr. Anderson at SUNY is a brilliant mind, an excellent teacher. Late 60's, quiet. Dr. Adams at St. Rose is equally brilliant, early 30's and a snit. Says whatever he feels like, to anybody. They keep him because they have to."

"Anderson and Adams. A pair of A's," he said. He recognized his first light comment in months. Perhaps he was healing.

"Your move, Jim." Aunt Emily said. She tended to her knitting. He'd better tend to his.

He looked at the board. He knew her style already, subtle and exquisitely hidden traps. Her execution was errorless. He was about to move when he stopped. She had shifted her strategy. Bold. Sudden. If he made one quick move, he would lose.

He was pretending to study the board while he watched her. No clues furnished. She spoke to him as if from a distance.

"Jim, do you remember the name of the person who left the tooth mark on your face?"

"Sure do. Little Margaret. Also known as Little Poison. Last name Hayden. Lived near us on Magazine Street. Know where that is?"

"Out Western Avenue, of course. You forget I visited many times when you were a boy."

"Sorry," he said, and meant it. He struggled, finally won the game. He didn't apologize. He'd earned it.

"What's next, Jim?" she asked.

"I'll be taking a math course with one of the two math teachers you mentioned. I've already found a small apartment in Menands. We'll see what Spring term brings."

"Can you manage a chess night here on Wednesdays?"

"Certainly. Happy to play with you." He meant it. He'd like to play her regular opponents, too. They must be one sharp group.

He chose the St. Rose course. Three early mornings a week. The rest of the days would belong to him.

Jim sat in the last row of the classroom. There were only 8 students and 30 seats. When Adams called "Chelsea" Jim replied "here." The tall, heavy teacher didn't even look up from his roll book. He checked off students, closed the book. He stared at them before speaking.

"I am Doctor Adams," the man announced, arrogantly. "I know math better than anyone in the world. As far as I'm concerned, you are all nothing. It is a privilege for you to be in the same room with me." He looked slowly at each student. A personal sneer. He moved away from the blackboard and towards the door. The class, mostly youngsters, tried to fathom his nastiness. The man pointed at Jim Chelsea.

"You, skunk head," he said. "I don't like your expression." As he turned his back, he chuckled at his own humor.

A knife flashed through the air, embedded itself in the door.

Adams stood motionless. When he moved to free the knife his hand shook. He was unable to loosen the blade.

The small group watched the pale man with the white streak in his hair walk to the room's front. He removed the knife effortlessly and shouldered Adams aside.

Chelsea continued into the hall, strode directly to the Registrar's office and withdrew from the class.

He registered with Dr. Anderson at SUNY that same afternoon. It was Monday. In five days he would move to Menands.

The Wednesday night meal proved different. There were only the two of them yet Aunt Emily continued bringing platters from the kitchen. She matched Jim bite for bite. When he let out his belt, she smiled.

"I'm gaining, too," she said. "I've decided to fatten you up."

"Where's the bride-to-be tonight?" he answered. "Have you run out of eligibles?"

"What a shameful comment to your poor old aunt, who is just trying to keep you from being lonely." The statement was delivered with a straight face. Then she chuckled.

"As a matter of fact, she'll be here in a few minutes. Her name is Hillary Stevens. She's my chess guide."

"Your what?"

"Chess guide. I can't beat you myself. I've called up the reserves."

Jim grinned as he spoke again.

"She's hardened and experienced, somewhere around the age of 78," he said, as they moved to the chessboard.

"You'll see."

She opened with white, and he followed to the first move. From the kitchen, a young woman strolled in. She was tall and slender. Her auburn hair, worn short, curled around a graceful neck. She moved a chair alongside Aunt Emily, looked at the board and commented.

"You started without me."

"Hillary, meet my nephew, Jim Chelsea."

"The knife thrower," Hillary said.

"News travels fast," Jim replied.

"The what?" Aunt Margaret asked.

Hillary seemed to stare at Jim's hair.

"There's an opening for a math teacher at St. Rose," she said. She covered her mouth with a hand, laughed with her eyes. Blue.

She spoke again.

"Emily, if we're the white, let's crush this nephew and move on to bigger and better things. We'll need a plan."

The two women held a whispered conference. Both giggled. Jim found himself smiling.

Over the next hour, the women chatted, conferred, occasionally shared a comment with him. They made their moves quickly. They told him Hillary worked as a reporter for the Times-Union. They enjoyed themselves.

"Mate," Aunt Margaret said.

"I surrender graciously," Jim said. "You two are a ferocious combination."

He thanked them both and went up to his room. He considered the loss. It was no accident. They had beaten him soundly.

He reminded himself to be careful. Especially of Aunt Emily. He wondered what she did during the day. He liked Hillary Stevens, by far the most interesting of the women who came to dinner. Nice blue eyes. Almost too attractive.

How did she learn about Dr. Adams? He already regretted the incident. He would dye the white streak.

On Thursday, he shopped Central Avenue. In the afternoon, he donned sweats and began light jogging in Washington Park. Later, the scale at Aunt Margaret's revealed five pounds added. Regular meals and good cooking.

Friday he moved to Menands. The stores had cooperated and his deliveries were prompt. Finished, he drove the Thruway, tuned up the BMW. He slipped into the Stuyvesant Plaza shopping center, found photos of the Adirondacks. Good shots, soon to grace his walls. At a nearby store he bought skis.

Two days later, he spotted a blue Volvo behind him. Again. A tail. If he had been careless he would have missed it. At home he checked doors, windows. Bought new locks. Installed them himself. Temporary.

Chess night. A final game. After, he would move on. Too bad. He liked Albany.

"Your cooking skills are impressive, Aunt Emily," Jim said.

"Compliments always welcome," she replied. "Let's step inside. My chess guide is due again. We work well together."

"I noticed."

Hillary breezed in as they set up the board. Jim nodded, received a smile in return. The blue eyes danced. She turned to the older woman.

"Do we give him a chance or simply annihilate him?"

"Let's give him a second chance," Aunt Emily said.

The banter was cheerful and pleasant. Jim relaxed.

The game began. The women played the white. He found himself fully challenged. He concentrated.

"Don't move," a man's voice commanded. "Anyone."

The voice was behind Chelsea. Hillary stared over his shoulder. Aunt Margaret rested the knitting needles. Her shawl covered her lap.

He could sense an intruder behind him. A second man appeared behind Hillary. Medium height. Work clothes. Masked. The man held an automatic, trained it on Chelsea.

"Don't do anything stupid," he said. Low voice. Harsh. Accented.

His partner came out from behind Chelsea. Tall, muscular, gray jumpsuit. His left hand held a gun pointed at the floor. With his free hand he smacked Hillary across the back of the head, a glancing blow. Its impact threw her face onto the edge of the chessboard.

Chelsea tensed.

"Your trail was difficult," the first man said. "It took a long time to find you," said the second intruder.

"Get out of my house," Aunt Emily said.

"Shut up," one man retorted. Both men looked at her as she spoke.

Simultaneously, a pair of knives flew across the table from Hillary. Each struck an arm holding a gun. The guns fell.

"Freeze!" Aunt Emily shouted.

Jim turned.

His aunt held a pair of shiny pistols. Steady. One aimed at each of the intruders.

"Don't do anything stupid," she warned.

The mop-up operation was fast, efficient, professional. A squad of large men arrived, cuffed the two prisoners and hurried them out of the house.

"Coffee?" Aunt Emily asked. The threesome sat near the chessboard. Everyone else had left.

"Yes," Hillary said. Jim nodded. An excellent idea. Aunt Emily poured.

"You know, Jim," the older woman said, "you're entitled to a few explanations. I guess now is as good a time as any."

He nodded assent. To his right, Hillary poured a small amount of milk into her coffee.

"Cool one she is," he thought.

"They weren't after you, Jim," Aunt Emily said. "You might say you were the bait. We knew they would follow you."

"We?"

"The company, Jim. The CIA. We all worked for the same people. You. Me. Nancy De Forest. Cheryl. Hillary."

"You knew?"

"Jim," Aunt Margaret said, patiently. "I recommended you in the first place. Did you think they just called up Georgetown and asked for names?"

"You've known all these years?"

"I've followed your career with interest. And pride," she added. "Rob Stuart told me you were the best he ever trained with the knives. At least until Hillary came along."

He turned to the younger woman.

"I admire your work," he said, sincerely. Her knives had nailed the two intruders with lightning fast accuracy. Over the rim of the coffee cup, the blue eyes danced.

"Don't be such a nerd, Jim," Aunt Emily said. She felt the embarrassment in his flat tone.

"You're going to do fine in Albany," she continued. "It's time to look around. Just as my playmate is doing. Just as I can, now. Those two were after me, not you. We had to show you the blue Volvo three times until you took action. Then they followed you, thinking you would lead them to me."

She laughed. Hillary laughed. Jim flushed.

"Jim," Aunt Emily said. "Neither of us could possibly have survived in Afghanistan. You're tougher, more determined and more resourceful. You look for different things than we do, but at least you always react."

"What does that mean?" he asked, more curious than annoyed.

"Take a good look at my playmate over there, while she tries to stop giggling. Incidentally, her name isn't Hillary. It's Margaret. Margaret Hayden."

"Margaret Hayden?"

"You'll notice on her right cheek a mark just like yours, Jim. Even as a a boy you hit back, or, in at least one instance, bit back."

He turned to the younger woman. Her coffee cup was on the table. She met his gaze, impishly, but her expression broke. She looked quickly at Aunt Emily and then back to him.

"From Magazine Street?" he asked her.

"Yes," she smiled.

"Also known as Little Poison?"

"In some circles."

"Perhaps you would be kind enough to escort Margaret home while an older woman catches up on her beauty sleep," Aunt Emily said. "But please be careful. I'm specially fond of her."

"Why is that, Aunt Emily?" Jim asked, mischievously, as he rose from his chair.

"Good chess guides are so hard to find."

8

The Mentors

Margo Matthews reached for the buzzing ivory phone.

She was working on a fashion article in her cramped Lower East Side apartment at 10:00 on a Saturday morning in May. After three hours labor she thought she might finish by noon.

"Matthews," she said into the mouthpiece, frowning at the interruption.

"Good morning, Margo. Ted Donaldson."

"Nice to hear from you, Ted." Margo snapped to attention. Donaldson's power as Features Editor of the New York Times was known to every free-lance writer in the city. Margo had completed two major assignments for him, earning substantial checks. More satisfying had been his hand-written notes praising her work.

"Read my paper today?"

"Glanced at the front page, Ted. It's on the table. Been busy."

"Last night an unknown American soprano debuted at The Metropolitan Opera in the role of Aida. She was an emergency substitute. Our critic and all the others gave Alexandra Vann great reviews.

"A star is born."

"Exactly. What holds my attention is her age. She's 24 years old, which makes her a child in the opera world. Hardly anyone knew she existed, including our critic. I'd like you to do a piece on her as soon as possible. Objective is a cover story in the Sunday Magazine.

You're much closer to her age than our critic and I think it gives you a big advantage. Are you available, Margo?"

"By all means."

"I counted on it. A messenger is on the way with last night's program from the Met and a two-page biography from her agent."

"What's the agent's name?"

"Georgio Cherubini Associates."

"Never heard of them."

"Neither have I, to be truthful. Ted Donaldson's openness made writers feel at ease.

"Thanks, Ted. I'll get right on it."

"Good pictures help. I admired your others."

"I'll do my best."

She settled the phone in its cradle and put aside the fashion article, which carried no deadline. She knew she faced a busy weekend. Though the Times assignment was a plum, Margo did not intend it to interfere with her own wide-ranging interests. At the moment duplicate bridge led her activities, including games at The Regency Club on 57th Street on Saturday and Sunday nights.

To honor her new commitment would require a hurried trip to the library for materials on opera, about which she knew little, and a steady reading schedule for the next two days.

In The Times' office, Donaldson welcomed a waiting opera critic whose facial expression spelled unhappiness.

"Who the hell is Margo Matthews?" the critic began. Donaldson's note to him had struck a nerve, disrupting the critic's plan for a lengthy Alexandra Vann interview.

"Relax, C.J." Donaldson said. "You're the best in the business and we all know it. Alexandra Vann is 24 years old and Margo Matthews a few years older. Birds of a feather, you know, and it might mean an interview no man could get, even if he's as good as you are."

C.J's smile assured Donaldson the situation had calmed.

"To answer your question, C.J.,Margo Matthews is a bright graduate of Columbia's Journalism School. I've been encouraging her since she was a student in my classes. She's a hard worker and uses her imagination. By the way, if you passed her on the sidewalk you'd certainly look twice. Tall, dark hair and wears glasses though I'm not sure she needs them. Good looks aren't her secret, it's her manner. I think people like her because she's pleasant."

"I see, Ted. Thanks for the explanation." The appeased critic returned to his own office. Behind him, Donaldson realized he might have mentioned Margo's figure, but he hadn't. He chuckled.

Many blocks downtown Margo Matthews was leaving for the library when a messenger delivered The Times' package. She closed the door and began to read.

Alexandra Vann, age 24. Only child of socially prominent family in Raleigh, North Carolina. Presented in the Debutante Cotillion at 18, graduate of University of North CArolina at 21. Her aunt, Louise Winstead, is a voice teacher who recognized the girl's potential and supervised her training. When Alexandra graduated from college, Louise Winstead secured a New York audition with Georgio Cherubini Associates, the firm which manages Alexandra's development.

For three years New York teachers selected by Cherubini tutored Alexandra. She sang overseas with small Italian opera companies. Her major career breakthrough occurred two months earlier in San Francisco, when she replaced an ailing star in the title role of Aida and earned stunning reviews.

The coincidence of two emergency replacements, each overwhelmingly successful, did not escape Margo's notice. "Helps to be lucky, doesn't it," she thought. "Worth checking."

Accompanying the brief biography were photographs of Alexandra Vann in the role of Aida. She seemed taller than the rotund women Margo pictured as opera singers. A glamour photo of Alexandra's face showed a straight nose, good teeth and dark hair. Margo reserved her opinion of the soprano's appearance. Publicity photographers were paid to lie, and New York's deserved their reputation as best in the world.

The material provided a minimum of usable facts. More research would be needed for a Sunday Magazine cover story. Margo's fingers walked into the yellow pages and walked out with a plane ticket to Raleigh on an early Monday flight.

"Good morning," she greeted the receptionist at Raleigh's daily newspaper, the News & Observer. "I've an appointment with the Society Editor."

"Right this way."

"Good morning, Mrs. Gardiner," Margo began. "As I told you, I'm doing a story on Alexandra Vann for the New York Times. I'm looking for background on Alexandra and her family. In return," she smiled," I'll provide you a copy of my story and lots of NY material as a basis for your own story."

"Really?"

"Promise."

"Done," said the older woman. "How can I help you?"

The briefing lasted an hour. Using the phone in Mrs. Gardiner's office, Margo arranged an interview with Louise Winstead at the Vann estate, and once in the taxi she reviewed what she learned in the newspaper's files, and from listening to Mrs. Gardiner's commentary.

Alexandra Vann's wealthy parents wielded power in both Raleigh and the state of North Carolina. They lived with their only daughter in a white colonnaded mansion outside the city, attended by a small army of servants.

Mrs. Amanda Vann marched in and out of committee meetings aware of her power and willing to use it. Few people challenged her. The few who dared learned about the fist of steel inside the velvet glove. Her husband, Axel, a bald banker twenty years older than his wife, was renowned for his cold personality.

"When Axel Vann looks at you he wants something," Mrs. Gardiner said. "If he doesn't want something he doesn't bother to look. It's that simple. The man radiates the charm of an ice cube."

The newspaper file gave up an unexpected tidbit of information. Alexandra Vann, the daughter of Amanda Vann's first husband, was adopted by Axel Vann at the time of his marriage to Amanda, a marriage which immediately assured Axel membership in Raleigh

Society. Alexandra was then two years old. No further details were on file, nor would they be forthcoming.

"No one here is brave enough or stupid enough to ask either Vann for details," Mrs. Gardiner had explained.

Margo put aside her notes to study the tall green pines beside the blacktop road. Spring sunshine tipped the pine tops white. Below, tree trunks stood at attention like silent dark pencils planted in bunches. The scenery reminded her of country lanes in upstate New York. She stopped the driver and snapped photos which might be usable in her story.

Margo's thoughts turned next to the woman she would soon meet, aunt Louise Winstead. So far, she had nothing to work with, nor had the publicity release from Georgio Cherubini Associates provided much information.

As usual when confronting the unknown, Margo felt edgy. She wondered if her blue print dress, comfortable white shoes and worn leather bag were appropriate for a vast Southern estate. She tried to concentrate and instead found her thoughts drifting to Saturday and Sunday night bridge games where her improving scores offered hope for the future.

The taxi driver reached an elaborate entry. Beside it, a black sign displayed the word "Vann" in gold letters. He turned his car between gates 12 feet high into a private road almost totally in shadow from centuries-old trees. He proceeded another hundred yards and stopped at a compact modern house. His passenger exited. He would wait until she signaled him.

The door of the house opened. A tall woman in her forties emerged. She wore a white blouse and pastel green skirt. She smiled pleasantly. Her feet were bare.

"Margo Matthews?"

"Yes."

"I'm Louise Winstead. How nice to see you. Please come in and be comfortable." The woman's voice surprised Margo. It was not the polite drawl of a Southern lady but sounded similar, at least in part, to her own way of speaking.

Margo returned the smile, an automatic response. She felt confused and hoped her nervousness didn't show. She had interviewed business leaders, politicians, gangsters, plumbers and mechanics. Each time she had some idea of what to expect. This interview had started on a different note. Wondering how to approach Louise Winstead, Margo recognized the return of her earlier tension.

She saw an old Honda parked on gravel behind the modest house. There was no garage. Inside, the home's furnishings were few and functional. A Steinway grand piano, its black top braced open, graced a sunken living room. Framed paintings crowded white walls reaching upward to a beamed cathedral ceiling. Two armchairs had been drawn beside a redwood butler's table, and on it waited a pitcher of iced tea and a pair of tall glasses.

"Sit where you'd like, Margo, help yourself to some iced tea and let's get at it," the older woman began. "I know you're here on behalf of the New York Times and the subject is Alexandra Vann. I'll answer most all proper questions. The others, the ones where you step on my toes, we'll know right away. I hit a toe and you move on to your next question."

Both women laughed. Margo relaxed. She settled herself in one of the chairs and quickly summed up the woman who faced her.

Louise Winstead enhanced a lively personality with dark eyebrows, nice teeth and untamed auburn hair gathered into a ponytail. Her eyes were alert. She tucked a foot under her as she adjusted her posture. A spot of blue paint on one hand suggested Louise painted the pictures on the walls. Margo would get to that if time permitted. At the moment the subject was Alexandra Vann.

"Tell me about Alexandra, please."

"Where do I begin?"

"Anywhere." An open-ended interview would give Margo the chance to listen and observe.

"Alexandra lived in the large mansion further up the road outside my window. Her parents are people of strong views, not necessarily inclined to allow for the frailty of children. One result was Alexandra spent a lot of time with me while she was growing up. In my twenties

I journeyed to New York as a voice student," Louise said, "and earned a degree in music education. This proved fortunate when I moved back to Raleigh, because private voice students supported me while I pursued what has become my major interest, painting."

Margo glanced at the large collection of framed art on the room's walls. Louise Winstead waited for her attention.

"You had to support yourself?" Margo asked. "Living on an estate?"

"It was necessary," Louise added. "Alexandra often dropped in while I was teaching. One day after my students departed she asked if I would play while she sang. It was then I first recognized the unique voice I helped develop to world class by the time she completed her college studies."

"World class? Your ear is that good?"

"I consulted with others, to be honest," Louise admitted. Experienced others."

"Names?"

"My toe hurts," Louise said. "Next question, please."

"Their advice then, if I may ask?"

"You may and I'll tell you. There was agreement on the best course of action, which was recommend Alexandra to Giorgio Cherubini Associates in New York for an audition. No promises. Take the chance and see what happens."

"What made you think Cherubini would audition her?"

"I maintain New York connections. It's where I sell my paintings."

"How did her parents react to your decision?"

"It was my recommendation, Margo, not my decision Alexandra decided she would go to New York. I suspect both parents were furious."

"But you don't know?"

"No, I do not. My relationship with my sister and her husband has been strained for some time. Factually, as you might write it, her husband and I no longer speak to each other."

"For how long?"

"Another toe hurts. Next question."

Margo sensed her questions were probing delicate areas. But so far Louise Winstead had been honest. The woman was obviously no fool, and her eyes, though friendly, were watchful. Time to shift gears.

"What did Alexandra major in at North Carolina U.?"

"Mathematics." A surprise.

"Why?"

"For one thing, she's a natural mathematics student. It comes easy for her. For another, her father would not pay for any college unless she chose a major he approved."

"He what?"

"He controls the money. As you might know already and I suspect you do, he's accustomed to getting his own way. All the time."

There was no bitterness in Louise's voice, but little warmth either.

"What did Alexandra want to major in?"

"Physical education."

"What?"

"Margo, I thought you knew. Alexandra is a fine soccer player, a swimmer and a golfer. In other words, an athlete. When you check her college yearbook, and I'm sure you will, you'll find her on the golf team, a major achievement at North Carolina U."

"Thanks for the compliment, Louise. The yearbook is on my checking list. I'm trying to absorb everything I can about Alexandra so I'll feel prepared when we finally get together."

"Is a date scheduled?"

"I called Georgio Cherubini Associates earlier. I'm to meet with them at 3:00 on Wednesday afternoon. If all goes well, they'll set up an interview with Alexandra on Friday."

Louise Winstead laughed. "If all doesn't go well?" she asked.

"I don't get the interview with Alexandra."

"Then what?"

"Out of spite I make up all kinds of lies about Alexandra, sell the whole thing to Playboy and Georgio Cherubini wishes he never heard of Margo Matthews."

Louise laughed again, this time almost uncontrollably, and Margo found the laughter contagious. When she regained her composure she asked the simplest of questions.

"What's so funny?"

"I'll tell you in a few minutes. Let's have more iced tea and let me show you my paintings. We'll get back to Alexandra."

"Fine." For some reason, Margo trusted this free-spirited woman. "May I first snap pictures of you in this interesting room?"

"By all means."

Margo worked fast but carefully. Louise complied with all suggestions and directions. She was easy to work with, and the colorful paintings behind her would accent the photographs. Margo replaced the Nikon in its leather case and the older woman again took the lead.

"I paint portraits and figures, as you see. I vary the sizes and enjoy the whole process. Most paintings are eventually sold, but I give some to people I like. Here, take this miniature figure study. It's yours."

Margo reacted with surprise and pleasure as she accepted the framed painting.

"Why, thank you, Louise. It's really nice and I know just where I'll hang it."

"If you think it's a bribe, it's not. I like you. Write what you want about Alexandra."

"I thought it. I admit it. I'm sorry."

"No apologies. You're human, that's all. Now, it's getting late and I've a painting to complete. I'll finish my comments about Alexandra and you can ask your final questions. Fair enough?"

"You'll like Alexandra. She's a good kid with a mind of her own. If you don't know her background she appears the same as everyone else. Her voice is truly world class, though I admit I'm prejudiced."

"Understandable."

"I've assembled some pictures of Alexandra which you can use, although I would like them back. We've even traveled together, which you might not have known. Italy, for instance."

"Where she sang with opera companies?"

"Where we played golf."

"You play golf, too?"

"Quite well, thank you. Now, any questions before I move you out so I can go back to my easel?"

"Can we arrange an interview with Alexandra's parents?"

No way. They'll put of off and put you off, and then do it again. Believe me. No way."

"Thank you."

"Next question."

"I appreciate the picture and your honesty, but something bothers me. If Axel Vann controlled all the family's money, how could Alexandra afford New York at the age of 21?"

"She received a college graduation present from Louise Winstead in the amount of $35,000, enough for a year or two of voice instruction if she managed carefully and was willing to defy her parents."

"You made enough money selling paintings to give her $35,000?" Margo asked. She thought of the aged Honda outside the door and the stark decor around her.

My toe hurts," Louise said. "Now I'll tell you why I laughed when you suggested you would make Giorgio Cherubini mad. It can't be done. I guarantee you will do well in your interview with Georgio Cherubini Associates, and I recommend strongly you talk with the managing partner."

"Why?"

"He can charm tusks from elephants. He'll charm you, too. I guarantee it. Now,go. Time's up."

"One final question, Louise."

"One final question."

"Is it Miss or Mrs. Louise Winstead?"

"It's Mrs." said the older woman without hesitation.

"And Mr. Winstead?"

"You've used up your questions, Margo. I've enjoyed meeting you. I'll walk with you to your taxi. We'll have to hurry. I do have a schedule."

Margo Matthews noted Louise Winstead's evasions but she didn't have time to dwell on them. She liked and trusted Louise. She also had a lot of work before flying home. She needed maximum preparation time for her Wednesday afternoon appointment.

Her subsequent investigation of Giorgio Cherubini Associates proved frustrating from the first moment she began it.

"Why, hello Margo Matthews, I'm pleased to meet you," said the opera critic of The New York Times. Ted told me of your assignment with Alexandra Vann. How's it going?"

"It's why I'm here, C.J.," she admitted. "What can you tell me about Georgio Cherubini Associates. They represent Alexandra Vann."

C.J. paused before answering. He seemed about to laugh.

"The firm's been in business 15 years and they're good at what they do. Not the biggest and not the smallest, but a nice business nonetheless. They don't represent stars, but if I were an opera singer needing work I'd probably want them representing me.

"Why did you smile?"

"Cherubini takes on new clients on a basis known only to them. Really a joke, though their opinions are respected. Someone scouts the talent, makes a call and the candidate is invited to show up. Once the papers are signed, all is well. But the principals in the firm are often unavailable and no one is ever sure where they are or even who they are."

"Which means?"

"At intervals the funny business, until next time."

"Georgio Cherubini puts up with this?"

"No one is sure who Georgio Cherubini is or what he looks like. Seven or eight people demanding interviews have been introduced to Cherubini, only to find out later it wasn't him but someone else."

"So?"

"Somewhere in Georgio Cherubini Associates is either a crackpot or a genius. I don't know which and I really don't care."

"Who runs the place?"

"The Managing Partner."

"What's he like?" Margo asked, remembering Louise Winstead's guarantee.

"The Managing Partner at Georgio Cherubini Associates is charming, friendly and obviously gay. He owns a wild sense of humor, wears an expensive diamond in his right ear and has received several plaques for generous contributions to AIDS research."

"His name?"

"Whatever he chooses to call himself," C.J. said, shaking his head. "I told you about his humor. Since he uses a different name whenever he feels like it, we call him the Managing Partner. He doesn't care and we don't either. Everyone's happy."

"That's all anyone knows?" she persisted.

"Oh, no. There's lots more. He's in his mid-forties, he reeks of expensive cologne and at the moment he shares an elegant East Side apartment with his steady companion, a fire lieutenant assigned to the Commissioner's Office."

"At the moment?"

"They seem to move a lot. Further, the Managing Partner is known to travel far and wide at unpredictable intervals. He's been seen in Tokyo, London, Rome and you name it. His explanations are classics. The man can make you believe anything he wants. An unusual talent."

Thanks, C.J." she said. "I've an appointment with Giorgio Cherubini Associates tomorrow. I'll keep you informed."

"Good luck. You may not need it but you'll enjoy the visit," was the critic's final, cheerful admonition.

At 1:00 on Wednesday afternoon Margo Matthews reviewed her store of information about Giorgio Cherubini Associates. The firm enjoyed a good reputation in the opera community as well as at the respected Juilliard School of Music. An opera critic for another paper supported C.J.'s comments about funny business. Margo noted this carefully. She also wanted an explanation for the two emergency appearances responsible for Alexandra Vann's success. She did not believe in coincidences.

"Rats" she said. Before proceeding further she confirmed a bridge date at The Regency Club for Friday night. She would not let her writing assignment interfere with her balanced private world.

At 2:00 she analyzed her approach to the Cherubini interview. She admitted to a bias concerning gays. Her own goals included marriage and children and one hopeful relationship had led to disappointment on learning the man was gay. After further thought she decided on an aggressive, inquisitive, persistent stance. She prepared a list of questions and the actions she would need to guarantee answers.

At 2:50 she rode a paneled Art Deco elevator to the third floor of an old office building near Carnegie Hall. A mature receptionist surrounded by framed black and white photos of costumed opera stars looked up and listened from behind an antique desk.

"I'm Margo Matthews, a writer working on an Alexandra Vann story for the N.Y.Times. I've an appointment at 3:00," she said, "presumably with Mr. Cherubini."

"I'll call inside if you'll wait just a moment," the woman answered. She indicated a ladderback mahogany chair with ornate carving.

The receptionist's brief, muted telephone call was followed by the appearance of a strikingly handsome man from a door beside the antique desk. He stood three inches taller than six feet and wore an expensive grey plaid suit, polished black loafers and a white shirt. The square of red silk which flowed from his lapel pocket accented his dramatic red tie. He walked to Margo. A gleam from the lamp beside her reflected off a large diamond in his right earlobe.

"Mr. Cherubini is not free at the moment," the man said. He smiled, exposing perfect white teeth. A tiny touch of silver at his temples accented his wavy dark hair. He was the handsomest man Margo had ever met.

"I'm the Managing Partner," the man continued. His voice was rich and firm, a voice which might belong to an announcer or an actor. "I'll be pleased if you'll accompany me to my office, and I'll try to answer your questions about Alexandra Vann."

He turned and led the way, leaving Margo no choice but to follow. His charm had reached her.

As she rose she added quick observations to her mental file. He displayed no gay mannerisms. When he neared her no hint of his trademark cologne reached her nostrils. Despite his stunning appearance she sensed he was fatigued. She was aware he had not introduced himself by name. She would cover that later.

Margo entered a high-ceilinged office, nicely carpeted and richly furnished. White lace curtains shielded a pair of windows behind the massive desk occupied by the Managing Partner. He waved her to a green leather armchair which faced his desk. She silently admired the dark mahogany doors in the middle of each side wall, and the gold keys with ornate scrollwork which protruded below brass doorhandles.

"Please make yourself comfortable, Margo," the man said, "while I introduce myself and make sure you enjoy your visit. "I'm Jim Morgan. Would you like something to drink while we chat?"

"No, but I'd like to tape our interview," she ventured.

"By all means."

His frankness disarmed her. She placed her tape recorder on a corner of his desk, noting a white manila folder centered on the unprotected wooden surface.

"That's a lovely outfit you're wearing, if I may say so," he said. "A variation of peach isn't it? It looks quite nice on you."

His eyes caressed the bolero jacket Margo wore over a matching bare-shouldered dress, carefully selected and part of her plan. The compliments sounded genuine and pleased her.

"May I remove my jacket? she asked. "I'm a bit warm."

"Certainly."

She draped the bolero jacket on the back of her chair. She removed her glasses and polished them with a clean tissue while she planned ahead. If she were to succeed she needed to control the interview, which might not be easy. Jim Morgan was indeed a charmer.

The door at her left opened and a tall man entered. The mustachioed newcomer wore a brimmed fireman's helmet, a black raincoat as long as his knees and high black boots. He carried an upright wooden pole with a grappling hook on it. Water dripped on him and off him and all over the carpeting as he clumped to the door on the room's far side.

Margo, momentarily surprised, enjoyed the scenario. It was genuinely humorous. She assumed the man was Morgan's companion, the lieutenant at Fire Department Headquarters, and she knew right away the whole scene was a put-on. As a journalism student she had attended many Manhattan fires. She knew every officer in the Fire Department stenciled his name in large white letters on the back of his black raincoat. The newcomer's raincoat bore no stenciling.

"Andrew, the Fire Department doesn't send officers from headquarters to fires," Morgan stated, exposing the scam without so much as a sideways glance. "You can't get my attention now, either, I'm busy." The fireman went through the door and closed it without saying a word.

"Margo," Morgan said, without changing expression or even acknowledging the startling interruption, "you need information about Alexandra Vann, about the role of Cherubini Associates in her development, and you'd like an appointment with Alexandra if you're to write your story properly. Am I correct?"

Margo stared. She couldn't have phrased it better.

"Yes."

"Im so glad we agree." Morgan's winning smile recognized they were on the same wavelength. If it weren't for the puddles across the carpeting she would have lowered her guard. What was it C.J. had said? "A genius or a crackpot?"

"In the order I think you'd like to have them, then," he continued, "I present you with the following:

"First, the address and telephone number of Alexandra Vann and our encouragement of your interview with her on Friday. She lives in Stuyvesant Town and expects your call. Ask her what you like.It will be one-on-one with no interference."

"Second, the folder I'm handling you contains the information in our file about Alexandra and the names of our people who work with her. It's yours."

He rose from his chair. Simultaneously, the door at her right opened and a tall mustachioed male figure appeared. Broad in the shoulders with a narrow waist and muscular legs, he wore nothing but a skimpy pair of white briefs. His features were rugged. He sauntered across the room between Margo and the desk and sat on a sturdy chair near the far door, again without saying a word.

Margo admired the newcomer's full head of dark hair. He was a few years older than her. He sat staring straight ahead, obviously determined to get Morgan's attention. For Margo, he was about to become a key contributor to the research she was accumulating.

Three times in the past several minutes Margo Matthews had deliberately leaned forward in her chair and adjusted her right shoe. She knew the move presented her breasts for male inspection. Each time her quick glance at Morgan's face found him oblivious, a man with genuine gay reflexes or a man with steely discipline. His eyes dismissed her ploy.

It was time to test the newcomer.

"Oh, it's Andrew, isn't it," she said. "We haven't met." She rose from the chair and turned to face him. She moved a step and pretended to catch her heel on a chair rung. She bent from the waist and glanced at Andrew, whose eyes enjoyed her breasts. He had passed her test. She was fascinated. He ignored her.

"I will not sit here any longer, James," Andrew announced. "If we're not out of here in ten minutes I will not cook for you tonight. And that's final," he said in a wimpy voice, and marched out of the room.

Margo listened alertly when Andrew spoke. The man may have played the same part before but his voice didn't ring true. In passing her test he also intensified her suspicions about the management of Georgio Cherubini Associates.

"I apologize for the interruption, Margo," Morgan said. "Andrew demands attention. But enough of that. You and I have work to do."

The winning smile reappeared. Margo Matthews smiled back. Her plan had worked. It was to her advantage to keep silent and let Morgan continue.

"Here's your folder," he resumed. "It includes both professional and personal information about Alexandra. Photographs too, from a young girl to today's woman."

He glanced at a gold Rolex watch.

"I'm sorry I have to run, Margo," he said. "It's been a pleasure meeting you."

"Do you have time for a few quick questions?"

"If they're quick, yes."

"Why do I have permission to interview Alexandra on Friday without you even questioning me?"

"Louise Winstead called. She liked you and enjoyed your visit. You must know she sent Alexandra here. Louise gave you permission. We simply communicated it for her."

"I see."

"And Georgio Cherubini? I'd like to meet him."

"I'm afraid you can't," Morgan said. "Georgio hasn't been well lately. In fact, he's out of the country. Perhaps when he returns we can arrange something."

"Thank you so much, Mr. Morgan," Margo said. "If I have any further questions I'll be sure to call you."

Friday's interview with Alexandra Vann progressed perfectly. The two women hit it off well. Margo completed a long, detailed story which she sent Ted Donaldson a week later, along with a series of excellent, exclusive photographs. Alexandra sang well and photographed better.

Ted Donaldson called as soon as he received Margo's story.

"Terrific job, Margo. Really professional. I got a personal bonus out of it, too. When C.J. read your story he started calling me your mentor. You know what? I sort of like it," he admitted.

Ted's compliments were heady reward for Margo, who knew she had completed a successful assignment even as she pondered a sequel. She resolved not to let go of Alexandra Vann or Louise Winstead or Jim Morgan until her journalistic suspicions had been put to rest.

She called Georgio Cherubini Associates to resume her research. She asked for Jim Morgan.

"Jim Morgan?" was the surprised response. "I don't recognize the name. Are you sure you have the right number? This is Georgio Cherubini Associates."

"Who's the Managing Partner?"

"Why, Georgio Cherubini," the woman said.

"May I speak with him, please?"

"He's out of town at the moment. Can someone else help you?"

"I'm afraid not."

Margo slammed the phone on its cradle.

"I'll kill those comedians," she shouted. Later, she realized the information for her story's sequel would be difficult but not impossible to obtain. She knew persistence would pay and her instincts and experience would serve her well. Her initial impulse matured into a crusade.

She resumed writing the fashion article and completed it Saturday afternoon. In the evening she appeared promptly at The Regency Club. The bridge club's owner was also her teacher. He met her before the game began.

"Your partner called, Margo. She can't make it tonight. If you don't object, I'll fill in."

"Object, Harry? I'm thrilled," she said. "It's a guaranteed first place finish for me."

"Not so."

"What are you telling me?" She fastened her attention to the gruff club owner, who chewed an unlit cigar. A retired clothing manufacturer, Harry enjoyed playing cards. He talked a lot, listened well and knew a lot about Manhattan happenings.

"The man who just came in is my good friend and he doesn't come often. I'm always glad to see him. He's also the best card player in the world, which means all we can hope for is second place."

"Where is he?"

Her eyes followed his nod to the club's entrance where several regular players clustered. Behind them, to her astonishment, stood the Managing Partner of Georgio Cherubini Associates and his companion, Andrew. Both wore slacks, open collar shirts and casual shoes. They chatted with each other.

"The two at the door, Harry?"

"Yes"

"Which?"

"The taller one. I'd bet the other guy's getting an education and a good one, too. Like I said, his teacher's the best card player in the world."

"What's his name?"

"Whatever he says it is."

"What does that mean?"

"In his line of work he doesn't want his name known, so he uses lots of names. Very convenient."

"His line of work?"

Harry looked over Margo's head, turned to make sure no other players were nearby, then stepped close to her and spoke in a hoarse whisper.

"You are looking at a man who can turn over one card, win or lose a hundred thousand dollars, and go home smiling either way. A rare breed. Like I told you, he's my friend. Excuse me while I say "Hello." Harry sounded pleased.

Margo's mind raced. The two men at the door made quite a pair. Both were good looking. One owned a super body and the other was overloaded with charm and talent. Could she write a story about such a unique twosome? She thought not. Who would believe it? But she would keep digging deeper until she learned whatever facts about Alexandra Vann she felt certain were being kept from her.

Harry was beside her. He held a list of the night's competitors.

"What's his name this time, Harry?"

"One I don't understand, to be honest with you. I've never known him to use it. It's his real name, which four people in town know, including me." The balding proprietor looked at her with a deep frown and chomped his cigar before thrusting the paper towards her.

She saw the listing. "James Morgan. Andrew Stewart." She heard Harry's voice say "If Jim hadn't told me to show you the names I would have changed them."

"Why, Harry?"

"To protect him. I'm sure he's helping the big guy he tows around. Jimmy's a genius who takes risks to help friends, but sometimes he forgets to protect himself."

The statement surprised Margo. If Harry was telling the truth, then Morgan had supplied his real name when she visited Cherubini's. Why? Harry drifted back towards Morgan and she pondered what she just heard. Her thoughts were interrupted by a tap on her shoulder from the club's assistant manager, Harry's wife.

"I must apologize, Miss Matthews, but Harry's gone. He's like that, you know, which means you have no partner. The game's getting under way and the only available partner is the big man with the mustache over by the door. I think his partner left with Harry." Behind her, people sat at tables waiting for the game to start. Margo's dilemma was solved when Morgan's partner approached her.

"We're both without partners," he said. "I'm Andrew Stewart. I didn't come here to play bridge," he continued. "I came to meet you and I have."

"I'm flattered."

"Have you eaten?"

"It's my business, Mr. Stewart, but I'll answer your question. I haven't eaten since lunch. I've been much too busy."

Margo sensed a dinner invitation rather than a bridge partnership. She found the man strange but attractive in a rugged way, and knew he might provide her the information she needed for her follow-up story about Alexandra Vann.

"If you'll join me for dinner I'll feel complimented," he said. She was not surprised. In fact, her curiosity was piqued. Why did he joke about meeting her, and how did he know she would be there?"

"Invitation accepted, conditionally," she said. "First I want to know your relationship with the Managing Partner of Giorgio Cherubini Associates."

"He's my mentor," came the prompt, pleasant response.

"Lead on, lieutenant."

"Captain," she heard behind his broad back. She followed him through the door and outside for a short walk in a misty drizzle which ended when he waved a cab to the curb.

Margo Matthews patiently extracted from Andrew Stewart the answers to most all her questions concerning Alexandra Vann during a relationship which began over dinner on Saturday evening, continued on an increasingly positive basis in early summer and included six trips to the Metropolitan Opera. By July 4th she had outlined her second story about Alexandra.

"Jimmy Morgan is a documented mathematical genius," Andrew explained, "as well as handsome, an excellent golfer and the best friend I'll ever have. Our relationship goes all the way back to grade school in Brooklyn, where he was two years ahead of me and lived with his aunt around the corner. Otherwise he was an orphan. We talked a lot, or I should say he talked a lot and I listened. Jimmy was a wild romantic. Maybe you know the type, always wanting to be a hero. Maybe some of it rubbed off on me. He truly knew music,especially opera. He'd memorized the scores and librettos of dozens of operas. It was fascinating listening to him.

By the time he was 15 Jimmy explored chess, checkers, backgammon and all forms of card playing. Anything related to numbers or cards was his forte, and he found an older man who educated him in the ways of professional gamblers. By the time he was 18 Jimmy was a top pro, specializing in poker. All forms of business have their degrees of excellence. Jimmy's genius meant he could win against the best players in the world before he was 21."

"Remarkable," Margo conceded.

"Like a lot of us in those days, Jimmy joined the Army reserve. At the same time he met a sparkling young woman who also loved opera. Their romance was short, followed by a quiet private wedding. Jimmy's aunt was dead and the girl's only relative at the wedding was her sister. They were from an old Raleigh family which had lost its money. The sister scrimped to come by train from Raleigh for the wedding."

"The bride's name was Amanda," Margo ventured.

"The bride's name was Louise."

"Wow"

"That's when all was right. Then it all went wrong."

"Tell me."

"The Army called up Jimmy. He couldn't wait to serve. He could support Louise on poker winnings when he was on leave. When he became a pilot the Army assigned Jimmy to the Far East, where he disappeared and was presumed dead. Louise was pregnant in New York, alone, with no money. She despaired."

"And then?"

"Louise returned to Raleigh and moved in with Amanda. Shortly after the birth of Louise's daughter, Axel Vann arrived, triumphant, with a lot of money. Axel wanted the family's society connections to make him respectable, and he met his match in Amanda Vann, a tough negotiator if there ever was one. Keep in mind Louise was almost a basket case, and neither she nor Amanda could support the daughter."

"I can't believe what you're about to say."

"Believe it. Amanda agreed to marry Axel if he would adopt Louise's daughter and provide for the girl's future the way neither she nor Louise could manage. He also agreed to provide a house on the grounds for Louise, and everybody agreed to keep quiet about the whole arrangement."

"Louise accepted conditions like these?"

"She was in a state of shock. She hardly knew the baby was gone. She survived on voice students Amanda rounded up, and the few dollars Amanda could get her. Axel Vann doesn't believe in anything beyond a deal's limits, and the deal did not include supporting Louise. He would have been just as pleased if Louise killed herself, and I understand she thought about it many times. If you know anything about Southern history, you know the strength of the women after the Civil War. Both Louise and Amanda were bred for strength and circumstances made them prove it."

"And then?"

"Four years later Jimmy Morgan escaped from an Asian prison where he'd been held after his plane crashed. He came back to New York to find his wife gone, his child carrying another man's name and his means of survival the same crazy sense of humor which preserved his sanity while in prison."

"Did he find Louise?"

"Certainly."

"But her name is Winstead."

"Louise Winstead Morgan. The girl was then five years old. Jimmy and Louise each needed years to get over their separate ordeals. In the meantime Louise discovered painting, and they both followed occupations better suited to a person working alone. What I'm saying, Margo, is they felt maybe Alexandra might be better off staying with the Vann's until the girl was old enough to handle the truth. Louise saw her regularly and Jimmy managed frequent trips to Raleigh. He was introduced to the girl as Louise's friend."

"I can imagine. I'm sure she figured it out, though. I interviewed Alexandra Vann. She's one smart young woman."

"They told her when she was twelve years old. She was surprised, pleased and then thrilled. She always liked Jimmy, as most people do. It's hard not to like him. It was Jimmy who taught her golf," he added.

"For sure," Margo said.

"Amanda and Axel knew about the disclosure before Alexandra was told. They received assurances no attempt would be made to change things. Even for someone like Axel it must have been hard."

"Tell me about Georgio Cherubini Associates."

"Jimmy won the business in a card game. He made up the name and he hired an old voice teacher with a mustache to make appearances when things were quiet. Between poker games Jimmy's humor keeps things dancing."

"The diamond ear ring?"

"Perfect cover for a man whose wife is unknown. Like everyone in the art's business he's lost clients and friends to AIDS. His big donations are in character for the part he plays, but they're also from the heart."

"The day I met him I thought he was tired."

"A three-night card game. He won. He was exhausted."

"Where do you come into this picture, captain? And why do you and Jimmy Morgan keep moving?"

"My wife was pregnant with our first child when she died, five years ago. I went into shock. I began taking wild chances, and you don't do that in my business. I went into a burning building and hauled out two firemen."

"A hero."

"I got them out. The building fell on me and when I got out of the hospital I ended up at headquarters on limited duty, which made me wilder. One day I bumped into Jimmy, and he talked me into moving in with him. He announced himself as my mentor. He calmed me down until I got my head on straight, and life's been a lot of fun with him ever since."

Margo looked calmly at the big fireman.

"Why did they promote you?"

"A hearing. I behaved myself and the people at headquarters like me. I was on the promotion list when I got hurt and I've been fine for two years. Promotion granted."

"You make Jimmy Morgan sound like he walks on water, Andrew. No one is that smart or that good. Not even your friend the genius."

She found Stewart's grin charming.

"I didn't say he's perfect, Margo. He can't cook and he's a terrible driver, and if he tried to draw a straight line with a ruler for the rest of his days he couldn't do it. As to your question why we move all the time, it's personal and I'm not going to answer now."

Margo accepted the rebuke. She liked Andrew Stewart and welcomed his attentions. She had every intention of prying from him the answers to all her questions about Alexandra Vann, and two weeks later the opportunity arose.

They had gone to another performance of Aida, and then ambled to a downtown cafe. The chance to discuss Alexandra after listening to her perform was too good to ignore.

"I really enjoyed listening to Alexandra tonight," Margo said. "She's a tribute to her mentor, meaning her father, of course."

"Jimmy's a born mentor. If you list his successes I guess you'd have to include me."

"Why did he tell me his right name, Andrew. Harry said he never does that."

"He wanted to play it straight with you. He wanted you to help his daughter, and Jimmy felt he wouldn't try to fool you with any funny business. He forgot to tell me, as you noticed when I did the 'fireman, fireman' routine."

"I'm still bothered by coincidences," she continued. "Both of Alexandra's replacement performances came at precisely the right time to advance her career. Will you tell me what really happened?"

"I don't know what happened but I'll risk an educated guess."

"I'm listening."

"The Board of directors of The San Francisco Opera Company probably includes a person who makes large contributions and also fancies himself an excellent poker player, a person who lost big and found himself offered an alternate way to satisfy the debt. It's even possible an organization s big as the Metropolitan Opera in New York might have a powerful director with similar leanings. It wouldn't surprise me at all, especially if they played cards with an expert mentoring his daughter."

Andrew's grin widened. He reached for his drink on the rough wood table and continued talking.

'If you need a great mentor, Jimmy's the man. Now I'll tell you why we keep moving. Jimmy's been scouting girl friends for me and he's most particular. We keep scouting locations while he checks out the neighborhoods because Jimmy knows me better than I do. I admit we were ready to move again when you arrived."

"Men are devious creatures, aren't they?" she asked in a teasing tone. The entire picture was clear and yet she felt frustrated; knowing the truth meant a story she couldn't write.

"Let's get out of here, Andrew. I need a walk to clear my head of mentors, mentors, mentors."

On a pleasant summer night they strolled East on 34th Street. Margo was relaxed. Beside her, the big man profited from a lesson his mentor, Morgan, drilled into him over and over.

"When the book is closed, Andrew, don't touch a page of it."

Andrew Stewart resolved never to tell Margo her editor friend at the New York Times, Ted Donaldson, fancied himself a poker player.

9

Soft Voices

"Move your foot, sir. Please, sir."

Donal Curran heard the woman's soft voice, so low she almost caressed him with each sibilant sound, yet he couldn't see her.

After retiring in New York and moving to Raleigh, North Carolina, Donal found himself with lots of free time. Some days he visited his daughter in North Raleigh. enjoyed lunch, and laughed with his four-year-old granddaughter, Sarah.

Other days he drove to the Oakwood area near downtown Raleigh and studied its classic Victorian homes. Many had been restored and now wore modern finery. Today, in warm May sunshine, he strolled to nearby Oakwood Cemetery, which he knew contained hundreds of Confederate soldiers, in graves marked by identical white stones which marched up and down a grassy knoll in strict military formation.

Donal liked walking in the cemetery. After reading inscriptions on many of the weathered stones around him he stopped to catch his breath. He sat on the grass beside a low marker which looked almost like white porcelain. "Annalee Simmons. Born 1845. Died 1875."

"Your foot, sir, if you please."

He moved his right foot six inches. As he did so he turned, slowly, first to one side and then the other. No one was there.

"Thank you, sir," the voice whispered.

When he retired Donal was chairman of Grover Cleveland High School's Speech Department. His trained ear recognized the low, cultured voice of an aristocratic Carolina woman.

He remembered hearing few r's from people of southern heritage when he first arrived in Raleigh. At the time he heard "Cahlina."

Later, he listened more carefully each time he heard 'r's' formed by a gentle delicate tongue. The sound delighted him. He regretted he heard it so seldom. A few days earlier he had thrilled to the voice of a wonderful white-haired docent wearing a navy blue suit and frilly blouse as she led a tour of the Governor's Mansion.

Donal pulled the brim of his white sunhat low around his head in case someone might see him talking.

"Are you Annalee?"

"Yes, sir."

"Why did you want my foot moved?"

"It blocked the warm sun."

"You can feel it?"

"Yes, sir. There's a bubble in the turf."

"Annalee?"

"Yes?"

"How old are you?"

"I stopped when I was thirty."

"Why?"

"I was tired of waiting for Rob. He was a Colonel. I knew he would never come back. When I heard he was here I joined him."

"Here?"

"With the other Confederate veterans, sir."

"How do you know, Annalee?"

"We talk, sir."

Donal Curran gulped. He shot a glance to each side and behind him. He neither saw nor heard a soul, though he really didn't care. The woman's wonderful soft voice had kissed his ears.

"Can you see, Annalee?"

"No, sir. I'm dead."

"Oh."

"But sometimes we can talk. I admit it's rare, sir, and only to one. I speak to my sister, Harriet, in the next grave. She speaks to the man beside her. It takes a long time but my message reaches Rob.

"What do you tell him?"

"It's not your business, sir

An aristocratic woman.

"Thank you, Annalee."

"Thank you for moving your foot, sir."

Donal Curran loved the soft 'r's' in Annalee closing message. He rose and approached the next low stone on his path, hidden from view by a blooming spring plant.

Harriet Simmons. Born 1847. Died 1896."

He was not surprised.

Donal completed his tour. He pulled his hat lower on his forehead as he neared the summit of a large hill. He pivoted, looked over his shoulder at the variations among the tall and low and grieving and silent markers behind him and walked towards the Confederate soldiers buried just inside the arched stone entrance to Oakwood Cemetery.

10

The Fanneran Reunion

Paul Fanneran started it. He looked at the calendar and saw his 50th birthday was two months off. Paul called his cousin Tim in New York. Tim just turned 50.

"Let's celebrate with a family reunion in Chicago," Paul said. "Since I live here, I'll sponsor it. We can get 'Johnny the bike,' too. He'll be 50 in a few weeks."

Cousin Johnny Cassidy's fondness for motorcycles was matched by his fondness for partying. If Johnny rode in from northern Illinois his sisters would come from California, Washington and Michigan. Other cousins were sure to follow.

"I'll bet we can get 40 people," Paul said. It'll be a grand occasion."

A dozen long-distance calls about the reunion reached my home in Raleigh, North Carolina. My wife, Babe, is Tim Fanneran's sister. We were preparing to go when my younger sister, Clare, called to tell us my 74-year-old cousin Liz, who's my godmother, was in suburban Chicago's Memorial Hospital with pneumonia.

Liz, who lives with her son Rick and his wife not far from Memorial Hospital, was moved there from upstate New York. Clare gave me Rick's number. When I called he said the hospital is an hour and a half from downtown Chicago. If we wanted to visit Liz Friday we should call on our arrival and then take the train. He would meet us at the Crystal Lake station and drive us to the hospital.

"Mom's pretty well over the pneumonia," Rick said. "She's not in great health but I'm sure she'll look forward to your visit."

"On Tuesday my older sister, Leslie, called from New York. She asked about our trip and I told her we would fly from Raleigh to Chicago early Friday, check into the Ambassador East hotel and then visit Liz before joining Babe's relatives at the Fanneran Reunion.

"Is that all? Leslie asked.

"Well, not entirely," I said. "In addition to visiting Liz the trip offers me special bonuses." I try not to tell Leslie too much, but when she insisted I had to explain what I meant.

I teach Art History at Meredith College in Raleigh. In my spare time I paint oil portraits. My plans included a solo visit to Chicago's famous Art Institute on Saturday, a visit which might prove the highlight of my year. If this wasn't enough the Fannerans' schedule included a Chicago White Sox baseball game Sunday afternoon. I enjoy the Fannerans, who would rather party than eat, but as Leslie knows, I revel in art and baseball. I was equally eager to see a White Sox game in the new Comiskey Park. At the end of my narrative Leslie sounded a negative note.

"Pneumonia is the least of Liz's problems, Barry," she informed me. "I was talking with Rick yesterday. Liz has hardening of the arteries and is rapidly losing touch with reality. She may not even recognize you."

Leslie tracks our entire family. She's always on the phone. She routinely interviews Clare and me and our brother, Joe. We all resist her intrusion into our lives. I admire Leslie's good qualities but she'd be more popular if she'd mind her own business. She's never liked Babe, either. Whenever something goes wrong Leslie blames Babe. I was glad Leslie would be in New York when we were in Chicago.

We began our trip Friday morning. By the time we parked at the Raleigh airport all ground fog had disappeared. When the plane took off we saw clear blue sky, a cheerful omen of good times to come.

Chicago in early May proved bright, warm and a bit windy. We taxied from Midway Airport to the Ambassador East, where we rode a small elevator to room 1734 and found on a mahogany table a card welcoming us to the Artist's Suite, three rooms filled with fine art reproductions. At registration I was assured of a moderate rate. I wondered about the suite.

We unpacked and headed for the train station, where I bought Liz a box of chocolates. Minutes later we were in a double-decked car with big windows. We saw a dozen stations in increasingly nicer areas during the long ride to Crystal Lake. In the inner city each station had trees near it. In the suburbs we saw open fields surrounded by trees whose leaves ranged in color from dark forest green to a green so light as to be almost yellow. Beyond the trees were small lakes and large houses on well-tended plots.

Rick met us at Crystal Lake. We rode with him until Babe spotted a flower shop and asked him to stop. She bought Liz a sizable potted plant. We resumed our ride and minutes later arrived at the hospital. Once out of the car Rick and Babe walked ahead. I followed, noting Rick's hair is a fine steel-blue and Babe's dark hair has lately added streaks of grey which take nothing from her lovely appearance. She's a most attractive woman.

When they reached the entrance I'd fallen behind. I like to look around. I reached a pair of clear doors and moved inside to where Rick was leading Babe to the elevator. I glanced to my left where a handsome blonde woman about Babe's age sat in an armchair near the reception desk, reading a newspaper. She looked at me and smiled. Her perfect teeth increased the wattage of a wonderful smile.

I almost staggered.

Before meeting Babe in New York 25 years ago I'd lived with an Irish girl named Irene Butler in Dublin, Ireland during the year following my graduation from art school. When I came home to New York Irene decided to stay in Dublin. Her choice, not mine. Once we separated she made sure there was no way I could reach her.

Two and a half decades later, 60 miles northwest of Chicago, I recognized her at once, as she knew I would. Her presence could not be a coincidence.

My pulse and mind raced. I continued walking to the elevator where Rick and Babe waited. I tried to pull myself together in the few seconds before I met my godmother.

We rode to the third floor. Rick led us to a nursing station, saluted the nurse on duty and faced to his right. Less than a dozen yards away stood a tiny, white-haired woman wearing a bright blue sweater and dark slacks. She stared at us.

"Hello, mom," Rick said. Liz straightened. In her youth she had not been a beauty. Illness had etched deep lines in her narrow face. When she recognized the threesome approaching her she smiled. After we greeted her Rick led the way to her room. Babe presented Liz the plant and I followed with the box of chocolates. Liz reached for my hand while Babe arranged the presents on the windowsill.

"I have to call work," Rick said. "I'll be back in a few minutes." In our short ride he'd told us he ran an electronics company 20 miles away. We watched him leave the room.

"Hello, doll," I began with Liz. I was rewarded with another smile. We'd always been on the same wavelength. We talked for 20 minutes before Rick returned. Liz was bright and lucid throughout,and I was able to keep her laughing. Ten minutes later it was time to leave. Just before we left Babe snapped two pictures of Liz and Rick and me. We all hugged Liz and headed for the elevator. I wondered if Irene was still downstairs.

When we reached the lobby the only person in it was a woman in a white uniform sitting behind the reception desk. Babe and Rick walked through the door and outside. The receptionist spoke to me.

"The woman who was here before left this for you," she said. She handed me a small piece of white paper with four numbers on it. 1764.

When I walked outside I was sweating. The paper with 1764 suggested Irene had a room at the Ambassador East, down the hall from Babe and me. I suspected Leslie had called Irene, and I cursed my sister's interference. When we reached Rick's car I wondered if I would survive the Fanneran Reunion. Irene was gorgeous. It would not be easy.

The train ride back was sort of quiet. Babe seemed preoccupied. She works hard at her job selling Raleigh real estate, and in her spare time keeps track of our daughters in New York. Marilyn is a lawyer and Amy a media expert. Both were coming to the reunion and staying at the Ambassador East.

When we reached the Artist's Suite a surprise greeted us. A basket of fruit sat on the table in our dining room, along with an envelope addressed by hand to Mrs. Barry Byrne. The note inside began "Dear Babe..." and welcomed her to The Artist's Suite. It was signed by the hotel manager, who offered her personal assistance in making Babe's visit successful.

Babe laughed. She had no more idea of what was going on than I did. We didn't dwell on it. We were due at Paul Fanneran's apartment in less than half an hour.

The Ambassador East is in the Gold Coast area of Chicago, three blocks from prestigious Lake Shore Drive. By checking a map I learned Paul's apartment was less than two blocks from the hotel. We walked to the corner and turned up North Stone Street. All five floors of the granite building beside us had been gutted. Construction equipment around it signaled renovation in progress. A sign inside the fencing read "homes...from $3 million."

We walked another thirty paces and reached Paul's building. A smiling doorman greeted us and led the way to an elevator whose total capacity was five people. He pushed the button for the top floor. A few seconds later the elevator stopped, the door opened and we were inside a small foyer. Beyond it, sounds from a three piece band playing loud Irish music welcomed us into a big living room where more than 30 people partied. "Johnny the bike" Cassidy stood roaring with laughter in the middle of the room, holding a drink in one hand while he wiped his thick gray mustache with the other.

"Why it's Babe and Barry" shouted Paul Fanneran, whose tall sister Pat stood beside him in a nicely tailored suit. Pat lives in Scottsdale, Arizona. Babe's brother Tim detached himself from a group of three glamorous women I later learned were Johnny's sisters

Valerie, Ursula and Elaine. Two were with husbands and a third with a friend but I never got the lineup straight.

Babe swung into action. She hugged everybody in sight and went off for a drink, leaving me with Paul's stunning wife, Molly.

"Did you have something to do with our suite at the Ambassador East?" I asked. "Everything, Barry," Molly replied. "Didn't you know I'm a promoter?"

I ambled through three rooms to the kitchen where a hired bartender presided. I asked for a martini, one of my weaknesses. A young woman distributing a tray of hors d'oeuvres bent her knees when she walked around the band. My daughters met me and showed off new dresses. Both were thrilled they came. A half dozen of the people around us were relatives their age they had never met.

"You girls are at the Ambassador East" I said. "Which room?"

We're in 720, which is great," Amy said. "The hospitality room up the hall is in 'Johnny the bike's suite. We were there before we came here. Johnny's wife, Beth, walked over with us. That's her over there, the woman in the white suit and blonde hair smiling at us."

"I've met Beth," I reminded her.

It was Marilyn's turn. "Mom asked me to bring the Fanneran family tree I worked on after you two went to Ireland last year," she said. "The Fannerans will probably make more changes."

"No doubt."

Maureen Fanneran, Tim's wife, appeared at my side and took my arm. Maureen is a beauty and a class act. "Isn't this place lovely, Barry?"

"Sure is."

"Come outside on the balcony with me. There's a clear view of Lake Michigan." I followed. Our views of the lake and Lake Shore Drive's moving headlights were impressive. Maureen turned me around. She pointed upward.

"There are two bedrooms and a bath up there. This place is a duplex penthouse," she said. "Spectacular, isn't it?"

"An understatement."

We went inside and Maureen drifted away. I saw stairs which led upward to the bedrooms, and sat for awhile on a comfortable sofa. I finished my drink and walked around, greeting people I knew and nodding at others. Five were relatives I would meet later on. Across the room, something about a stylish cousin named Jane Fanning reminded me of Irene.

The guitar player picked up a mike and began singing "Danny Boy." In the next five minutes he produced the worst performance I'd ever heard. He knew some of the words and some of the tune and faked the rest with disastrous consequences. I reacted by going to the kitchen and gulping down a second martini. When I put down the glass I could see Irene's face. Around me the party was in full swing. The drinks may have helped, but no one else noticed the guitar player's assault on "Danny Boy."

I thought of another martini. Irene's face reappeared.

Normally I'm circumspect with my in-laws, but martinis warp my judgement. My year in Dublin with Irene had begun slowly and built up to a sexual stratosphere. I wondered why she was in Chicago. I was willing to find out.

"If you'll excuse me, Maureen," I said to Tim's wife, "I'm going to leave quietly. Babe is happy surrounded by all her relatives and you know she'll be the last to leave. If you'd make my apologies I'd appreciate it."

"No problem, Barry. I understand."

Minutes later I was in the lobby of the Ambassador East. I called room 1764. Irene answered.

"Hi," I said.

"Where are you?"

"In the lobby."

"I'm waiting"

When I reached 1764 the door was ajar. I marched in, closing the door behind me. When I turned Irene rushed into my arms. She smelled great. In bare feet and wearing a white shower robe she fit perfectly in my embrace. She wore the perfume I used to buy her, a musky scent called Wilde Swan. I love good perfume.

"Well," I said, after we kissed three times. "Your welcoming party has conquered America. Can we sit down?"

"Let's."

I looked around. A plaque beside a full mahogany bookcase identified her accommodations as The Author's Suite. We moved to a sofa in the living room, where I noticed an almost empty glass on a coffee table. A small bottle of vodka and an open tonic bottle stood beside the glass. A surprise. Irene hadn't been much of a drinker.

"You're into vodka and tonic?"

"I'm not into meeting husbands, Barry. I needed the vodka to fortify me, but I'm not apologizing. I'm thrilled you're here."

"Meet two-martini Byrne," I laughed, for the same reason. "I'm not apologizing either. I'm thrilled to be with you again. Now tell me when you talked with my sister, Leslie."

"I've talked with her for years, Barry. Ever since she visited us in Dublin. I knew about Babe and your two girls. Leslie told me last year about your brief visit to Ireland, and a week ago she told me about Chicago. Leslie's never been a fan of Babe's, either. She wanted us to marry so she could come visit Ireland."

"It figures. Since you know all about me, tell me about you," I said, running a hand across a bare shoulder beneath her white shower robe.

Irene spoke of life in Dublin with her husband, Brian Fallon, a quiet and likable accountant by whom she had two boys. A hysterectomy in her thirties meant no more children, and both boys were already out on their own. Brian went off to work each morning and Irene stayed behind in a small studio where she illustrated children's books. The money she earned was hers to keep. Usually it went on short trips to the continent. Brian disliked traveling.

"I'm not unhappy with Brian," she said, "and I've had no affairs with anyone since you left. When I told Brian my sudden urge to visit the Art Institute in Chicago he said "go ahead." Here I am. If only it were that simple," she added.

"Which means?"

"It means I'm almost unable to control myself in the company of the married man who still haunts my dreams. There's more to my visit than that," she said, "but I can't wait any longer, Barry. Please." She dropped the shower robe from her shoulders and I gasped. Her meaning was clear. Her mood matched mine exactly.

We almost ran to the bedroom. Afterwards, we agreed to meet at noon Saturday at The Art Institute. I dressed quickly and rushed up the hall and into The Artist's Suite. I showered to remove any lingering scent of Wilde Swan, and minutes later I was sound asleep.

In the morning I realized I'd slept like a baby when I should have tossed and turned with a guilty conscience. Once awake I felt elated and guilty at the same time. It's difficult to explain. I looked over at Babe's dark head and wondered how or if I would get through the next two days.

I stood up. My mind raced across the activities scheduled for Saturday. I wanted more of Irene without discovery by Babe, Marilyn or Amy. I preferred to be ignored by all the Fannerans, in itself impossible. I looked out a window for the crowning disaster of a heavy downpour and a sunny sky surprised me. Perhaps there was hope.

We breakfasted a few blocks away with cousins from the West Coast. The food was excellent and the group included Maureen and Jack McNamara, a handsome Chicago couple who met and married in New York. Maureen McNamara and Maureen Fanneran struck me as the two prettiest grey-haired women I've ever seen.

Babe and I returned to the Ambassador East. Her plan was to lunch with our daughters at a P.J.Clarke's grill within easy walking distance, followed by an informal tour of the Gold Coast. Knowing I was off to The Art Institute, she reminded me I was due back no later than 2:30. A hired bus would take us to Chicago's Comedy Theater for the long-running Irish play "Flanagan's Wake." The bus was Johnny's idea, its driver a biker pal who owned a Chicago bar. All 42 of us could travel together.

A doorman called me a taxi. On the drive up North Michigan Avenue we passed Marshall Field's famous store and crossed Paul

Harvey Drive, where the Chicago Tribune Building glared across a bridge at the building housing its lesser-known rival, the Chicago Sun-Times. Pedestrian traffic on the sidewalks spilled into each intersection. At The Art Institute I left the taxi and crossed the avenue in a crowd of lively teenagers. When I marched up the steps of the Institute, beside its's guardian lions, Irene was waiting. She wore a simple beige dress with comfortable brown shoes, and carried a leather bag. Taking my hand, she led me through the door. She pulled me aside and kissed me without letting go of my hand. She smelled great and I felt the same.

"Let's enjoy every second, Barry," she said. "You lead, I'll follow. Like old times."

For an hour and more we sampled as much of the Institute's enormous collection as possible. Renoirs, Picassos, Monets and Gauguins seemed everywhere. Toulouse-Lautrec and Edgar Degas added verve, and the face on an 1878 portrait by Edouard Manet got gold stars from both of us. Strategically placed Rodin statues, bigger than life size, were easily recognizable. A check of my watch brought our visit to a sudden end.

"It's time, Irene. Back to the Ambassador for me, and then 'Flanagan's Wake' at the Chicago Comedy Theater. After 'Flanagan's Wake' all the Fannerans go by bus to the Greek Islands Restaurant on South Halstead Street. If there's some way for me to catch you by midnight, expect me." We kissed, firm and friendly. I waved to her and sprinted for a cab.

I reached the Ambassador with enough time to shower before the bus left. Babe recited her morning's activities.I was pleased to listen. She was glad I enjoyed the Art Institute. We joined the group in the hotel lobby, where our daughter Marilyn came over to ask me about my morning. When the bus arrived Marilyn and I sat together. A short ride brought us to The Chicago Comedy Theater, where Molly Fanneran distributed tickets for 'Flanagan's Wake.' Ushers handed us Stagebill magazines. We were early enough for most of our group to sit in the first three rows. After I leafed through the Stagebill I glanced back, shortly before curtain time. Every seat in the small theater was occupied.

'Flanagan's Wake' proved a wonderful outing. First-rate slapstick comedy by a talented and experienced cast had everyone roaring with laughter. When the lights went up we filed outside and milled on the sidewalk, waiting under a marquee for our bus. I stood off to one side, staring across the street at an unusual building to my right. An office building 20 floors up from the ground, it was topped by an elaborate network of gothic spires, as if a miniature St. Patrick's Cathedral had been dropped on it from the sky. It drew my amused attention.

I dropped my eyes to see a neat blonde in a yellow dress and high heels strolling up the sidewalk towards our group. It was Irene. I almost panicked. Instead, I walked a few steps toward her, took her by the arm and turned us both to face the strange building. I was thrilled by her touch and scared by the situation. I pointed at the building and said "If you don't know what it is, shake your head and go on. I had to touch you. I hope you enjoyed the play."

"I don't know what it is," she said. "It's one of a kind, and yes, I really enjoyed the play." She shook her head and smiled. Without a word or a backward look, she resumed walking turned the corner and was lost from sight.

"Who was that, dad?" asked Marilyn at my side, her blue eyes staring into mine. She was so close she might have heard my whispers.

"Someone who didn't know what that odd building is across the street," I replied, "because she's a tourist like us. It might be an office building with a church on it or a church with an office building under it. What do you think?"

"It's the Chicago Temple building," Marilyn said. "It's in all the guidebooks. Do you always stop women you don't know on sidewalks and ask questions?" she persisted.

"Doesn't everyone?"

Our bus arrived before she could answer. I was grateful. We sat together on the ride to dinner. Marilyn rode in silence, checking out all of downtown Chicago on her first visit. She is one smart woman. I hoped she accepted my explanation.

At the Greek Islands Restaurant our private room wasn't ready. Everyone headed into the bar, where bartenders served drinks for the next half hour without requesting payment. Fanneran bar traffic was heavy, indeed, and when our room was finally ready I could only imagine the bar bill.

Food was plentiful and nicely prepared. A costumed young belly dancer showed lots of skin when she arrived with her accompanist. She performed her ages-old routine with enough turns, twists and fillips to satisfy the most critical watcher. She seemed unsurprised when Tim Fanneran invited himself to accompany her, and pleased at his genuine and jovial bare-chested performance while cameras flashed all around them.

When she and her accompanist left the room waiters walked in to serve dessert. Tim rose and demanded attention. He held a manila folder in his hand and his smile was contagious.

"We're here on this grand occasion because we're proud to be Fannerans," he roared. "Here with us are wonderful people who wish they were Fannerans, and fortunately for them, we can designate each of them tonight as 'Honorary Fannerans'

He waved the manila folder and took out a certificate.

"In honor of Charlie Kronke, the greatest Fanneran party-person of all time, I bestow honorary Fanneran membership on his lovely widow Mary Lou Kronke, who is here from Aurora, Illinois to accept this special recognition."

A beaming Mary Lou rose to accept. Her daughters Eileen and Patricia cheered her, accompanied by loud clapping from Babe. Charlie and Mary Lou had come to Raleigh many times with festive groups heading for the Carolina shore.

Tim presented Honorary Fanneran certificates to everyone eligible. Molly Fanneran's hand-lettered certificate read "Most Outstanding Fanneran," a well-deserved honor. My certificate honored 'Barry Burn." The Fannerans mean well but sometimes I wonder.

The bus came at dinner's end for the ride back to the Ambassador East. Once Babe was inside she hauled out her chart of the Fanneran family tree and announced we were off to the hospitality suite.

"I saw four changes which have to me made on this chart last night, and heard two two more in the afternoon today," she said. "I'm meeting Marilyn and Amy and we're going to get this thing right. You're welcome to join us but I don't think this is one of your projects, Barry."

We took the elevator to the seventh floor. About half the group was sitting around, drinks in hand. Music played from a hi-fi. I was pleased to see relatives in their 20's from around the country enjoying each other's company. Babe was right, though. Her family tree isn't one of my projects. I had other things in mind.

A trip to the lobby and a call to Irene preceded my arrival in her suite. We moved quickly and fondly into the bedroom. I enjoyed Irene to the fullest, and again savored Wilde Swan perfume. We created mutual treats until, finally, we rested.

"Barry, I'd like you to to listen for a few minutes," Irene said, because there's something I have to tell you."

"Good news or bad?"

"I don't know, Barry. I'd say it's the sound of footsteps."

"You have my attention."

"Fine. No interruptions. Okay?"

"Okay."

"When you and Babe spent a day in Dublin last year you met Babe's young cousin, Maeve, for a drink. Your tour went to Wexford where you visited Maeve's parents, Noreen and Frank Butler. Noreen's maiden name was Fanneran and she's as interested in the Fannerans as Babe."

"Mmmm." I said.

"You returned to Raleigh, painted an oil portrait of Maeve and sent it to Noreen and Frank. Everyone was thrilled."

"Mmmm"

"You probably didn't know Frank Butler is my cousin. He never met you years ago but he certainly heard your name. Did he mention me to you?"

"No."

"I didn't think he would. Frank's one of nature's noblemen. Well, a few weeks ago his daughter Maeve visited me. She saw my portrait, the one you painted and signed 'Brian Boru.' Maeve thinks her portrait is amazingly similar to mine.

Hers is signed 'b.b.' She knows your name is Barry Byrne. When she wondered if Barry Byrne and 'Brian Boru' could be the same person I said "it's most unlikely."

"Whew."

"Noreen and Frank are coming to New York in June, when their son Dan's wife is due to give birth to their first grandchild. You'd better plan ahead, Barry. Babe will want to meet Noreen and Frank in New York, which means you'll be there, too. The family tree will come out as soon as you say hello.

Do you hear the footsteps, my dear?"

"I hear them loud and clear. Since my style for painting lovely blondes has never changed I thank you for alerting me. Now, kiss me again before I leave."

"I'll kiss you more than once, my Brian Boru, for these are our final minutes together," she whispered in the sweet Irish brogue I hear when I close my eyes. "I've enjoyed every minute. I wish I could give you a gold memento but here is what I have."

She handed me her admission ticked to The Chicago Art Institute.

"Thank you for a wonderful memento. I'll think of you every time I see it," I said. "Since I have my own Institute ticket with me, please take it with you." I handed it to her.

"Wait, Barry." Irene ran into the bedroom and came back with a pen. She circled the "I" on her Institute ticket in green ink, then did the same on mine.

"Do you see what we have, Barry? Irish eyes." She laughed and I laughed with her. Irene's fey sense of humor is delightful and contagious. "Keep the pen," she added. "Aer Lingus doesn't need it."

I took her in my arms and held her. Minutes later I reminded her the Fannerans would have Stadium Club privileges at the Chicago White Sox game Sunday. If she could get a ticket I wanted her to know where I would be.

"I'll be walking around the entrance to the Stadium Club during the seventh inning stretch," I said.

"Barry," she said, finally, "you have to go. How about a quick shower here followed by you riding to the lobby in the elevator to the left of my door. Once in the lobby, take the other elevator back up and maybe, just maybe, it will be empty when you need it."

I accepted Irene's suggestion. On reaching the lobby I saw suave Frank Cassidy and his wife, Chris, hurrying towards the elevator to my left. Chris, the mother of two young men, looks like a successful red-haired actress. In the winter she teaches grade school at Lake Tahoe and in summer runs a par 3 golf course which earns her a new Cadillac every Labor Day. The Cassidy's reached my elevator and the door closed. Minutes later I took the empty elevator to The Artist's Suite, where Babe had just climbed into bed.

"I'm tired, Barry," she said. "Let's wait until we get home."

I knew what she meant.

"Mmmmm," I mumbled. The lovely Irish blonde in the suite down the hall had exhausted me. Wondering how much luck and energy would be needed to survive the final day of The Fanneran Reunion, I turned off the bed lamp.

Sunday morning began with a visit to the hospitality suite. A round of goodbyes thanked the half dozen young Fannerans who'd flown in Saturday to attend the family dinner. Mike, Courtney and Albert from New York mingled with Chicago cousins Meredith and Jennifer. Pretty girls surrounded me. I took pictures along with everyone else, hoping my future paintings would benefit from the lovely models. Paul Fanneran and Tim clustered in a corner with Johnny the bike. Each of the three shared a monumental hangover.

Plane times and schedules were discussed, with half the delegates heading for O'Hare Airport. Paul and Molly corralled Babe and me and drove us to the White Sox game in their sparkling new Lexus RV. Brilliant blue sky lit up our route, allowing all of Chicago to put its best foot forward. We enjoyed the shifting scenery, from the towers of the Gold Coast to the long rows of houses with yellow vinyl siding further along the ride. When we arrived at Comiskey Park's parking lot our daughters stood waiting. Both have inherited good looks from their mother. When they walked with Babe and lovely Molly they drew stares from every direction. Paul, like his cousin Tim a tall man with greying hair, possesses a ton of charm. He circled to my side. Above us, a light breeze tossed the flags high atop the stadium. We merged with the crowd along the walkways and went through a series of numbered gates to the special entrance which welcomes holders of Stadium Club tickets.

We boarded an elevator. A quick ride was followed by a short walk to a bar, a series of tables and a row of folding seats facing a glass wall high above the playing field. Uniformed waitresses flitted about. Game time was a half hour away. To our left a wooden ledge ran across the glass wall, with groups of chairs scattered beside it. Two dozen customers rested food and drink on the ledge and looked through the glass on rows of seated fans outside and below them. Concrete steps descended downward to the pipe railings which circled the green grass of the outfield.

I checked my ticket. It entitled mer to one of the outside seats and meant I could enjoy the near-capacity crowd. Behind me the rest of our group ordered food and drink, while through the glass I saw a giant illuminated scoreboard on the far side of the stadium. It listed White Sox players and the opposing Oakland team by number and position.

"Quite a sight, isn't it?" I asked my daughter Marilyn, who stood beside me.

"It's really something, dad. I see you came prepared." She pointed to the black binocular case strapped across my shoulders.

"I like to see everything," I explained. "I always bring them along." They might help locate Irene, too, a fact I didn't bother to mention.

Marilyn moved away. I went outside and looked for my seat while enjoying the sun's warmth. The seat was on the end of a row, a pleasant surprise. In a few more minutes the game would start and I was excited. I love baseball.

Amy and Marilyn arrived and sat in the seats beside me. Warmups ended and the first pitch was thrown when Amy explained the empty seats all around us. The others of our Reunion remained in the bar.

At intervals during the game I scanned the stands casually, sometimes using the binoculars. I didn't see Irene. I returned my attention to the game.

The White Sox tried gallantly to win. By the middle of the seventh inning they trailed by a score of 3-2, thanks to a home run by Frank Thomas, perennial all-star. When the home fans rose for the traditional seventh inning stretch I excused myself.

"I think I'll just walk around," I said. "Be back in a few minutes."

"Leave me the binoculars, dad," Marilyn said. I handed them to her before descending the concrete steps to the corridor outside the Stadium Club entrance where a smiling Irene stood waiting. She wore a pastel green dress and dark leather shoes and, simply stated, looked gorgeous.

"I'm thrilled to see you here," I said. I took her in my arms and kissed her thoroughly. When she stepped back I told her how wonderful she looked, and her presence made my day a triumph.

"Thank you, my Brian Boru." A tear appeared in one of her blue eyes, and then the other. She turned her back. Looking at me over one shoulder she managed a smile. She waved an immaculate piece of white lace, touched it to her eyes and walked away.

I watched until she disappeared before returning to my seat in the upper reaches of the stadium.

"You dropped this when you left, dad," Marilyn said, handing me the Aer Lingus pen. "Where did you find this?"

"I really don't remember. Somewhere along the way" was the best I could manage.

Marilyn inhaled once or twice as if short of breath, then returned her attention to the game. The action on the field slowed and she scanned the crowd with the binoculars.

"Dad, take these binoculars and look over there," she said, suddenly. "See that woman in the green dress? Doesn't she look like the woman you spoke with on the sidewalk yesterday? You know, the pretty blonde in the yellow dress who spoke with a brogue?"

"A brogue?"

"Dad, I was right behind you. I heard her."

I took the binoculars and pointed them where she told me. I was unsurprised to see Irene's lovely features. I decided to seem hesitant.

"I'm not sure it's the same woman, Marilyn, though there's certainly a resemblance. I'd guess it's just a coincidence. Happens a lot, you know." At that moment the sun disappeared. Around us experienced fans rose, took sweaters from around their waists and put them on. I felt a chill though I wasn't certain what caused it.

I handed Marilyn the binoculars and patted her on the shoulder. "Let's enjoy the rest of the game," I said. "You know how much I enjoy baseball."

She looked at me, then returned her attention to Irene. When she put down the binoculars she shook her head. I didn't relax until the game ended. Predictably, the White Sox lost 3-2 with the homer by Frank Thomas absorbing some of the sting.

We ambled up to the Stadium Club and said our goodbyes. Marilyn and Amy were leaving later from O'Hare Airport. Paul and Molly drove Babe and me to Midway. Hours later we were home in Raleigh.

Wednesday night Babe enjoyed a long telephone conversation with each of our daughters, who live in different parts of Manhattan. Amy loved the Fanneran Reunion and was glad she went to Chicago. Marilyn was equally pleased. After her long conversation with her mother she asked to chat with me.

"Dad," she began, "you came back after the seventh inning stretch of the White Sox game on Sunday smelling of perfume. It was the same perfume that lovely blonde wore on Saturday. I'm absolutely sure."

"Really?" I asked.

"She had a brogue, dad. Did your Aer Lingus pen come from an Irish airline?"

"Are you starting a court case, Marilyn" I asked. "How can I get you to defend me if you're also the prosecutor?"

"I don't know how you did it, dad, but it's over and I'm glad. The blonde was really gorgeous. I'm willing to leave well enough alone if you are, sort of between us, if you know what I mean."

"I think I can figure it out, Marilyn," I said.

"Good night, dad." She hung up.

Babe said nothing to me about her conversations with either Amy or Marilyn. However, when I returned from my afternoon class Thursday afternoon I was astonished to find a different Babe waiting for me.

The new Babe was a trim, smiling blonde who shall go unpainted until well after she redraws the Fanneran family tree with Noreen and Frank Butler in New York when their first grandchild is born.

In silence and in solitude, I reflected on the Fanneran Reunion. Two strings remained untied.

One was easy. I sent my sister Leslie a box of chocolates she'll never figure out.

The other seconded my surrender. I sent Marilyn a large, expensive bottle of Wilde Swan perfume.

11

Red-Haired Women

Wendy Forbes waited patiently until the doorbell rang. Her clothes were packed and ready. Her ride to Duke University Graduate School had been arranged by her cousin, Marilyn.

"Farrell's okay," Marilyn said, "but I don't have time for losers. He's lost his job. He's a beer drinker, too. I think he only liked me because I have red hair. Whatever, he's moving to Florida. Do well at Duke, Wendy."

Wendy opened the door. The man who faced her wore chino slacks, white shirt with short sleeves, and sneakers, all appropriate on a warm August morning. He was tall. Strands of sandy brown hair hung down over his right eye. She didn't know his age but she guessed he was under thirty.

"I'm Farrell," he said. "Just call me Bee. Are you Wendy?"

"Yes, and I'm ready."

"Good."

He carried her two bags. She draped clothes on hangers across her arm. Downstairs, he lifted the bags into the big trunk of an old gray Cadillac. She saw his bags were already in the trunk, along with several taped cardboard cartons.

They made two more trips upstairs. Finally, after rearranging the trunk and the car's back seat, they found places for all her possessions.

Today's ride from the Forbes apartment near New York's old Forest Hills tennis stadium to Duke University in Durham, North Carolina, would occupy their entire day.

He pulled out into the traffic on Queens Boulevard. The flashing bulbs of a bank clock showed 9:15 a.m.

They rode slowly in silence through the final chapters of the morning rush hour. On leaving Manhattan and reaching the Jersey Turnpike traffic thinned and the Cadillac's speed increased noticeably.

They were further south when Wendy realized the man beside her had spoken hardly a word. Idly, she tugged at a lock of her thick, dark hair. Perhaps it was up to her to break the silence.

"This car rides well, Bee," she began. "It's comfortable, too. Have you had it long?"

"Two days," he said. He continued concentrating on the road, without turning towards her.

She waited.

End of conversation. She'd tried, but he wasn't talking. She wondered if he was hung over. She shifted her attention to the trees, grass and occasional office buildings they passed.

At a toll plaza Farrell handed the collector a bill. He received change and turned to her.

"If you like, play the radio," he said.

Wendy selected a station with music. "Okay?" she asked. He nodded and they continued without talking with the radio substituting for conversation.

As they continued southward Wendy frequently changed the radio's settings as station signals faded out and were replaced by newer, closer stations.

They passed an electric sign which flashed a green arrow.

Washington, D.C. was ahead. Wendy turned to Farrell with an announcement.

"I can drive, too," she said. "I'd be happy to. I'd like to drive for awhile if you don't mind, and it would give you a break.

"A big car like this?" Farrell asked.

"My father prefers big cars," she said. "I love to drive them."

"Terrific. We'll switch after lunch." He sounded like he meant it.

He slowed at the next exit ramp and they drove to a suburban restaurant. Wendy was grateful it wasn't a fast food outlet; her low budget promised plenty of those in her future.

Lunch opened Wendy's eyes about her chauffeur. He talked and smiled and joked with her.

He told her his name was Boylan Farrell but he'd never liked Boylan, his mother's maiden name. He didn't like 'Boy' either. In school he signed his name 'B. Farrell' and answered to nothing else. After fourth grade almost no one knew his real name, including her cousin Marilyn.

Farrell's older brother Andrew was the family's favorite son. Of late Andrew had begun using 'A. Farrell' and 'B. Farrell,' stressing B as inferior to A.

Wendy found listening to him easy and encouraged him to continue.

He'd done well at the bank, only to find his entire department eliminated.

Marilyn had been unimpressed with the explanation for his job hunt and she had written him off, too. Andrew Farrell made so much noise about his younger brother's two big losses it was time to head south, before B.Farrell beat the stuffing out of A. Farrell and their parents threw him out anyway.

Time was on his side. He was young enough for a fresh start. He sold his BMW, bought the old Cadillac and banked the difference for expenses while he hunted for a new job.

"One more thing," he said while Wendy laughed at a further comment, "I like the taste of beer, but I never drink when I'm driving. Since you're driving now, I can have a couple of beers here. I'd like to pick up a few for future reference while we're off the main road, and then we can be on our way."

"Fine with me, Boylan Farrell," she said.

"I'll take the check," he replied. "I know we agreed to share expenses, but it's the least I can do when traveling with someone so very young."

They laughed together and went out to the car.

Wendy adjusted the chrome-edged leather seat and drove to a nearby store. Farrell emerged with two six-packs of canned beer. He made space for them on the crowded floor behind the passenger seat.

She handled the big sedan well. She tested the car's response by edging the speedometer needle into the middle seventies. The car had power to spare and Wendy enjoyed driving fast.

After they passed Richmond, Virginia, traffic lightened to an occasional car. Farrell dozed. The red needle on the dash climbed upward. Wendy glanced in the rear view mirror and saw a black car overtaking them. It closed the space between them so fast she guessed its speed at close to 90 miles an hour.

The black car moved beside her and slowed. She saw it was a Camaro. The teenager driving it waved triumphantly as he looked over at Wendy. The wave cost him control of his car.

The Camaro veered to the right. Wendy spun her steering wheel to avoid a collision.

The Camaro shot ahead. The Cadillac careened off the lane, teetered on two wheels and turned over. Its forward momentum plowed a furrow in the grass before the car halted, upside down and at an angle to the highway. Steam spewed from the engine. The four large wheels continued to spin slowly.

Farrell's head caromed off the windshield and snapped back. He was momentarily stunned. When his vision cleared he saw he was upside down, held in place by his seatbelt. He could see Wendy beside him, unconscious. Her head lolled to one side.

He tried to think clearly. He undid his seatbelt and righted himself. A part of the Cadillac's roof had compressed so he could not get to Wendy. The inside of the car smelled of beer and his clothes were soaked with it. He tried forcing open the passenger door, which resisted his best efforts. He could see the smoke clouds thrown up by the engine, and he was aware of the danger of fire.

He smashed the door window with a shoe and climbed out, cutting his hands in the process. He hardly stopped to inspect them.

Once outside, he broke Wendy's window, too. He had no time to remove all the jagged glass around the window frame. He reached in and began working on her seatbelt. Finally, she was free. He lowered her to the car's roof, still inside the car.

He fought the weight of the driver's door, trying to open it as he became more conscious of the fire danger. The door hardly moved. He stifled the beginnings of panic and pulled the door open far enough to maneuver Wendy's unconscious form through.

He cradled her in his bloodied hands. At least she's breathing, he thought, though the slant of her head seemed all wrong to his troubled inspection.

Two big truckers took her from his arms and he slumped to the grass. He heard a siren in the distance before he passed out.

Farrell opened his eyes. He'd dozed and waked for many hours. This time he stayed awake. His head hurt. He was on his back in bed, under a white sheet. He turned his head slightly and realized he was in a hospital, somewhere.

He tried to move his arms and stopped. Heavy bandages extended from above his elbows to his fingertips.

He remembered Wendy lying on the grass. He wondered about her.

The room's door flew open.

"He's awake now, the bastard," a voice said. It was Marilyn, rushing through the door.

"You rat, you bumbler, you drunk," she shouted at him in rapid-fire fashion. A white-uniformed nurse rushed in behind Marilyn and grabbed her. Marilyn wrenched away and continued.

"You lunatic, you menace, you jackass. I hope they give you a hundred years on the DWI. I hope they lock you up and throw the key away," she yelled before the nurse led her from the room.

Boylan "Bee" Farrell wondered what was next.

The nurse returned. A grey-haired woman in starched white hat, she signaled him for silence with a finger at her lips. She closed the bedroom door as she left.

He ached. His head hurt and the bandages on his arms made even slight movements painful.

The nurse re-entered.

"How's Wendy?" Farrell asked.

"She'll recover," the nurse said. "No marks on the outside but she can't remember everything. We call it aphasia. Bump on the brain. All of her memory or some of it may come back. Good chance at her age. School's off for this year, that's for sure."

"Oh," Farrell said. He remembered Marilyn's comment about the DWI charge. He thought about his defense, the testimony of a young woman who might not want to admit she'd been driving, or might not remember.

"Ouch," he said, trying to move. The nurse watched him from her post near the door.

He glanced at the wall, where a calendar showed August dates and below it "North Hospital, Raleigh."

"Mr. Farrell, the nurse said. "Wendy's family is badly upset. They've given strict instructions you're to have no contact with her."

"Not surprised," he said. He realized he might as well begin on his defense now.

"Nurse, I have a message for you," he added.

"Yes?"

"She was driving."

"Oh. No one thought of that."

"Why not?"

"You were soaked in beer, and the trooper thought DWI. Then Marilyn flew down. She was very upset and she yelled about your beer drinking, in case you didn't guess."

"I guessed," he said, "but did Marilyn think Wendy flew out of her seatbelt, like Peter Pan?"

"If you're telling the truth, Mr. Farrell," the nurse said, "Wendy's whole family might owe you an apology."

"Tell me about it," Farrell said, watching her surprised expression. "Then tell them about it. And while you're at it, I'd like a cold beer. In a can."

He closed his eyes.

Someone turned the room's doorknob and the noise woke him. The nurse entered, followed by a short,older woman. The newcomer's eyes were heavily made up. The woman was smartly dressed, but what attracted Farrell's attention was the deep auburn color of her hair.

"Mr. Farrell," the woman said in a husky voice, sitting on the hard chair beside his bed, "nurse Myers thinks you've been falsely accused. I'm Lois Gordon, and I'm a real estate agent in Durham. Whether you know it or not you're going to need treatment for the next month, maybe longer. If you let me, I'll find you a place to stay."

Farrell was grateful. Also suspicious. He felt capable of handling his own affairs. Her suggestion made sense and as always he was fascinated by a red-haired woman.

He turned to find her dark brown eyes staring at him. He couldn't tell whether she was simply trying to help him or had some other motive.

"Fine," he said. "And thank you, nurse Myers, I appreciate your help."

The two women started to leave. The nurse looked over her shoulder at Farrell. "I'll work on the beer," she said.

"Cold. In a can," Farrell specified.

For the balance of the day he was poked at, examined, interviewed, sized up and x-rayed. The trooper accepted his explanation of the accident. Doctors advised close watch of his many cuts, guarding against infection. He agreed to remain in the area after his release. Despite the headache, Boylan Farrell's recovery seemed free of major problems.

He enjoyed his hospital dinner.

Afterwards, nurse Myers visited. Visiting hours were almost over and she knew no visitors would come for him.

They both turned as the door opened. Wendy Forbes stood in the doorway. She wore a white hospital gown which contrasted sharply with her thick dark hair.

Boylan Farrell, unemployed, homeless and aching, behaved like a gentleman.

"Come in, fair maiden," he said. "We've been expecting you." He was pleased she wanted to see him. He was equally pleased by the loose lines of her hospital gown.

"Perhaps I'll leave," nurse Myers said.

"Perhaps there's a can of beer in the building?"

"Perhaps," said the nurse. She left, leaving the room's door slightly ajar.

Wendy Forbes sat on the hard chair by Farrell's bed.

"Boylan Farrell," she began, "I've a few things to tell you."

"Tell."

"First, thanks for getting me out of the car and taking Marilyn's abuse. I know she's embarrassed. Can we apologize?"

"Accepted."

"Second, you'd better get used to my family," she continued. "We're devious. The real estate agent who visited you is my aunt Lois. She does work in Durham but she was also checking you out."

"Shocking."

"And Boylan Farrell I'd also like it if you help me remember while I help you forget."

"Forget what?" Farrell asked.

"How I deceived you. After listening to Marilyn I didn't want to like you," she said.

"You didn't want to like me?" he said, his tone obviously laden with mischief.

Wendy ignored his comments. She put two hands to her head. After a good pull, the wig of dark hair slipped to the floor, replaced by long, shining red tresses which reflected the lights from above.

"I'm sorry, Boylan," Wendy said. "I was devious, too."

They sat and looked wordlessly at each other. Soon, Wendy's patience evaporated. She'd apologized and the man had said nothing. She picked up the wig from the floor and turned to him in exasperation.

"Don't you have anything to say, Boylan Farrell?"

"I most certainly do," Farrell said. He sat up in bed and yelled. Loud.

"Nurse!"

As he suspected, nurse Myers waited outside the door.

"Yes, Mr. Farrell?" she asked as she entered, one hand still on the doorknob.

"Make that two cans of beer," he instructed her. "cold beers, if you don't mind." He turned his attention to Wendy. He looked at her fondly. "Might as well get her young and train her right," he said.

12

Grateful Chorus

When I was a girl people living in rural farm communities in Eastern North Carolina enjoyed few entertainment choices. Arrival of a carnival was invariably cause for celebration.

Early on a sunny August afternoon I joined my three older sisters in welcoming John E. Frakes traveling carnival to Old Hanover, N.C. We milled around in the dirt and watched big men carry red wooden panels from a half dozen trucks. They unloaded dirty canvas tents wrapped in heavy ropes and opened them, and a rectangle of tents soon occupied the perimeter of our fairgrounds. I watched with excitement, taking in every move, awed by the arm muscles of men who wore sleeveless undershirts, and who, when they walked near us, smelled of sweat.

My reverie was interrupted by my sister, Shirley.

"Time to go home, Annie," she said. "Dinner time." I turned, following her the few short blocks to our home, excited as only a nine-year-old could be.

We lived in a big white colonial centered on a corner plot with a large green lawn. Rockers lined the porch which surrounded our house on three sides. The garage which held my father's Buick sat in the back of the yard. As owner of the Old Hanover drug store my father provided us a comfortable living.

At dinner we talked about going to the carnival on Saturday, only two days off. Later, when my sister Shirley and I were drying dishes we heard a knock at the front door.

"I'll answer it," I shouted. I raced to open the door.

A man and woman faced me.

The woman was huge. Four times wider than me and much taller, she wore a flat straw hat with s black band. The hat sat like a small island on her enormous sea of greying hair. Her faded print dress with red and white flowers hung shapelessly to her ankles. She carried a bulging shopping bag in each hand and watched me in silence.

The man beside her wore a pair of black pants and an aged white shirt. Taller than the woman, he was the skinniest man I'd ever seen. His thin and narrow head, almost pointed, was too small for his body. He, too, held a shopping bag in each hand.

I stared, motionless, at the couple's odd appearance. The man spoke to me.

"Can we meet with your mother?" he asked, in a rich, deep voice which frightened me.

"Ma," I yelled. I ran inside. My mother passed me on her way to the door. I stood on the far side of the living room, waiting to see what would happen.

Minutes later my mother led the strange man and woman through the house to the kitchen. The floor creaked at each step the giantess took. Neither she nor the skinny man looked at my father or me or any of my sisters.

Mama returned at once.

"We're having guests for the night," she said. "I'll take care of it. Just leave us alone." She returned to the kitchen, closing the door behind her.

"Well, girls," my father said. "We'll see what happens. In the meantime, let's enjoy the night air on the porch."

Ten minutes later my mother came outside.

"Annie, you and Shirley come with me. I need your help carrying blankets and sheets."

We followed instructions. She had us make up the bed in our guest room, which she said was for the man. The woman would sleep on the kitchen floor because she was too heavy for any of our beds.

"Who are they, ma?" I asked.

"She's the Fat Lady in the Carnival and he's the Pin-Head Man. The owner has no money and can't pay them until Saturday's show. They asked if they could stay with us tonight. They're hungry, too. They're eating in the kitchen, and when they finish they'll stay here as our guests. In the morning they'll leave, after breakfast. I'll have food they can take with them. Tomorrow night they'll sleep in one of the tents."

"Wow, mama," was all I could say.

"There's more,' mama said. "Tell your father and sisters when I call you're all to come into the living room. Not before. When you do, sit. Don't say anything."

"Why, mama?"

"Just do as I say."

I was bursting with curiosity. Shirley and I looked at each other. We repeated Mama's instructions when we reached the porch.

A half hour later mama joined us.

"Come in now," she said.

We hurried to our living room., where mama assigned each of us a seat. Some of the room's furniture had been moved.

Our piano now rested against the far wall. The skinny man sat on the bench and faced the keyboard, presenting us a view of his back. The heavy woman sat erect on the floor beside him. Her broad back hid her features.

We made bustling sounds as we took our seats. We looked at mama, who waited until we were in place before she spoke.

She smiled.

"As you see, we have guests tonight," she said. "Their names are Roseanne and Henry and we are pleased we can help them. Usually they are known only by their carnival names. Roseanne is the Fat Lady and Henry is the Pin-Head Man. They are grateful for our hospitality and will thank us with their singing which most people don't know about. They prefer we look at their backs because they tire of people staring at them, though they know folks can't help it."

Mama paused. She smiled again and clapped. She nodded and we clapped, too.

The strange couple's singing delighted us. The man's deep tones blended with the sweet voice of The Fat Lady. After they sang 10 songs for us we applauded their beautiful duet. I've been a lot of places since and heard many famous singers. Some were as good. None were better.

When they finished, Mama waved us out of the room before caring for our guests, who left early in the morning.

Saturday we went to the John E. Frakes carnival, along with everyone else in Old Hanover. When I found the tent featuring the Fat Lady and the Pin-Head Man I entered, stood to one side and stared. The Fat Lady sat. The Pin-Head Man stood near her. When I moved she nudged him and rippled the fingers of a gloved hand. He looked where she pointed and they smiled at me. On impulse I returned the smile before merging into the crowd.

When I finished school in Old Hanover I went on to college. I moved north and for many decades worked in Massachusetts. After I took early retirement I returned to Old Hanover.

Now I live in the same house where I grew up. Shirley and I keep order. The carnival doesn't come around any more, of course, but on quiet nights I go into our parlor. If I listen carefully I sometimes hear Roseanne and Henry singing their Grateful Chorus.

—⚍—

13

Hugon Karnowsky

I was 12 years old in 1950.

My father moved himself, my mother and me from the Ukraine to a two-family brick house in Jackson Heights, a bustling neighborhood in the New York City borough of Queens.

We lived on the first floor of our rented house. The O'Brien's lived upstairs. All the houses on our block looked alike. Most of them held lots of kids with Irish names.

I was big for my age. After a few introductory fights I got along fine with the other boys. Many of them were named Bill or Jack or Kevin. Among the girls were quite a few Maureens, Eileens and Catherines. We all attended parochial grade schools.

Most of the kids thought Hugon was a funny name, for no one in their family had ever been named Hugon. Additionally, it didn't help much to be Hugon in the 1950's when Russian immigrants were viewed with suspicion.

I loved Irish names. They all sounded sweeter than mine.

My father was descended from Russian nobility. His father had been a general and as a young man my father considered a military career. He knew a lot about the military but as luck would have it he ended up a pastry chef in a New York hotel.

"Leaders lead and followers follow," he told me. "You will be a leader." I was uninterested.

"A good general or good leader always takes care of the troops first," my father said. "Take care of the troops and they'll take care of you." How right he was.

One Irish girl and her name held a particular fascination for me. I made it my business to talk with her as often as I could. This wasn't easy because Mary Margaret Nolan was always running from somewhere to somewhere else. I met her first when she was 10 years old. She had a pretty nose and the nicest smile I have ever seen.

She was one of the five Nolan children who lived at the far end of our block. Mary Margaret achieved high grades in school, laughed a lot, and participated in every game going. Her dark hair was naturally curly. Her large blue eyes were topped by thick dark lashes. When she smiled her mouth displayed perfect teeth. Her skin was as smooth as a newborn baby's.

Mary Margaret was hard to find except when I drifted to a quiet spot behind our house where I liked to draw.

Then she would appear at once.

"What are you drawing, Hugon?" she would ask. When she learned I only drew people her question changed to "who are you drawing now, Hugon?"

It might be a politician from the cover of Time magazine, a popular movie star or a face from a family photo. She sat beside me and watched, unaware I slowed down to lengthen her visit. Once I drew her profile, paying special attention to her nose. When I finished I signed the drawing "Karnowsky."

"Oh, that's a fine job, Hugon," she said. She reached for my pencil and put a neat "MM" in front of "Karnowsky." She looked me in the eye when she said "I always like what you draw, Hugon. I initialed it so we could be partners."

Her comment made me almost as happy as her nearness. Seconds later, she raced off to the next stop on her busy agenda.

When I graduated from high school my father decided I should go to a college with an ROTC program. He felt I should participate in military activities before choosing my career path. I went to a college in Massachusetts with an ROTC program. ROTC surprised me. I liked it.

Two years after I began college Mary Margaret earned a scholarship to a Philadelphia college. I saw her at the few intervals when our semester breaks coincided. She grew into a lovely young woman. Once she asked me to draw her picture and I did. When I finished she initialed it as before, and handed it back.

"Keep this one, Hugon. I'm going to be a nun. You'll have something to remember me by. If I wasn't a nun I'd chase you in a second," she added.

I didn't know then whether to be flustered or disappointed. I was busy with my own plans. On graduation from college I applied for active military duty as a second lieutenant in the infantry.

I qualified for an elite corps of Special Forces troops. We saw a lot of behind-the-lines action. On a night parachute raid I carried a badly-wounded black sergeant on my back to a pick-up point almost a mile away. Later, my commanding officer reprimanded me for ignoring his order to leave the sergeant behind. Sergeant Jackson survived, however, and the commander relented. He didn't put a formal reprimand in my officer's performance file. The Army awarded me a citation and a medal which I sent to my father in New York, along with Sergeant Jackson's letter of thanks.

Months later I led another night raid. This time I wasn't so fortunate. An enemy soldier with a machete dropped from a tree. His first swing sliced into my nose. He began a second slash when a shot from beside me struck him. His machete slowed but didn't stop. It slid against the side of my neck. I heard a second shot. I passed out.

I didn't regain my senses fully for two weeks. When my head cleared I faced a surgeon who sat beside my bed in a military hospital in Japan.

"You were lucky to be saved from the man who cut you," he said, "but your Army days are over. Now, we'll be working together so you're presentable in civilian life."

"Which means?"

"You choose the nose you like best and I'll see how close I can come. The process requires months. Once it's done your neck wound should be healed. The scar won't be pretty and I'd suggest a full beard. It's up to you."

I asked for a pencil and drew a picture of Mary Margaret's nose.

"Here's what I want," I said.

The nose-building process required a number of skin grafts. They weren't fun. When the neck scar healed a full beard hid it. I put together a packet of drawings and applied for a job as editorial cartoonist with newspapers around the country. The News & Observer in Raleigh, North Carolina, had an opening. We agreed on a salary. I moved to Raleigh.

A small apartment, a car and a few clothes got me started. I began a heavy reading program, which seemed to be the best way to begin my editorial career.

Two surprising letters reached me. One was from Sergeant Jackson. He reminded me the soldier who saved my life was Ben Heard, which I knew. He informed me Ben was his cousin, which I hadn't known.

"I told him to try getting into your unit," Jackson told me, "for I knew you'd look out for him as well as yourself. Funny how things work out, isn't it?" he added.

Funny isn't the word I would use.

The other letter was from Tommy Nolan, who lived on my block in Jackson Heights. Tommy's a fire lieutenant.

"Your father gave me your Raleigh address, Hugon," he wrote. "I met him in the supermarket. He looks well. Mary Margaret is also in Raleigh. Did you know that? She's Sister Mary Hugon, a Notre Dame nun assigned to St.Raphael's parish."

I usually attend the Russian Orthodox church but made an exception the following Sunday. A copy of the parish bulletin at St. Raphael's said Sister Mary Hugon was director of Faith Formation, whatever that meant. A call to the rectory was more rewarding. I learned Sister Mary Hugon regularly attended the 10 o'clock Mass on Sunday and sang in the choir.

My seat at the next Sunday's 10 o'clock Mass was on the end of the third row.

Sister Mary Hugon was easy to recognize. She was even more attractive than I remembered. I didn't think she'd recognize me with my new nose and full beard, but she did. She left the choir before Mass ended. She was ready for me when I left the pew.

"Hugon, I knew you'd come. Tommy wrote me you were in Raleigh. All I had to do was wait."

"I hope my new nose looks familiar," I said. In case you didn't guess, it's yours. Now we each have something of the other's. I have your nose and you have my name."

"Tommy said you'd been hurt when you were in the Army," she continued. "You seem fine now, and if so, I'm glad."

"I am fine, Mary Margaret, if I can still call you that. Now about you? Do you like the life of a nun?"

"I like it when you call me Mary Margaret," she replied, "and I love my work. I can't imagine doing anything else."

"I guess I'll just have to wait," I said.

I waited twenty-five years. I never missed a ten o'clock Mass on Sunday. We talked with each other every week. We aged together.

Her funeral was held last week at St.Michael's Catholic Church in Cary, a Raleigh suburb. The bishop presided. Mary Margaret will be buried in the Karnowsky plot in St.Agnes Cemetery. When my time comes I'll be buried beside her. The bishop married us before the wasting disease took her life. A special dispensation, you might say...

...for Hugon Karnowsky.

—ɯ—

14

Albany Man

The capital city of the state of New York is Albany, which sits on the west bank of the Hudson River one hundred sixty miles north of Manhattan and reminisces about its heyday, which occurred in 1910.

Albany is a wonderful place for people who don't like big cities and don't mind a climate which gets mighty cold in November and stays cold until early April. In spring and summer Albany's climate is delightful. Many fine parks and the rich greens in the surrounding mountains exert a powerful presence on the people who live there.

My father and mother grew up in Albany. As he had a clear idea of where he would pursue his career as an attorney he whisked his young bride a thousand miles away almost as soon as the last piece of thrown rice hit the pavement outside St. James Church.

My parents enjoyed a happy and congenial life. I'm their only child. My decision to attempt a career in professional baseball disappointed them until I hurt my pitching arm. Now I'm a lawyer and happy at it but the career change wasn't an easy one. My parents manipulated me at every opportunity though even as a youngster I was determined to think for myself. Despite their attempts at controlling me I made my own decisions. I'm glad we resolved our differences later on a friendly basis.

My parents are dead, buried in Albany as they wished. I acknowledge my obligation to visit their grave. As each visit means a two thousand mile trip, my visits are widely spaced. My wife has accompanied me twice but she prefers staying home with our small children.

I'm a regular bridge player. I play once a week at my bridge club and I make tournament appearances. My wife plays, too. We're capable but not exceptional players. I enjoy bridge.

When I go to Albany I visit cousins who like to compare living in Albany with life in my city. Everyone enjoys these get-togethers. If I have time I go to the Albany Bridge Club for a game. The director always finds a partner for me.

In March I learned Albany would host a bridge tournament on an August weekend.

This explains my visit to the Albany Bridge Club on a Friday afternoon in summer, seeking a partner for Saturday and Sunday. My arrival in Albany the previous Monday allowed me to exchange pleasantries with numerous cousins, visit the cemetery and still have time for bridge. My wife chose to stay home. Her absence meant I relied on getting a partner for my bridge from the Club director, a tall man with shrewd eyes who now led a short man to where I waited.

"Mr. Fanning," said the director to me, "meet Mr. Slade." You'd better talk over your approach and if you agree you'll be partners. As you know, the tournament is held at the Armory. First session tomorrow is at 1:00 p.m.

Having discharged his obligation, he left us.

Slade's greeting to me was a nod of the head. He looked to be 65 or older. He wore tan slacks, brown shoes with laces and a tan shirt with short sleeves which exposed freckled, skinny arms. He owned a long, straight nose. His jaw seemed firm, and above it a wide mouth separated a pair of parentheses which ran from nose to chin. He wore no watch. His grey hair, neatly combed, was parted on the side. His glasses were framed in silver and through their lenses I could see dark blue eyes, though I wasn't sure of the color. Slade watched me, unsmiling. Then he spoke.

"I'll play your system, whatever it is," he mumbled, bluntly. "Don't worry about me. Don't ask questions. Understand?" He paused and watched. A few seconds later, since I hadn't said anything, he added "We'll do fine."

I've heard worse introductions. I outlined my system and he listened without a word until I finished.

"I'll see you tomorrow," he said. I watched him walk to the door. His movements seemed awkward. He didn't look back.

Saturday's schedule at the Armory included an afternoon session and another at night. We finished second in both sessions, the best record I've achieved in any tournament. Slade mumbled as on Friday, looking at me only when necessary. During the pauses I wondered about him. When our night game was completed the little man had played six hours of errorless tournament bridge.

Our Sunday performance repeated Saturday's, including my highest score ever. Yet my 'nice play partner' comments to Slade generated nothing but grunts. His icy demeanor and 'no questions' attitude frustrated my urge to ask him his first name or at least to join with me in celebrating our results. I knew no more about him than I did on Friday except he wore a silver ring on his right hand which featured a bird in flight. To my eye the bird resembled a falcon.

"Thanks," Slade said as he turned over the last card. "Thanks." He rose and left the table without even looking at me. I watched him slog his way to the door of the Armory and disappear.

Monday morning I drove my rented car out Menands Road to the cemetery for a few quiet moments of reflection before continuing to the airport. An old-fashioned cemetery set in rolling hills, with plentiful trees and winding gravel lanes, St.Agnes displays a variety of large and small marble monuments chiseled in styles which changed over more than 100 years.

I enjoyed touches from the sun's fingers as they reached me through the tall trees. Lush grass surrounded me on all sides as I sat on a convenient stone marker. I appreciated the gentle, cool breeze which preceded the day's heat. Later, my flight proved smooth. Tuesday I was back at work. outwardly relaxed but still excited by my tournament bridge success.

I found my curiosity about Slade increased each time I reviewed the previous week. I knew I would be sorry if I didn't make an effort to check further on the little man with the falcon ring and the mumble.

"Oh, hello Mr. Fanning," said the director of the Albany Bridge Club. "Congratulations on your terrific results with Mr. Slade. Looks like you two got along just fine."

"Thank you. Thank you especially for finding him for me. In fact, he's the reason I'm calling you."

"Oh, I didn't find him for you," the director said.

"You didn't?"

"No. He came to me and asked for you. All I did was bring him over."

"He asked for me?" I said.

"Yes."

I wondered if he heard my intake of breath.

"Do you have a first name or an address or anything else about Mr. Slade?" I continued. "I'm more than a little curious, as you might imagine."

"Just a moment, Mr.Fanning, I'll see if there's anything here in writing, though I can tell you I never saw him before Friday. He just walked in."

The line went quiet. While I waited I wondered if one of my Albany cousins had played a joke on me, or perhaps knew Mr. Slade from somewhere and heard me talk about bridge. It made sense. I'd wondered about it before I called.

"Mr. Fanning?"

"Yes?"

"I can give you Mr.Slade's first name, which is Sidney, and his address if you want it. That's all."

I jotted down the address, thanked the director and hung up the phone. My next call, to the national headquarters of the American Contract Bridge League in Tennessee, frightened me.

Sidney Slade is a famous member of the Bridge Hall of Fame and a former resident of Albany, New York.

His address, 2700 Menands Road, appears on my bills for care of my parents' grave.

Sidney Slade died ten years ago and lies under a headstone with a falcon on it, which I recall seeing in St. Agnes Cemetery, slightly to the right, and just behind, the stone marked "Fanning."

15

Panis Angelicus

"In the morning," Julia Pryzborski thought. "In the morning I'll write my sister Eileen. She became a nun when we both had a choice. After I married Ed, my choices were few. Now, my daughter Maureen has given me a problem I can't solve alone. Eileen was always better at solving problems. I wonder what she'll say if I ask her help. It's the first time I ever asked, thanks to my being so independent. I wonder if she'll help me."

Julia finished cleaning the kitchen and went to her bedroom. In the mirror over her dresser she saw a woman of fifty with greying hair, a straight nose and the lines life etches early on the face of a working widow.

Julia's work meant piano lessons every day, choir practices two nights a week and her position on Sunday mornings as organist at 10 o'clock Mass. She loved music. It had helped her recover after Ed's untimely death five years earlier. Music thrilled her less now than it used to, except on rare occasions which involved Gregorian Chant or her favorite hymn, Panis Angelicus.

Julia's oldest child, Joe, a fine athlete who once played in the Red Sox chain, lived on the other side of Providence with his wife, Rose. They were parents of two boys named for Rose's brothers, Lou and Tony.

Julia's next child, Tom, a pilot, lived in Chicago with his wife, Helen. Married for a decade, they were childless. Julia's third and last child, Maureen, finished high school in Providence ten years ago and moved to New York. After securing a secretarial job she enrolled in college at night paying all her expenses herself. On graduation she accepted a job in the personnel department of a large insurance company.

Of Julia's three children, Maureen was the least talkative. A slender girl whose quiet disposition marked a fierce competitive spirit, Maureen never shared her plans with Julia. Once a plan succeeded, however, Maureen provided Julia the details. For Julia the relationship proved frustrating and fascinating.

Julia maintained contact with her children by phone and mail. She seldom wrote her sister. She visited her grandchildren dutifully and every second year Tom and his wife celebrated Christmas in Providence with Julia, joined by Ed, his wife and two boys. Christmas in Providence never included Maureen, whose litany of excuses seemed endless.

Before her marriage Julia's name was Julia Ellen Kiernan. Despite her recent frustrations she still nursed a strong desire for a grandson named Kevin or Patrick, to preserve her Irish heritage.

Maureen's occasional mention of socials in New York never hinted at marriage. Julia forced herself to be patient. Her tall daughter who inherited blonde hair from her father and a stubborn streak from her mother valued her privacy. Julia respected her daughter's determination to go her own way, a lifelong habit so strong Julia had not tried to obstruct the move to New York.

Julia glanced at the digital clock on her dresser. It displayed 9:28 p.m.in large green numbers on a black background.

"I can't put it off any longer," She thought. "I've got to write tonight to my sister, the noted Mother Superior."

She put on a robe and slippers. Minutes later, she began.

Dear Eileen,

As I write you the clock beside me edges towards ten and I'm fully charged. I know I won't sleep. I may explode. It's Sunday night in Providence. When I tell you what happened today you may understand why I must write you now.

This is about my daughter, Maureen, your goddaughter. The quiet one, who lives in New York.

At 8:00 in the morning today my phone rang.

"Mom, it's me, Maureen. I'm in Providence with my fiancee and I'd like you to meet him. His name's Casey. We're on a tight time schedule, Mom. I'll explain when I can. We'll see you at church after ten o'clock Mass, but then we have to go across town. We'd like to have dinner with you tonight at the house if it's okay with you."

"Of course it's okay with me," I said.

The phone clicked, Eileen, and I sat there. It's been years since Maureen came to Providence. Now, on less than two hours notice, I'm to meet her and her fiancee. At church, Eileen. What do I wear? What do I say? I don't know if Casey is his first name or his last name.

Did I panic? Of course I panicked. I don't know what you would do, Eileen. My panic lasted about ten minutes and then, well, it was time to get on with it. I decided to wear a simple grey dress and a strand of pearls. Get the job done, give nothing away and see what happens.

I went to church for the ten o'clock Mass, early as usual, and went upstairs to prepare for the choir's arrival. I felt overdressed for choir but ready for Maureen's fiancee.

"Good morning"

The pleasant voice startled me. It belonged to a smiling man about thirty who walked toward me. He looked like John F. Kennedy, Jr., tall and with the same wavy hair. His relaxed and friendly smile told me he liked me and wanted me to like him. He wore a tuxedo with tails, certainly different from what members of St.Matthew's choir usually wear to Sunday Mass. He held out his hand to me.

"I'm David."

"Julia"

"I know. I talked with the pastor and asked if I could solo with your choir. He said it was okay if you agreed."

"What do you have in mind?"

"Panis Angelicus. It's my favorite," he said. He saw my look of concern and smiled his winning smile.

"Don't worry about the tuxedo," he said. "I have to wear it later. As to Panis Angelicus, I spent 6 years as choir director and soloist at St. Paul's Seminary in New Jersey."

"You're a priest?" I asked.

"Almost a priest," he said. "Changed my mind after 4 years in the Seminary. Took me another 4 years to leave New Jersey."

David and I had a few minutes to discuss his voice, its range, and the handling of the hymn. He knew Panis Angelicus, all right. I hoped he sang well because when he stood up everyone in the choir would feast on his good looks. I didn't think it would be possible for me to forget about Maureen and her fiancee waiting downstairs, Eileen, but this young David made me forget. He was as likable as a man can be while staying focused on what he was doing.

I introduced him to the members of the choir and he smiled pleasantly. Mass began. He sat on a wooden folding chair beside the organ. When the time for his solo arrived he stood up and faced the altar, unseen by the congregation below. I played the organ without looking at the keys, watching the back of his head in the mirror over my keyboard. He began singing. Around me, the choir listened and watched.

"Pah-nis Ahn-gel-icus" he sang out, loud and clear and dominant. His trained voice was magnificent. As you know, Eileen, I love the hymn. I've seldom heard it sung so well and never heard it sung better. When David finished, he turned, his smile reflecting his own pleasure, and sat down on the wooden chair facing the altar.

To my astonishment the choir applauded. At Mass, no less, which didn't seem to bother anyone. I applauded, too, and then we all heard the spontaneous applause which floated upward from the congregation. At the altar Monsignor Ricci turned, looked up at us and smiled, joining the interruption with a silent clapping of his own hands.

Mass ended. David waited politely beside me, watching as the choir filed downstairs. He indicated I should go first and he would follow. Only then did I remember Maureen and her fiancee.

I reached the main floor and looked through the milling crowd in the sanctuary for Maureen, wondering if she was outside. I saw David's tuxedo vanish to my right before I could ask for his name.

Outside, the sun shone brightly on a picture-perfect scene. No clouds in the sky, lots of bright colors on women dressed in Sunday-best clothes. Little boys and girls chased each other on the sidewalk. To one side, Monsignor Ricci chatted pleasantly with an old parishioner.

Eileen, I was a happy woman. I glowed from that wonderful Panis Angelicus, even while searching for Maureen. I found her and gasped. She stood in a navy blue suit with an ironed white collar, and beside her, holding her hand, was the tuxedoed David who charmed all of St. Matthew's.

"David Casey?" I asked myself. "With his looks and voice? Is God getting ready to play another trick on me?"

Things progressed so fast I could hardly keep up. Yes, Maureen's fiancee is David Casey, or to be precise, David K. Casey. He grew up on the other side of Providence, near the golf course. He's been an undertaker in New York since leaving New Jersey. His plan is to buy a place here and move back to Providence, which he truly loves. I think the tuxedo had something to do with the undertaking business. He and Maureen had to hurry off and I raced home to figure all this out.

Eileen, you know my circumstances. You know I've always wanted a grandson named Kevin, and now you know my daughter has returned with this fiancee whose middle initial is undoubtedly K for Kevin. In fact, I'm sure of it. To top it off he's the best Irish tenor I've ever heard.

Dinner was perfect, so far as I could tell. Afterward, David and Maureen flew to New York. Their wedding will be here in Providence in three months, and you'll certainly be invited. This is why I need the favor, Eileen.

Tell God not to do anything funny. Let the wedding happen so I can stop holding my breath. You get through to God better than I can. All I've ever wanted is a grandson named Kevin, better if he has an Irish name. Kevin Casey? Wow! I've done my best with Ed's Polish sisters but if God cooperates they may have to adjust to an Irish in-law. Again.

Thanks, Eileen. Pray hard. I guarantee you'll love David.

Fondly,
Your sister, Julia.

—◦◦◦—

Dear Maureen,

Although I'm now the Mother Superior of our order, I'm never too busy to write my favorite goddaughter. I'm sure you'll enjoy my letter, especially since I claim full responsibility for sending David Casey to you. Isn't it nice he came to visit his sister at the convent just before he moved to New York? Nice he grew up in Providence, too. If I had faced a choice of vocations as a young woman, my dear, and a David Casey was around, my choice would have been sheer torture.

However,

I write you now because in your busy schedule you forgot to inform your mother of a few details which may need some delicate handling.

She adores David Casey, as most people do. In the hubbub of your quick visit no one told her why David wore his tuxedo. She presumed it had to do with his becoming an undertaker. She was amazed by the Panis Angelicus, as I told you she would be. Last but not least, your mother has always wanted a grandson with an Irish name, ideally

Kevin. Isn't it nice David's full name is David K.Casey? Is the picture clearing, Maureen?

I presume in your excitement with David you forgot to tell your mother you were off to St.Josephat's Polish church in North Providence, where David would sing at the Polish Mass. The tuxedo was for the formal party afterwards for his mom, who was born Wanda Rompalske. Did you mention to your mother David's career as a singer takes him all over the country but he likes being an undertaker when he's not traveling? Finally, Maureen, it might be a good idea for your mother to know David's middle initial is "K" for Kasimir and not Kevin. David's K salutes his Polish ancestry.

I don't think your father's sisters will have a problem with your marriage into a Polish family with an Irish connection, Maureen. It worked out nicely the first time. But plan ahead. If you become mother of a girl, whatever name you choose will be fine. But a boy? Can your mother cope with David Kasimir Casey? Could she handle David Kevin Kasimir Casey? Or even David Kiernan Casey?

Let's enjoy a laugh or two, Maureen, and then we'll figure out how we'll calm your mother. In the meantime, I'll write and tell her God is on her side because he, too, loves Panis Angelicus.

Sincerely,
+ Mother Superior, Sister Eileen
+ (Your devious godmother)

16

New York Eye Glasses

Cramped deep in the old armchair where he'd found sleep in pre-dawn hours, Arthur Fields opened his eyes. He glanced at his wristwatch. About eleven, mid-morning on Friday. Stiffness in arms and shoulders replaced the previous night's almost unbearable neck pain.

Outside, piles of shoveled white snow in the community courtyard reached knee level. The ice underneath had not melted. Would another cold day loom ahead in the worst New York winter of Arthur's five decades?

Mixed notes of a taped Rachmaninoff concerto drifted across his small, rectangular living room. Stacked books, tilted at odd angles, filled a sofa facing the room's casement window. A collection of unmatched and unstained pine boards rested against the blue wall under the window. A folding table near the boards held glue bottles, hand tools and pieces of wire. Black and white keys of a portable piano keyboard and a manual with home study lessons rose beside the darkened TV screen which connected Fields to the outside world.

His ruined neck confined him to the suburban Queens apartment, a sentence aggravated this winter by a siege of snow and ice from Christmas through mid-January. After ten years in the corner apartment he seldom reflected on the days before his divorce.

His disability erased job opportunities. Frequent neck agonies made pain and insomnia regular companions. Recovery lasted a day or two, longer if he was lucky. Medical bills chewed into his modest disability check.

Arthur Fields preserved his sanity by swapping jokes with the retired husbands who shared most of the courtyard's 14 apartments. In good weather his deep voice and booming laughter echoed on communal grass. Health permitting, he crafted wooden birdhouses which a friend sold at flea markets, an important assist in his unending struggle for a balanced budget.

Arthur's end apartment guarded one side of the horseshoe-shaped courtyard. People could look into his uncurtained first floor window, but he avoided even a wave unless necessary. His schedule with all its aggravations could not overcome a lifelong fondness for privacy. He distanced himself from neighbors, especially nosy ones.

Of late he'd seen few neighbors. They stayed inside and avoided injury from a fall on the ice coating the courtyard's concrete walk.

Fields ran a hand through his greying blond hair. He edged across the carpet to his narrow kitchen and dismissed as unimportant the sink full of unwashed dishes. He absorbed the room's warmth, grateful for a perfect thermostat, often a problem in the old brick buildings where some neighbors reported odd temperature fluctuations.

The buzz of his cordless phone jarred him.

"Hello?"

"Mr. Fields?"

"Yes?"

"This is Lydia Lawrence."

Both call and caller surprised him. Arthur knew Lydia Lawrence only by sight since her move to the far corner of the court in August. Tall, dark-haired, younger than himself, she often hurried by in an unbecoming grey sweatsuit and peaked cap. The retired men referred to her as "The Fat Woman."

"Yes?" he repeated. He grasped the phone and paced to the uncurtained window, surprised by sunshine and the many water streaks on the sidewalk below.

"Otto says you're well-read, Mr. Fields. Or is it 'Bird' which is what he called you?" Her voice seemed hesitant.

"I'll kill Otto," Arthur said. "He thinks he's funny. But I do read a lot. What can I do for you?"

"Do you use glasses when you read, Mr. Fields?"

"Yes. Why?" Her question held his attention.

"I've something I'd like you to read over, if it's not too much trouble. The sun has melted the sidewalk ice and it's a short walk in our courtyard. I live in the middle unit at the end of the court, the one with the red door. Would you come over and do me this favor, Mr. Fields?"

Arthur hesitated. He needed no involvement, least of all an unattached woman. If she proved difficult he would have problems avoiding her. But it was sunny and he hadn't been out in days. He saw puddles on the sidewalk, confirming her statement about melted ice. He decided to risk a visit.

"Yes, I'll come over in a little while," he said.

"Thank you. Don't forget your glasses."

Arthur wrapped a scarf on his neck before zipping his jacket. He wore a green plaid shirt and wrinkled chino pants. He chose his steps with care as he approached the red door ahead.

He saw a white shade and lace curtains on the window, and recognized the apartment as identical to his own. At night its thick beige drapes denied outsiders a hint of the inside decor.

He rang the doorbell. At once, the door moved inward.

"Come inside Mr. Fields," she said from behind the door.

He walked three steps into the apartment and heard her close and bolt the door behind him.

Arthur Fields was prepared for almost anything, but the scene he faced defied his imagination. Worse, the room's temperature was well into the 90's. He reached for his jacket's zipper as he began to sweat.

The walls were bare. A tan sofa overflowed with clothes. Two grey sweatsuits topped the pile. An exercise machine with a treadmill and a pair of ski poles stood idle against the narrow far wall. Two new armchairs flanked a polished table near the window, guarded by a plain brass floor lamp. An army of full brown supermarket bags, each closed, occupied every available inch of the uncarpeted wood floor. A slightly unpleasant aroma, somewhat familiar, wafted to his nostrils.

He glanced into the kitchen. Its contents were even messier than his own. Opened boxes and cans sat on a white washer and dryer, with unwashed dishes beside them.

Arthur Fields' first reaction verged on panic. He turned to look at Lydia Lawrence and his second reaction topped the first.

She wore a flimsy white gown and no shoes. Having closed the door behind him, she reached to lower the window shade. Sunlight flowing through the window outlined her figure and it was obvious to Fields she wore no clothing under the gown. She reached up and yanked at the shade, which resisted her. On her third attempt it finally loosened.

Arthur's eyes focused on full breasts and long, slender legs. His mind told him to get out the door as fast as possible. Confused, he stood and stared. Maybe when she moved in she had been fat, but those days were long gone. Her figure was as perfect as any man could imagine.

She turned and saw him staring.

"Oh," she said. She looked down at her thin gown, suddenly aware of its transparency. Her face reddened.

"Sit anywhere," she flung at him as she fled into the bedroom. When she came out she wore a belted robe with matching slippers. She carried a brown manila envelope. Only a pair of red dots on her cheeks suggested she was not at ease.

"Thank you for coming, Mr. Fields," she said.

Arthur sat in one of the new armchairs. He wondered what might come next, as well as how fast he could get out of the apartment. He saw the red in her cheeks. He felt he was part of a performance, a feeling intensified by his thought her eyes watched him too carefully.

"This is my bill of sale for this apartment," she said, still standing. "I presume you have one for yours, too."

"Yes, I do," Arthur answered. He found it difficult to concentrate on her words. She sat on the other side of the polished table and one creamy calf was exposed when she moved the robe. He uncased his glasses. Her eyes didn't blink. He felt rivers of sweat running down his back. He hoped she would lower the thermostat but felt certain she wouldn't. He resisted another glance at the exposed calf. He wondered if he should stand up, zip his jacket and go home.

"Would you read this agreement?" she asked, "and then tell me how much I paid for this apartment?" She handed him the papers. At the same time, Lydia Lawrence slapped both pockets of her robe as if searching for something.

"I can't find my glasses, Mr. Fields," she said. "Let me borrow yours for a moment, if you don't mind." She took his glasses without waiting for a reply. She rose, rested the glasses on her nose and walked to a wall thermostat.

"Oh," she exhaled. The sound was an odd mixture of a word and a sigh. In fluid moves she changed the thermostat setting, continued her walk and vanished into the bedroom, closing the door behind her.

After a short interval she returned. She handed Arthur Fields his glasses.

"Thank you, I apologize for the delay." She sounded truly apologetic and Fields noted the tension had gone out of her voice.

"Please read now, Mr. Fields," she added.

He read without interruption. The price had been above the current market and he valued her apartment below it.

"In other words, Lydia," he said, "If you try to sell now you're certain to take a substantial loss." He noticed he'd stopped sweating. The heat level was falling but he didn't trust his neck.

"I have a question for you, Lydia," Arthur said. "Didn't you know what you paid?"

She took the papers back without answering. She flipped the robe's edge so it covered the bare calf, a gesture so automatic he suspected she'd not noticed his glance. She swallowed, still mute.

"Mr. Fields," she said. "I'm grateful to you for helping me but you should know I want no involvement with you or anyone else in this courtyard. As far as I'm concerned this will be your one and only visit to my apartment. I say this so you know my feelings, not because I dislike you or any of our neighbors. Do I make myself clear?"

"Absolutely," Fields answered. "I'm not offended. I feel the same way myself." He looked again at the full brown supermarket bags and the clothes on the sofa. He inhaled the familiar but unnamed aroma. He recalled the disaster in the kitchen and added to himself "I couldn't agree more."

She smiled.

"The answer to your question is really 'none of your business' she said, but you've been nice enough to help me. I didn't buy this apartment. My attorney bought it for me after my...unpleasant... divorce. I really wasn't myself for awhile. I'd also added 40 pounds. If it hadn't been for her, I don't know what might have happened to me."

Arthur Fields nodded. He was familiar with reactions to an unpleasant divorce.

"Since you won't be coming here again, Mr. Fields, let me add two comments. Let's be friends and call me Lydia."

"Fine, Lydia," Fields said. "Call me Art or Arthur but certainly not 'Bird' as Otto tried to tell you."

"Okay, Art," she said. "I've passed your window a few times when I've gone out. We keep similar hours and your keyboard suggests we both like piano. Is that so?"

"Why, yes," a surprised Arthur Fields replied.

"Let's talk about piano when the weather warms."

"Fine."

Back in his own apartment, Arthur tried to analyze events with little success. He spent the afternoon cleaning his kitchen, vacuuming, and reestablishing contact with the world.

At five, he saw a trio of young men walk by his window, escorting an empty wheelbarrow. On their return trip the barrow was full of brown supermarket bags. Arthur stepped outside onto his cleared steps, closing the zipper jacket as the temperature began its nightly drop. The trio returned with their barrow as Fields waited.

"Hi, guys," he said.

"Hi, yourself," said the oldest of the men.

"Sale on brown bags?"

The trio stopped. The speaker looked over his shoulder, and, satisfied no one was watching, stepped closer.

"Funniest thing I've come across this winter," he began.

"Oh?"

"Woman fell up her icy steps a month ago and broke her glasses. New here. Couldn't see the phone book, doesn't know anybody on this courtyard. She's been bagging garbage for a month. She couldn't even set her thermostat, would you believe?"

"You don't say," Fields remarked. "Is she all right?"

"Oh, yeah. She called us and we brought her food, detergent, stuff like that. Picked up two pair of glasses for her. We're getting rid of the garbage now. She's tired, though. You should have seen the living room."

"I can imagine," Fields said. "How did she get to call you?"

"You know," the man said, "I never thought of that. How could she read the phone book?"

"Probably something creative," Fields said. "Women are good at things like that."

"I know, pal. Well, we're on our way."

Arthur went inside, tossed his jacket on the sofa and slouched into his old armchair. In a few weeks New York's worst winter would be history. Then, as always, lovely Spring would arrive.

Arthur thought about the afternoon's scene. He was grateful for the warmth and the chance to get outside. And then he roared his loud, booming laugh.

"She wanted me for my glasses," he said aloud. "Too blind to read the phone book, too proud to ask for help. Couldn't see the thermostat. Got my number from Otto and worked it out."

"For your glasses, Fields," he reminded himself, not your charm." He chuckled again. He knew now she owed him a laugh or a joke or a pleasant smile at the very least. He would collect when the weather warmed. He pictured her earlier, standing beside her window. It would be worth the wait.

—⚏—

17

Storefront Studio

"I'm not going to give you the painting and that's final," the artist said.

A tall man, he wore an unbuttoned blue smock on which smears of yellow, red and other paints announced his profession while protecting an old grey sweatshirt and a pair of faded blue jeans. He towered over the blonde woman despite her chic leather heels.

They were about the same age, middle thirties. She was neatly dressed in the height of fashion. His worn sneakers indicated either a severe money problem or total disinterest in what he wore.

"But it's my face. I didn't know you would display it all over New York," she said.

"You were paid for posing," he reminded her.

"I told you I'd buy it from you."

"I couldn't sell it to you now if I wanted to," he said. "It belongs to someone else. I'd appreciate it if you would go away. You're disrupting the people who just finished class."

Behind him a dozen painters dismantled easels and cleaned brushes in the storefront studio on East 18th Street.

"Buy it back. I'll pay for it," she demanded. "You know I only came down here on a whim. I didn't know you were famous. In fact, it was the last thing I might have thought."

"I know," he admitted, removing the blue smock and draping it across the back of a paint-spattered wooden chair.

161

"I volunteered to pose because your model was sick."

"You kept the fee."

"It was a joke."

"Not to me it wasn't. If the model keeps the money the painting's mine. I'm entitled to show it anywhere I want and do with it what I want. I have. Someone else owns it now, as I told you.

"I said I'll buy it back."

"No way."

She changed her approach. She replaced the demanding tone with something more reasonable, hoping to get her way.

"Tell me who owns it, George. Maybe they'll sell it to me. Is that possible?"

George sat down on a wooden folding chair. Its low seat pushed his knees up almost to his chin. He spread an arm across the back of the chair beside him.

"Look at you," he said. "The fashionable Mrs. Allison Sherman, queen of Park Avenue, come to make demands in her usual way. She wants what she wants when she wants it."

"That's not fair, George," the blonde said. "I don't have to take that from you or anyone else and I wouldn't, except I want the painting. Badly."

"I've noticed," George replied. "The answer is still 'no'."

"I'll pay $9,000 for your painting, George. It's a fair price," the blonde said. "I know it's your going rate for a head and shoulders portrait."

"You're right about the price," George admitted, "but wrong about the portrait. If it's any consolation to you, you won't be seeing it around New York any more."

He rose to his full height. He flipped the blue smock across his arm and walked across the ancient wooden floor to a chrome clothing stand. He hung the smock on a wire hanger with more care than the shapeless garment merited.

He turned. Allison stood behind him.

"George," she said. "I'll ask you as politely as I can. Would you please tell me who owns the painting?"

George eyed the blonde for a moment or two. He waved her back towards the wooden chair, pulling another close to it so they could sit together.

"At least." she thought, "he's talking to me. There's a chance he'll change his mind.

"Mrs. Sherman," George began. "I'll tell you a little story. You may know it already, but I'll tell you anyway."

"George, no stories, Allison said.

"Your choice," he replied.

"What about the painting? Would it kill you to tell me who owns it?"

"Not really, George said. "I've thought about it some more. I've decided I'll tell you who owns it."

"Wait until I get my pen, George, the blonde said. "The address is important." She removed a gold Cartier pen and a piece of folded ivory paper from her leather shoulder bag.

"This really means a lot to me, George," she said. "I'm not flattering you when I say you painted a perfect likeness."

"I know," George said. "Are you ready?"

'Yes."

"Mother owns it. You can go visit her any time, Allison."

The blonde jumped up from the chair. Anger marked her features.

"You bastard," she said. She slapped the pen and paper hurriedly into her leather bag.

"You haven't visited her in ten years, sister dearest," George said. "She wondered what you looked like. Now she knows."

George shook his head. Allison marched out of the storefront studio and slammed the door behind her.

18

Billy Doon

My name is Billy Doolin. I was born in Raleigh, North Carolina, and lived there until I was ten years old.

My father's name is Mack. He's six foot five and weighs 240. My mom, Cynthia, stands almost six feet tall. I was an only child, a short, skinny kid, but I knew I would grow tall. I wasn't big but I was smart.

In Raleigh we lived not far from Millbrook High School, near the school's basketball coach, Charlie Spangler, and his son, Buck, who was my age.

I attended the same school as Buck Spangler and his friend, Alan. Both were much bigger than me. At lunch they thought it funny to take my peanut butter sandwich and then stomp on it. Then they would eat big lunches. Often I went home hungry and angry. My father sensed something wrong and asked me if I had a problem. I told him I was mad at two boys in my class.

"Don't get mad, get even, son," he said, "but it's best if you do it on their terms, whatever they may be."

"What do you mean?"

"Well if they think they're good baseball players, you play better. If they think they're smart, you get better grades."

"Why is it better, dad?"

"Beating a man at his own game gives you maximum satisfaction. Believe me."

"Thanks. I didn't know that."

My father is a carpenter who works for himself. When we lived in Raleigh unexpected asthma attacks meant he couldn't work a schedule. He could always pay our rent but at times food money didn't amount to much. Buck Spangler and Alan took my sandwiches because they knew I was hungry. They thought it great fun. They called me "Billy Doon" too, venting more of their humor on me.

On my eleventh birthday we moved to Charlotte, where a doctor prescribed medicine which cured my father's asthma. Our food supply increased. I grew bigger, stronger and taller and discovered my special talent for basketball. I read all the books on basketball in our local library, including Mr. Spangler's "Man To Man Defense" He insisted zone defenses were always the wrong choice.

"I never let my team play a zone defense no matter what the score," he wrote.

I read his book carefully. Towards the back he admitted man-to-man defenses had a major flaw. A superior offensive player could create unsolvable problems for even the best man-to-man defense.

In Charlotte, my school's team achieved small success until I began playing. My arrival changed the team's attitude and we won regularly. I'm not modest but I'm not loud, either. I just worked as hard as I could as often as I could. We won. I kept growing bigger and stronger until I was almost the same size as my father.

The summer following my junior year in high school my father's business prospered. I continued to do well in school and on the basketball court. My mother's father died and left a substantial estate. I received a personal bequest of several thousand dollars.

In school, I talked with our coach, asking advice as to how I might improve my basketball.

"The toughest league in the country is probably the Harlem Summer League in New York," he told me. A summer in it would either guarantee a college education worth thousands of dollars, or ruin you."

"Oh?"

"For you it would be even tougher. Most Harlem players are black while you are a good-looking blonde. You wouldn't be the only white player but your appearance would challenge them. They would greet you with hard fouls, elbows, knees and the works. It would be up to you to take it all and give back more of same. It's been done."

I entered the Harlem Summer League, using my bequest as an investment in my future and hoping I made the right choice.

Before I left for New York and a cousin's extra room my father accepted a management position with a Raleigh construction company.

"When you come back from New York we'll have to look for a new house. It means you'll have to change schools your senior year," he reminded me.

My coach proved accurate beyond my wildest dreams. In my first two games in Harlem I was pushed, shoved, grabbed, elbowed and fouled in every imaginable manner. I decided to survive. I pushed, shoved, grabbed, kneed, fouled back and scored, early and often. I learned how to position myself, to move easily with and without the ball. I received lots of good advice.

At summer's end my Harlem coach paid me a great compliment.

"Doolin, you can play on my team anytime. Thanks for coming."

Returning to Raleigh meant I would play high school basketball. In the library I learned Charlie Spangler still coached Millbrook High School's basketball team. The Raleigh News & Observer quoted him as expecting his coming season to be one of his all-time best, if not best ever. His team featured his son, Buck, and Alan, too.

It was then I made my plan and carried it out.

A week before my father began searching for our new house in Raleigh he drove me from one high school to another. At each, I kept an appointment with the school's basketball coach and recited my position.

"My name is Billy Doolin," I said. "I'm trying to decide which of several Raleigh schools I'll attend in the Fall. I play at a high level, my grades are excellent and I'm no trouble.

I'll provide you with a great basketball reference and my transcript will delight you. It sounds too good to be true and it is. There's a price. I have one request and if you're willing to grant it I'll enroll in your school."

"Which is?"

"When we play Millbrook High School you follow my game plan."

"You want to be coach?"

"I didn't say that. You be the coach. It's your job and I'm a high school student. I assure you I'm a major basketball talent and you get it if you follow my game plan. Millbrook."

"Any special reason?" one man asked. "Charlie Spangler's the Millbrook coach. He's one of the best. You want to match wits with Charlie?"

"You have the picture," I said. "If you can live with my request I'll try out; otherwise, thanks for listening.

My first three visits were turndowns.

Park Ridge High School's coach, Larry Francis, looked me in the eye and laughed.

"Son, I love your nerve. If what you say is so you can play here. We don't have a bad team. I'll follow your game plan at Millbrook, whatever it is. One game isn't going to ruin me. I've been here thirty years and maybe it's time I try someone else's game plan. Will it work? Last year Millbrook beat us by 15 points."

"I think so, coach. I'll share it with you after I enroll."

It's something personal, isn't it, Doolin?"

"Coach, I think I'll like Park Ridge," I said.

"Park Ridge High School is in Raleigh's far northwestern corner. My parents found a home they liked there and we moved, satisfying all of us.

My senior year at Park Ridge proved a lot of fun for Coach Francis and his winning basketball team. I blended into his system, followed his requests and achieved good grades. My name appeared in all the box scores as the team's leading scorer. Park Ridge's rise to undefeated status was totally unexpected. After a dozen games we were to play Millbrook at their gym in early November.

The two teams came out to warm up before a packed house. Buck Spangler looked over at his opponents, laughed, and trotted over to his bench for a word with his father.

"Hey dad. Know who's on the Park Ridge team? Billy Doon. Remember him?"

"Who?"

"Billy Doon. He used to live near us. Me n' Alan used to take his lunch away from him, send him home hungry," he laughed.

"There's nobody on Park Ridge with that name, Buck" his father said. "I've got all the box scores. Pay attention, will you?"

"The big sissy in the corner, dad. Number 10"

In the Park Ridge locker room, coach Francis had explained the odd plan presented by Billy Doolin.

"When we have the ball, you give it to Billy and everyone goes to the far corner and stays there until the point is over."

"Why, coach?" asked one of the players.

"Charlie Spangler's teams must play man-to-man defense. This means one player, alone, has to defend Billy. Billy thinks it can't be done, especially if Buck Spangler gets the job."

"You guys met?" a kid asked Billy"

"You might say that," he replied.

The game began.

Millbrook's fans laughed when they saw four Park Ridge players run to a far corner each time Park Ridge got the ball. The laughter stopped when Billy Doolin scored every time he got the ball. At the end of the quarter the score was Doolin, 14, Millbrook 8. At halftime, Doolin 31, Millbrook 19. Doolin had been careful not to let Buck Spangler foul out.Many moves rehearsed in Harlem left Spangler groping for empty air. Twice Doolin scored on thunderous dunks which would have broken Spangler's fingers if he hadn't pulled them away at the last possible second.

In the Millbrook locker rooom at halftime, Charlie Spangler saw a defeated team. A full half remained. His only choices were to go to the zone defense his team never practiced or watch Buck's continuing humiliation.

Charlie walked over to where his son sat hunched on a bench, exhausted and beaten.

"For a joke you and Alan took this kid's lunch away from him, Buck?" he asked.

A nod of the bowed head gave him his answer.

"Many times?"

Another nod.

"We'll play the second half with the same defense we used in the first," Charlie Spangler said, with an eye on his son. "Maybe we'll learn something."

Park Ridge won easily. Billy Doolin scored 71 points, the highest total ever achieved against Millbrook. With two minutes to go, Doolin asked a pleased Larry Francis to take him out. The coach granted his request.

A horn sounded the game's end, and most of the Park Ridge team sprinted for the locker room. In front of them a lone player sat on a bench the Millbrook team would pass on its way to the locker room.

It was Billy Doolin, eating a peanut butter sandwich.

19

Little Brat

Mary Harrington grew up in a neighborhood of similar houses which marched across New York's Queens County to wildly different cadences. Each house featured beside it twin rails of concrete which led to a backyard garage. Her family included two brothers who played football and baseball and fooled around with cars. In 1952 she was 15 years old.

The small, house with its bats, balls and wrenches lured boys to it like bees to honey.

When Mary spied on masculine activities, the boys hooted and dismissed the brown-haired, freckle-faced girl with "beat it brat."

Sometimes they grabbed her ponytail. When feeling generous they let her watch them work on cars. Their successes often ended with the roar of an engine and a playful shake of the ponytail, followed by "how about that, brat?" as they waited for her admiration.

College was unnecessary. Mary matured, married, settled nearby and raised two boys of her own.

When her boys were sick, she distracted them with card games. Computers arrived. She absorbed the manuals in the quiet of daytime. She challenged herself with a series of programs for top players, an expertise which impressed neither boys nor husband. Their eyes opened wider when she fixed a car brake or tuned its motor.

Her hair grayed. On advice of a colorist she chose blonde. The boys married; job changes propelled one to Chicago and the other to

Jacksonville. Her parents were gone. Her brothers retired and moved to Florida. Then, her husband sickened and died.

Months of mourning followed.

On a sunny Spring morning in Queens, Mary H. Morrison decided it was time for future planning. Perhaps warmer weather would help move the clouds which misted her vision. She had no real need for the large house. One retired brother lived somewhere near Miami. The other son and her only grandson beckoned from Jacksonville. Perhaps a move toward them would help recharge her vitality.

Three months later, she drove her Buick to a motel near LaGuardia Airport. Mary settled into her room and reviewed her recent accomplishments.

She had sold the big house. She missed the garden where she spent many happy hours yet rejoiced at her escape from a house which needed constant cleaning and expensive maintenance. She owned a generous bank account and was free to do as she pleased.

Later, for her own amusement, she toyed with computer programs on her new laptop.

Tomorrow meant excitement. A drive to Florida with stops along the way to investigate whatever intrigued her. A forecast of ideal weather seemed a good omen.

She glanced in a mirror. She saw a woman with pleasant expression and firm skin, her maturity accented by delicate sun needles at the corners of hazel eyes.

Her wavy blonde hair, gathered at the neck in a youthful ponytail, rested on an ivory silk blouse with pearl buttons. She stood 5'5" tall in beige leather pumps, shoulders back, and in one hand held new sunglasses.

Mary smiled. She struck a movie star pose, positioned the glasses near her chin and tilted her head.

"Ravishing, my dear," she murmured in a throaty tone. "Simply ravishing."

Morning began with a fresh shirt, faded blue jeans and new white sneakers. She emerged from the motel and drove off on bumpy, potholed roads. At a busy intersection she pulled the Buick off the macadam and onto the lot of a Chevrolet dealer. It was not her first visit. She had thrilled for years to the growl of high performance Corvettes. Now she would tame one herself.

The dealer personally brought the tan Corvette through the showroom door. She felt a rush of excitement. She stifled impatience as he handed over her warranty and reexplained the car's special traits. She could hear the low rumble of the two-seater's power plant and wanted to rush off at once.

The dealer preceded her to the car. She watched her bags being stowed. A mechanic idled the motor and she listened with practiced ear. The man strolled around the car and handed her the keys.

"Lady, this car's a beauty," he said. "Good Luck."

She drove out. The car's quick response pleased her. She was dismayed when three deep potholes rocked the Corvette's wheels.

By noon she was far from New York. The New Jersey Turnpike disappeared behind her. She delighted in fingertip control of the surging tan Corvette with its quick acceleration and instant response. Near Baltimore she stopped for a break, still uncertain of her destination. With extra driving she could make Charleston, a city The National Geographic found eternally interesting.

The break relaxed her. When she resumed she began noticing vanity license plates on other cars. "TEETH" read one, probably a dentist. "BOBZBENZ" on a Mercedes was as easy as "LUVCATS;" "SEW WHAT" drew a grin.

She heard the unwelcome front end noise for the first time as she shifted lanes on I-95 south of Richmond. An hour later, her ears caught the warning again after she passed a truck. Ahead of her she read 'FORTUNAT8" on the back of a black Honda.

She stopped at the next cloverleaf and checked her maps. She saw Raleigh's location and chose it as the closest city with skilled Corvette facilities.

She followed signs from I-95 to Raleigh. She was grateful for smooth roads which were kind to her new car. An inquiry located a large Chevrolet dealer with good reputation.

"I've checked it carefully, ma'am the service supervisor said. "I'm glad you told me about hitting those pot holes, because I'm certain I've located the problem." Bill McClure, a decade younger than Mary, smiled easily. He wore an open collar shirt with short sleeves and the same chocolate color pants she saw on his mechanics.

"Can you fix it?" she asked.

"Yes," he replied. "an important piece of your steering assembly needs replacement. It's covered under your warranty and won't cost you anything."

"I'm so glad I checked," Mary answered, relieved. "How long will it take?"

"Two or three days until I can get the part," he said. "I wish sooner, but we have little call for that part and we don't stock them here."

"I need a place to stay. I've never been in Raleigh before, though it seems nice enough," she added, truthfully. "Do you have any suggestions?"

"If you can afford it, the Hotel Marion's pretty nice. I pass it on my way home and if you wait I'll be pleased to take you there."

She was grateful for the suggestion. Bill McClure drove her and her luggage to the Marion Hotel and she thanked him for his kindness. She watched as he drove off in his small sedan. The plate read "CARS."

A reservations clerk told her how lucky she was to find a room available. Only a late cancellation made it possible.

"We've a full house this week," he explained. "Regional Bridge Tournament." His comment gave Mary an idea. She would be in Raleigh another day or two. She'd never tried a bridge tournament. It might be fun.

She settled into her room, freshened up and returned to the hotel lobby. At an information table a trio of busy women answered questions from a stream of visitors.

May I help you?" a bright-faced woman asked in a pleasant tone. A card on her shoulder identified her as Donna.

"What do I need to enter a bridge tournament?

To begin, a partner. I can take care of that for you after I know how well you play and how many points you have."

Truthfully, I play bridge well," Mary said, "but I don't have any points, whatever they are. I'm traveling south from New York. I'll be staying in the hotel for two days and thought I might try the tournament while I'm here."

"Oh, you're from New York," the woman said. "Wait here. "I'll be right back."

She returned with a tall man who wore a dark blue shirt, blue slacks and sunglasses with amber lenses. His thick hair was grey and a slim mustache rode his upper lip.

"Maybe Ted can help you," the woman said. "He lives in Raleigh but he gets along well with New York people. Just repeat what you told me."

Donna turned away. The man looked at Mary, smiled and introduced himself.

"I'm Ted Gahling," he drawled. "Pleased to help."

"I'm Mary Morrison." She recited a simple version of her trip from New York and the surprise problem which led her to the Marion Hotel. She mentioned long hours with computer bridge programs and the fascination they held for her. He was easy to talk with and a good listener.

"I own a good memory, Mr. Gahling," she added. "It might be a help in this tournament."

"Ted," he corrected.

"Ted."

"I'll partner you tonight," he offered unexpectedly. "After that it's up to you. We can find you someone else if you like."

Mary hesitated. She looked at people bustling in both directions on the carpeted hallway. She realized how little she knew of the whole process. Ted Gahling's offer contained an escape clause, too.

"Agreed," she said.

"I'll talk to Donna. She'll help you sign up. I'll meet you here at 7:30. Game begins at 8:00. He walked away without looking back.

Mary strolled the busy lobby and then returned to the information table. Donna soon led Mary to a room where an afternoon session was ending and in few words explained the procedures.

Ted Gahling arrived promptly and at 8:00 they were seated in a large room.

People came to their table, then left. Mary found the bustle stimulating. Following Ted's instructions proved child's play. Card games had always been her forte. A look around the room informed her she could wear anything she wished.

"How did we do?" she asked Ted after the final card was played.

"Well enough I'd like us to play tomorrow, Mary. Think before you answer, though. With morning, afternoon and evening sessions it's long and tiring."

"Well, Ted Gahling," she replied. "If you can do it, so can I."

"I'll meet you at 8:30. Game begins at nine." He left in a single, fluid move. She watched as he strode through the door. When she rose to follow she felt fatigued and was grateful sleep was near at hand.

In the morning she visited the hotel's restaurant. Waiting for breakfast she reviewed the previous evening.

Ted Gahling played almost errorless bridge. At intervals he nodded encouragement to her. He seldom spoke. Late in the evening she became aware he avoided eye contact. Twice she thought he was staring at her neck, which puzzled her.

She wore no jewelry, and other than a small childhood scar her neck looked like everyone else's. She concluded she was mistaken, probably misled by his tinted glasses.

"May I join you?" asked an unseen newcomer. Donna seated herself before Mary had time for a reply. A waiter arrived with Mary's order "Looks good to me, waiter," Donna announced. "Make mine the same."

Mary welcomed Donna's company. She felt uneasy alone, though the quiet room was far from crowded.

"You had a wonderful game with Ted Gatling," Donna said. "I admit I was surprised when I posted the score sheets."

A light flashed in Mary's memory. She heard Ted's name as different than earlier, though she still wasn't certain.

"Where are the score sheets, Donna?"

"On the wall where each game is played. Computer scoring makes it easy and fast. Part of my job is doing the postings."

They completed their breakfast with a minimum of talk. Donna had to hurry. When she left, Mary visited the site of the previous evening's game. She saw her name and Ted's listed on a printout. A series of numbers followed but she ignored them. She looked again at the two names: Mary Harrison, New York and Ted Gatling, Raleigh.

Why did 'Gatling' stir her memory? She didn't know, and "Ted" meant nothing. Of that she was certain. Until she cleared the nagging doubt she would keep the man at arm's length.

They played in the morning session. Mary concentrated on bridge with an occasional oblique look at her partner. He still avoided eye contact. If he looked at her neck, she didn't see him.

They finished a few minutes before noon.

"I have to rush off, Mary." Ted said. "My son watches our business while I'm here. I'll be back before the 2:00 o'clock game."

Mary went to her room to freshen for lunch when a clue clicked in her memory bank. She reached for the phone and dialed her brother Joe in Miami.

"Joe Harrington," the cheerful voice answered.

"It's Mary, Joe," she said. She explained her presence in Raleigh.

"Nice city, Raleigh," Joe said. "Like it a lot."

"Joe, do you remember when I fell and cut my neck, back when we were kids?"

"Sure, Mary. You were being bratty, as usual.

"Which means?"

You poured oil over my friend's tools. He was chasing you with a snowball when you tripped over a tree branch."

"Tell me about him, Joe.

"Sure, Mary. He felt terrible when you fell. But mad, too, if you know what I mean. He wanted to get even." Joe paused, then resumed. "One of the funniest guys I knew, as well as one of the smartest. His funny stuff livened up a lot of parties. I liked him, Mary. Good guy. Family moved away."

"His name, Joe."

"Gunner."

"Joe, do better," she said, impatiently. "What was his name?"

"Gatling, Mary. Like in Gatling gun. Easy to remember."

"Thanks, Joe. Can you remember his first name?"

"Everybody called him Gunner, Mary. He even called himself Gunner. I'm not sure I knew his first name."

"Is it possible he was named Ted?"

"You know, Mary, I think that's it. How come you're so interested?"

"Thinking about the past, I guess. Don't you, Joe?"

"Sure, Mary. Everyone does."

"Thanks, Joe."

Mary felt flustered as well as satisfied. She could hide in her room and send Ted Gatling a message. Donna could tell him she didn't feel well and would not play again. Another two days and Raleigh would become a shadowy memory.

Yet the man had treated her kindly. He was a note from her happy childhood. There was less happy music as time went on. She decided she would keep her knowledge to herself and enjoy the rest of her stay. She would partner Ted Gatling while discreetly watching his every move.

They completed the afternoon session and wandered into the hall together. Ted Gatling halted and faced Mary.

"Here's a map of Raleigh, Mary. And the keys to my car. No reason you should be stuck at the Marion all the time you're here. Drive around and see Raleigh. Car's parked outside. It's an open Jeep, so dress casual."

He handed her the keys. Surprised and speechless, she could only stare, mute for a minute.

"If you like, I'll drive you myself. Either way it's up to you. Next game's at 8:00 tonight."

"You trust me with your car, I trust you to drive, Ted," she said, after hesitating. She would be alert but wary.

She wore jeans and had no need to change. Once through the doors of the hotel, July brightness welcomed her into heat which reflected off a sea of concrete. Dozens of four-wheel vehicles were parked in the hotel's lots. She trailed Ted as he threaded through them. He stopped behind a black Jeep.

"Here it is, Mary. Try that side."

He moved to the driver's door. She looked at the spare wheel mounted on the Jeep's back and automatically to the plate below it.

"BUD-LITE"

She climbed inside the Jeep and fastened her seat belt, wondering the meaning of the car's plate. Beer drinker? Bar owner?

He drove well. She could hear a slight miss in the Jeep's motor. He turned into the highway and wind ruffled her hair. He passed similar cars with drivers who looked like teenagers, invariably with young blondes in the passenger seat. She felt her years disappearing.

'I'll drive, you ask," Ted said. She saw downtown, colleges, churches, numerous neat homes with pretty flowers. He responded to her questions without looking at her. His comments were few and brief.

At 7:00 by the dial on the Jeep's dash he turned into a restaurant parking lot.

"We're pushing for time. Service here is unusual. Fast." he smiled. "On me."

They ordered and the food was excellent. She decided to satisfy her curiosity with a technique remembered from girlhood.

"Tell me about yourself, Ted," she said.

"Not much to tell, he drawled." Me and my son and a small business. You tell me about flowers. You like 'em? They're more interesting than me."

Before she knew it, she'd launched into her favorite topic. They finished eating and reached the Marion with minutes to spare.

Afterwards, she found someone had slid an envelope under her room door. Bill McClure would stop for her at 8:00 in the morning on his way to work. The Corvette waited.

The decision was hers. Stay? Or be on her way? She knew now Ted could thicken his drawl or make it disappear whenever he chose. She knew little more about him than two days ago, and the license plate added to the mystery. She decided to stay another day.

The Corvette purred perfectly. She maneuvered it back to the Marion and checked at the desk. The clerk assured her the Corvette would be safe outside. Donna appeared, carefully holding a gift-wrapped package in both hands.

Ted Gatling left this for you, Mary. He's sorry he has to take care of business today. He won't be able to play."

Mary saw a clean white envelope tucked under the package's silver spangled ribbon.

"How nice. Thank you, Donna. I'm sure you're busy. I'll open this upstairs."

She pulled the envelope from under the ribbon and opened it. Empty. She frowned. She opened the bow and parted a white forest of tissue paper. She saw a new oil can with a long, thin spout. A business card hung on the spout.

"Gunner's" flowed across the card's middle. An address and telephone number followed, with "T.Gatling, Prop." on the bottom.

She turned the card over.

"Enjoy Florida, Brat," she read.

Her multiple reactions were immediate and intense. She was angry and frustrated and surprised and finally, challenged. He'd known all along. But she didn't give up easily. She would repay Ted Gatling and a plan quickly took shape in her mind. She knew exactly what she needed.

She headed for the Marion's Gift Shop where she'd seen Raleigh maps, She found the area of Ted Gatling's business.

In the busy lobby, a crowd of bridge players prepared for the morning session. She waited at the information table until Donna recognized her and came over.

"Ted Gatling's business," Mary asked. "Near the corner of Six Forks Road and Concord?"

"On the corner," Donna confirmed with a brief, puzzled look.

"Thanks."

Feeling both calm and mischievous, Mary went out to her Corvette. The morning sunshine was brighter than before. She drove until she found a hardware store where she bought wrench, pliers, a screwdriver and a metal box to put them in. At a gas station she bought a quart of motor oil. A supermarket provided a supply of breadcrumbs and a box of riceroni. Mixed together inside the metal box, the recipe would be hidden. When placed inside the back of a Jeep, license plate "BUD-LITE," curiosity would do the rest. She smiled at the thought of Ted's face when he began to clean them. No mechanic would pass up free tools.

Next step meant locating his bar. "Gunner's" had a nice ring to it. Probably a neighborhood tavern. The Jeep would be parked outside or around the corner.

Her first surprise was the tree-lined route leading to Six Forks Road. She saw pleasant greenery on either side but no stores or malls. When the Corvette reached its destination, tall trees overran three corners of the intersection. The traffic signal was red, and she waited. The single possibility was the depressed far corner, its building far below street level. She could see only a long, black rooftop.

The signal stayed red longer than usual. Across the way, many cars coming towards her turned towards the rooftop and disappeared. The signal changed and she moved the Corvette forward. At her left she saw a low, sprawling collection of four buildings. Full parking lots wrapped around three sides. She had no option except to turn into the sloped driveway where the other cars disappeared.

She read the sign on the nearest building. "Gunner's Nursery." Flowers? Many cars at close quarters demanded her full attention. Her Corvette was vulnerable. She found a spot on the far side and parked.

Trees and shrubs were everywhere. It was the biggest nursery she'd ever seen. Men and women walked among colorful shrubs, banded trees and hanging plants. Small trays of potted blooms framed the walkways.

Gunner's Nursery teamed with customers. Signs proclaimed a special sale. If it weren't for her errand the flowers would tempt her. She shook her head. Locating the Jeep was her first priority.

She sighted the black vehicle behind one of the smaller buildings. Getting close to it would not be easy.

She wondered how she would carry out her plan when her mind suddenly sent her a clear and surprising message.

"BUD-LITE" ... flowers! The best license plate she'd seen. She laughed aloud. She couldn't help it.

"I thought you'd show up," said a voice at her elbow.

"Did you really?" she replied. He faced her. He wasn't wearing his sunglasses. She could see his eyes were blue.

"I was certain," he said. "How certain? Follow me."

She had little choice. She followed to where two latticed chairs waited, side by side.

"You knew all the while," she accused.

"It's not a federal offense," he reminded her.

"The oil can was a low blow."

"Can you think of a better way to get you here? Probably waiting to hit me when I'm not looking."

The comment was so close to the mark she said nothing. She realized, suddenly, she wanted to fight with this man, with his funny sense of humor and his calm and patient ways. But how to say so?

"What now?" he asked.

"Any suggestions?" She smiled at him, trying her best to send the message she wanted him to receive.

"If I make enough noise inside I can play bridge," he said. "After all I own this forest."

"You'll need a partner."

"If she'll stay in Raleigh, I hope."

"Yes," was Mary's reply. "Now you follow me. I want you to see my new car. Then we can go to the Marion."

"I've already seen your new car," Ted said.

"What do you think?"

"You'll know in a minute."

"What makes you think so?"

At the Corvette Mary prepared to enter when Ted spoke again. "Take a look at the front," he suggested.

She saw it as soon as she looked. In the middle of the front bumper a neat frame enclosed a vanity license plate.

"LIL BRAT"

She was unfazed.

"We'll go to the Marion in this car," she said, firmly. "I rode in yours yesterday. The engine needs tuning. Fortunately, I brought the tools with me.

—m—

20

Business Buffet

Raleigh's Chamber of Commerce hosts a business buffet each month in cooperation with one of the city's trade groups. Attendance ranges from a low of 100 to a high of more than 200, depending on the site selected and the appeal of the sponsor.

Penny Brown attends every buffet. She believes she needs to meet new people to succeed in real estate sales. At the age of 28 Penny has been selling houses for two years. Her preliminary results are encouraging. She studied carefully before entering real estate. She estimated she would need five years to become established. After budgeting her savings carefully she is prepared for a slow but steady rise. She is always cheerful and keeps learning all the time.

Late in the afternoon of an unseasonably warm Tuesday in March she enters the paneled elevator of a downtown office building. Though her ride to the building's top floor is brief she finds time to smile at the three men and two women en route with her to a business buffet in the elegant surroundings of The Cardinal Club.

Her fellow riders cluster in age from 25 to 40. Dressed in conservative business attire, they are men and women who favor dark colors. When they leave the elevator the group walks soundlessly on grey carpet to the corridor's far end.

At the door to The Cardinal Club two tables face arriving guests. A sign on each identifies today's sponsoring groups as The Raleigh Chamber of Commerce and Rex Hospital. Penny fills out a card, finds her name badge, picks up a package of material about Rex Hospital and enters. Around her, a stir of people stands chatting. A certain electricity of expectation is in the air.

Quickly and efficiently Penny surveys the crowd. White-jacketed waiters spoon hot food onto small plates. Early arrivals take food to a dozen tables. Each table holds four chairs with padded leather arms which lend the table a touch of distinction.

Beyond the dark glass of the windows and well below window level, the city's lights come on. Above the city, in The Capital Club, maroon carpeting helps mute noise. Piped-in music is fragile and cheerful. Near the ceiling of Penny's room each of 32 chandeliers holds a small crystal light fixture at the end of a thin brass arm.

A long bar with two bartenders provides free drinks to a thirsty group. Penny knows there is a second room beyond this one, where she will find another bar and a duplicate buffet table. She knows the overwhelming choice of drinks will be white wine. In most instances no one will overindulge, in part because of the business nature of the gathering, and partly because it ends at 7:00 p.m.

She walks to the bar and then sips a glass of white wine while she looks around. The crowd exceeds 200 by a good margin. She has met a number of guests on other occasions. She exchanges a nod of recognition with those who make eye contact with her.

"Hello," she says to the man who stands beside her. She eyes his badge. "I'm Penny, Jim," she says with a smile. "Is this your first visit to our buffet?"

"Yes. Nice to meet you," Jim says. He's in his late 30's and tall, wearing a dark suit, conservative tie and gold-rim glasses. In a few minutes Penny has given him her card and pocketed his, which names his as president of a small start-up electronics firm. His card will go in her file and he will receive her monthly newsletter for the next two years.

Penny completes her buffet effort by 6:00 o'clock. She takes the last of her wine to an empty table to enjoy a brief rest before leaving. A figure approaches the table from behind her, and suddenly she's no longer alone. A man puts his glass of white wine on the tabletop near her and sits down.

"Hello, Penny Brown," he says.

She looks at his thin face with its regular features and takes in his pleasant smile. His hair is white and wavy. He wears a navy blue suit, white shirt and a gold tie she knows is expensive. She guesses his age as past fifty and suspects he has a wife somewhere, a wife he has no intention of mentioning. He exudes charm. She warns herself to be careful.

"I don't know your name but you know mine. Have we met somewhere?" she asks.

"No, we haven't he says. "You can see on my name badge my name is Paul Connelly. No middle initial." He smiles again, the same warm and winning smile as when he sat down.

She looks at his badge and says nothing.

"I'm in real estate just as you are, Penny Brown. I'm also a builder. You can look me up. I'm about to build a giant new development in the Wake Forest area. I need a smart, hard-working real estate person to work with me on this. Two months ago I sent out my friends and told them to ask around for the smart, hard-working real estate person I need. Three of them came back with the same name...Penny Brown. I came to see for myself. I've watched you all night. You are, to put it mildly, for real."

"Thank you," she said. "Yes." She felt saying 'yes' to this man might be a big mistake but she couldn't help it. She wanted him to like her.

"I'd like you to take this card," Connelly said, "and check up on me any way you can. Talk to competitors and your fellow agents. Go visit the newspaper. If you satisfy yourself I'm on the level we're even because I'm satisfied you're the person I want. Call me. We'll set up a meeting, and see what happens."

"Oh," said Penny Brown. She watched Paul Connelly walk gracefully away from the table, leaving his wine behind.

A month later Penny Brown became a business associate of builder Paul Connelly. She made a fortune with him in Wake Forest but it wasn't her greatest surprise.

Paul's hard-working son Jamie echoed the smarts of his successful father when Penny arrived on the scene. He invited her to check him out, and a year later invited her to become Mrs.Connelly. He checked out well, and she added "I do" to her list of responses.

Five years later the older Connelly admitted to his daughter-in-law he'd told her but half the truth. He'd sent out his friends to look for a business associate OR a wife for his son, Jamie, who had a tendency to work too hard, trying to please his father.

"He thought he needed to please me," Paul explained. "I didn't need pleasing at the time and I don't need it now. I appreciated what I heard about you and decided it might be more fun for both of you if Jamie liked pleasing you."

"So you're guilty, guilty, guilty, aren't you, father-in-law of mine?" Penny asked.

"Yes," Connelly said. "Now what?"

"I insist you add Rex Hospital to your large donations list," she replied. "And you might also send a dollar or two to The Raleigh Chamber of Commerce."

"Why?" he asked.

"Because it will make both of our lists the same," she said.

21

The Resume'

On a June day near Long Island's Mineola courthouse a woman clad in a tailored beige suit paused on the bright sidewalk of a narrow street. She wore black-framed sunglasses. Once she verified the address of the storefront law office beside her she twisted its scarred doorknob.

A blonde secretary looked up from a desk in a small room. "Yes?"

"Is attorney Delaney in?" the woman asked.

"Yes," she is."

"May I speak with her, please? It's a business matter."

"You are speaking with her. I'm attorney Kathryn Delaney. I'm also secretary Delaney. How can I help you?"

The blonde sat taller on a wheeled chair and surveyed her visitor's face, which was framed by a navy straw hat with a broad brim. The woman held a new leather portfolio worth a month's office rent. She smiled, exposing twin rows of perfect white teeth. Her smile seemed impersonal.

"May I sit down?"

"Certainly."

The blue-eyed attorney watched through contact lenses as the slender woman sat beside her. She guessed the woman's age as late 30's. A hint of expensive floral perfume floated across the desk.

"My name is Suzanne Murray," the woman said. "I'll get right to the point. You've been recommended to me. I've a copy of your resume'. There are many ways of checking and I prefer my own, which is why I'm here.

"I see."

"I'm familiar with attorneys. Your time is money. I'd like your next two hours," she said. "In return, I'll pay you $200. Is that acceptable to you?"

"Yes," Kathryn agreed. Her law degree and her 32nd birthday had arrived on the same day. She had waitressed her way through law school and practiced less than a year. Her morning was free and so was her afternoon.

"Fine." The visitor removed four fifty-dollar bills from a pocket in the leather portfolio and placed them on the desktop.

Kathryn ignored the money. She noted the graceful fingers which removed the straw hat, and watched the same pale fingers fluff a head of wavy brown hair. Kathryn saw flecks of grey at the woman's temples. The dark glasses cast ebony shadows on a thin, straight nose.

"I've an assignment for you," Suzanne Murray said, "but first I must feel certain you can handle it."

Kathryn's eyes steadied as she met the gaze of her visitor. An unusual beginning, though the money looked real. She glanced down. Her own restless fingers tapped a beat on the desktop.

Suzanne Murray removed a red binder from the leather portfolio and began reading.

"From John B. Daley and Company, Confidential Investigations," to Suzanne Murray: Here is the resume' of Kathryn M. Delaney and the background report you requested, along with our bill. We hope you find our work satisfactory and we stand ready to serve you. Signed, John B. Daley."

She turned her head.

"I've read you Mr.Daley's letter in case you think my visit is casual, Kathryn. I assure you it's not."

Kathryn nodded.

"I'll read you the highlights of Mr. Daley's report," Suzanne said.

"You're the daughter of Kevin Delaney and Mary Kate Delaney, obviously of Irish descent. You grew up in Queens and graduated from Catholic schools with above average grades. Right?"

"Yes."

"You began working while in high school, including an imaginative period when you decorated sweatshirts using slim hand-held paints."

Kathryn admired Daley's thoroughness.

"After graduation you managed a children's clothing store in Queens while attending four colleges at night, finally graduating with honors from Manhattan's Baruch College."

"You earned your law degree with excellent grades while living in Long Beach, N.Y., and struggling with marginal jobs such as waitress, bartender, process server and short order cook."

She paused.

"Accurate?"

"Perfect," Kathryn replied.

"I'll conclude by stating Mr. Daley's investigators used devious ways to prove you're creative and you're smart. But I need more information before proceeding. May I explain?"

"Please do."

"I'm an only child," said Suzanne Murray, "and I've always resented it. I believe the way to whole people is family background. This report tells me you come from a large family. I'd like to know about your family relationships, especially with your parents."

Kathryn's keen hearing detected a break in the modulated voice beside her. Her instincts warned her against revealing too much. At the same time, Suzanne Murray's presentation piqued her curiosity.

"Understatement is a lawyer's best friend," Kathryn reminded herself. She applied a sense of discipline by stilling her hands.

"Your request is odd, Suzanne, but I've heard odder," Kathryn began. "I've one brother, Tommy, as you may know. He's the youngest. He's twenty and has dark hair. My sister, Maureen, is older than I am by a year, and my sister, Amy, is four years younger. Maureen's hair is fair like mine, and Amy's is like Tommy's. I chose blonde six years ago. It lets me have fun with color." Describing hair colors seemed an easy way to identify the others.

"Who's you favorite sister?"

Kathryn thought this an unusual question. She waited before answering.

"Well, I'm closer to Amy because Maureen and I are on different wavelengths. We argue more and then make up, to be truthful," she said.

Suzanne Murray produced a quick, tense smile.

"We're up to parents, Kathryn. Let's start with your mother."

"Mom's friendly and very attractive. She's also a good athlete."

"She sounds like fun."

"She is fun. She's one of a kind." Kathryn's liking for her mother bubbled in her voice.

"Did she work, too, Kathryn?"

"Yes. Part-time for a heart specialist while we were in school. Later she became a paralegal. Now she sells real estate."

"She sounds fascinating. Which of you is her favorite?"

"I don't think she has one," Kathryn said. "She treats us all the same. If you knew mom you wouldn't ask the question."

"Where is she now. In Queens?"

"No. My parents sold the Queens house and moved to North Carolina. They live in Raleigh."

"I see."

Suzanne Murray rose from the chair and walked a few steps, stretching her arms as she did so. She noted travel posters on the office walls and flowering plants with red, yellow and green buds which smiled on small tables. She ran a hand through her thick, dark hair.

Kathryn also stood. She studied Suzanne's every move. The well-dressed visitor was the taller of the two, and thinner. Kathryn reminded herself to cut back on french fries. Suzanne returned to the deskside chair.

"What about Kevin Delaney?" Kathryn.

"Dad?" Oh, he's probably your typical father. You know, pays the bills and goes to all the family affairs. Helps with this and helps with that."

"His job?"

"Office manager for the Chase Bank in Manhattan.

"In most families with more than one daughter, Kathryn, one is the father's favorite. Are you his favorite? Is it Maureen? Or Amy?"

The questioner's focus on 'favorites' made Kathryn's smile an effort.

"Suzanne, if I may call you Suzanne," she said, "We've all asked the same question since we were little girls. I asked dad myself, and I'm sure Maureen and Amy did, too. He told us we were all his favorites. He treats each of us as special. If he has a favorite he sure keeps it quiet. But that's like dad. He's really sort of dull. I don't think he's done much interesting in his life."

As soon as the words were out Kathryn felt like kicking herself. Dad had treated her great. She hadn't meant to sound critical.

"Thank you, Kathryn," said the voice beside her. "I appreciate your frankness."

Kathryn tugged at a blonde curl and leaned back in the chair. She looked on her desk with its framed family photo. She checked her watch. It was an hour since Suzanne Murray first walked through the door.

"I'm convinced, Kathryn," said the visitor. "You've got the assignment. In the next fifteen minutes I'll be honest with you for a very good reason. Once I go out the door we won't see each other again. Does that surprise you?"

"Hardly," said the young attorney. "I don't surprise easily." She presented Suzanne a professional smile while she thought about what she'd heard. Something didn't add up. Suzanne Murray's eyes fastened to Kathryn's face. It made her uncomfortable.

"You're as poised as they said," Suzanne continued. "but keep in mind I'm like everyone else. Some things I can talk about and some things I can't."

"I'll buy that," Kathryn said, pleased she had passed whatever test the woman gave her.

"Your assignment concerns my resume'" Suzanne said. "I've reduced it to one page. The page ends 7 years ago. After that is my concern, not yours. I do not have a money problem, unless having too much is a problem. I don't live in this area and I'll be on my way in half an hour."

She removed the sunglasses. Kathryn saw clear blue eyes beneath long, dark eyelashes.

"When I leave, Kathryn, please contact the law firm of Frohn, Konner and Maltby, which is over on Jerico Turnpike. Ask to speak to Mr. Frohn. He'll verify what I tell you."

Kathryn listened.

"I gave a bank draft to Mr. Frohn. It's for $15,000 and it's made out to you. It's to pay for your time and efforts in investigating my resume'. Mr. Frohn will also provide you with additional background materials. Specifically, something on the resume' is untrue, yet I cannot discuss it with you. Mr.Krohn's associates and Mr. Daley's investigators found the resume' perfect. It isn't. I'm willing to try one more time. Your assignment is find the flaw. Wen you find it -- I'm confident you will -- Mr. Frohn has a second bank draft for you in the amount of $40,000."

"$40,000, Kathryn said. "Why so much?"

"When you find the flaw, Kathryn, you'll need an explanation worth $40,000. Believe me. Now, I must be going."

Suzanne took a sealed white envelope from her portfolio and placed it on the desk.

"The resume'" she said. "Good luck, Kathryn." She reached for Kathryn's hand. Her smile had warmed. "May I look around before I leave?"

"Feel free."

Five minutes later Suzanne stepped out of the office without a backward glance.

Kathryn picked up the four green and white fifty dollar bills from the desk while in her mind she reviewed the odd assignment.

She would do her best. Whatever the outcome, $15,000 would pay a lot of rent.

"What can be hidden in a one-page resume'?" she asked herself. She locked the office door. She smiled as she inhaled a trace of floral perfume.

From her desk she removed a new white sweatshirt with a grey-stenciled eagle on the front. From a cabinet she removed three dozen thin magic markers, each a different color. In the next hour Kathryn's talented fingers produced a plumed eagle in startling hues. She folded the shirt and reached for a yellow legal pad. She wrote down every observation of the interview just ended. Long ago she had learned the trick of keeping fingers busy while her mind raced.

The resume' seemed routine. Suzanne Murray, born 38 years earlier in Manhattan, was the only child of Richard and Sheila Murray. She attended parochial schools in Manhattan, followed by graduation from Manhattanville College. She earned teacher's certification, followed by a dozen years teaching English in a Manhattan high school, followed by a shift from teaching to editorial work at two publishing houses.

She had resigned from the second publisher 7 years earlier without explanation. Her salaries had been moderate. She listed a single Manhattan address and no hobbies.

A visit to Frohn, Kenner and Maltby seemed in order.

"Thank you for waiting, Kathryn," said Abel Frohn. "Suzanne Murray has given me a bank draft and an envelope of family pictures for you. Also, copies of our investigation of her resume' and a similar investigation by Daley and Company."

Kathryn looked around the room. Chairs upholstered in camel leather sat on conservative dark carpeting, while mahogany desks added to a sedate atmosphere. Bland and typical of prosperous law firms, Kathryn thought, mentally contrasting Frohn's neutral office with the bright colors surrounding her own desk.

"My client has been specific in her instructions," Frohn continued. "I can't say much more, other than hope I see you again."

Kathryn packed all her newly acquired papers in the trunk of her aged red Nissan sedan. Before driving across Long Island's ribbons of concrete to her apartment in Long Beach she deposited the Murray bank draft. On reaching home she put aside the newly-decorated sweatshirt and prepared dinner. Her hands catered the food. Her mind worked on the resume' assignment.

A month later Kathryn sat in her Mineola office with her sister, Maureen.

"Why are you bugging me, Maureen?" she asked.

"Listen," was the reply. "I enjoyed the lunch, even though it's not easy to get here on the train from Manhattan. I'm not bugging you, either. I simply asked why you spent a month on a one-page resume'. Don't you have anything better to do?"

"You're bugging me, Maureen," Kathryn said. She put a Jimmy Buffet CD in a player. Vases of fresh roses scented the air. The music interrupted their exchange and both women quieted.

"I'll walk to the train, Kathryn," Maureen said when the disc ended. "Call me when you're coming to Manhattan."

Kathryn watched the door close behind her sister. Her mind returned again, as so often in the previous four weeks, to Suzanne Murray's resume'.

Both John B. Daley and Abel Frohn had verified each item on the resume'. Their reports included conversations with neighbors, teachers, publishing supervisors and fellow workers. Both reports were detailed and in total agreement.

Suzanne Murray lived with her parents in an elegant townhouse on Manhattan's upper East Side. She was described as quiet and intelligent. She seemed to work because she wanted to rather than from a need for money. Many interviewees suspected she was personally wealthy, though none knew her well. She made no reference to a personal life, nor could anyone recall mention of a boy friend. Her parents died a year apart, some dozen years earlier.

Several former associates remembered a mention of travel when she returned from vacations, though no details were provided. She enjoyed an excellent reputation in teaching English and had earned the respect of her supervisors at the publishing houses. No one had seen or heard from her in the past 7 years.

One clue, possibly an important one, stared at Kathryn from the pages of Daley's investigation. He had traced Suzanne Murray's social security number to one on an income tax return filed from the American Embassy in Paris by Mrs. Adam Elliott, wife of the American Charge d' Affaires.

"There are no secrets," Kathryn said, "but this isn't much help. I'm not going to France."

She listened. Jimmy Buffet ended his performance. She enjoyed the mixture of floral scents in the small office as she reached for her magnifying glass. Perhaps another study of the few pictures provided by Suzanne Murray might yet unlock the mystery.

The earliest photo showed a couple holding a small baby. Another, taken in grade school days, portrayed the same smiling couple holding hands with a skinny, serious, dark-haired girl. A cap and gown shot identified the family at high school graduation. In addition, the collection of color pictures included individual portraits of father, mother and Suzanne dated a decade earlier.

Kathryn put down the magnifying glass. She scanned the ruby red polish on her manicured nails. Perfect, as usual. Kathryn took pride in her beautiful fingers. A good manicure helped display them.

"The town house?" she asked herself. It brought a seven figure price around the time the resume ended. Presumably, the money went to Suzanne Murray.

She reached for the notes written immediately after their meeting.

"Why questions about my family?" she wondered in disbelief. "Especially the questions about favorites. What could they mean?"

After five trips to Manhattan in the little Nissan and many hours of mental anguish Kathryn still lacked a solution to the problem. She wondered if an order of Enzo's fine spaghetti in Bayside might help her think. She could picture her steaming plate as Enzo brought it to the table. Maybe she would ask Amy along, an added expense now possible because of Suzanne Murray's generous bank draft.

She decided on a final summary of the problem before calling Amy.

"What do I know best?" she asked. She looked around the room. The answer leaped at her. "Color."

"What about my family?" came next. "She's never met Maureen, me, Amy or Tommy. She doesn't know mom. That leaves dad. Dad? Hardly. But who else?" She had examined resumes of her father and mother with great care, to no avail.

"Color, color, color," Kathryn said. Her fingers drummed on the desk. She looked down and saw the black handle of her magnifying glass and the sparkling lens which distorted the photos beneath.

"Color," she repeated.

In the paperback novels she enjoyed in idle moments, heroes favored shouts of "Egad" in mid-crisis, while heroines yelled a beloved's name at a sudden turn of events.

Kathryn's mental awakening more closely resembled a wisp of air floating through the mail slot at the bottom of her office door.

Color. Two brown-eyed people do not produce a blue-eyed daughter.

She spun the magnifying glass. Richard Murray possessed brown eyes, as did his wife, Sheila. Beside them, Suzanne Murray's blue eyes verified their description in the interview notes on Kathryn's yellow pad.

Kathryn knew what had to be done. For the next six days she became a virtual whirlwind. She knew what to look for, and where.

In Manhattan's Hall of Records, she checked two dozen birth certificates issued on the day Suzanne Murray was born. Then she checked Suzanne's. All but one followed a similar format on well-aged paper. Suzanne's had been completed later, on newer paper and in slightly different format. Suspicions verified.

Educational background provided another clue. Parochial schools. In Kathryn's girlhood New York's Cardinal frequently chaired appeals for his favorite charity, The New york Foundling Hospital. The Foundling Hospital also handled most Catholic adoptions in Manhattan.

"Yes?" asked the elderly nun, identified by a plain desk plate as sister Francilla.

"I requested this interview for two reasons, sister," Kathryn began. "One reason is business and the other is, uh, personal." She hesitated before resuming. Her palms were sweating. "Both reasons involve a baby I feel certain was born here 38 years ago."

"Yes? What would you like to know?"

"First, sister, how long have you bern at The New York Foundling Hospital?"

"Almost 40 years, though sometimes I feel I began yesterday, if you know what I mean."

"Yes, I do know," Kathryn said. She smiled. "I'm an attorney who's been commissioned by an unusual client to check into her background. Her path has led me here."

"Yes?"

"I'd like to know what you can tell me if I give you a baby girl's adoptive name?"

"I can tell you very little, young woman," said the nun. "For instance, only the adoptee is entitled to know the name of the true parents. There isn't much I'm allowed to tell you. These are delicate situations."

"I understand, sister. In this situation, though, it's also important to me personally. Very important," she added. Kathryn wondered if the nun detected her nervousness. "If I give you the family's name, would you please check your records for me?"

"If you'll give me the date of birth and the name of the adoptive parents, I'll look at our files," she said.

"Birth date, thirty eight years ago next month," Kathryn stated. July 9th. Adoptive parents, Richard and Sheila Murray of Manhattan."

The nun's posture remained erect. Kathryn detected a flicker in the serene dark eyes.

"Be patient, Kathryn," said the older woman, rising. "It will take me a few minutes. I'm not as young as I used to be." She rose. Her black shoes made not the slightest sound on the white tiled floor of the small office.

"How do they walk without making noises?" Kathryn thought. She remembered the question from high school. She hoped her nervousness disguised her cleverness. If the nun returned with a labeled folder the question was answered, even if no comments were offered. The rules were strict and Kathryn held little hope an experienced nun would make such a mistake.

Her wait seemed endless. When the nun reappeared Kathryn's hands moved nervously. She tried to still them but she couldn't. The nun's empty hands confirmed Kathryn's judgment.

"I've checked the files," sister Francilla said. "As I told you, there's little I can tell you without permission from an adoptee. You did say there's a personal reason for your question. May I ask what?"

"I'm not sure I can tell you, sister. It's only a guess and a wild one and I'll have a lot of work to do if it's accurate and I'm not sure what answer I want." Kathryn rattled out the words, too fast. Her mind raced faster. She felt confused and disoriented. She shook her head. "I, uh, can't tell you, sister. I'm really embarrassed but I, uh, I just can't."

Sister Francilla stared at the young blonde's clear complexion. She saw a single, unexplained tear inch under a corner of Kathryn's eye. The nun's experienced gaze recognized an emotional struggle.

"My dear Kathryn," the nun said. "I've been here a long time. Perhaps I can help you, but only a little."

Kathryn pulled three tissues from her bag and wiped her contact lenses.

"On the date you mentioned," the nun continued, "a young woman experienced a difficult birth. I was still new here and as a trainee I assisted. Fortunately for the mother, she survived. Unfortunately, she would never again have another child."

"Can you tell me whether the baby was a boy or a girl?"

"A girl, a healthy girl."

An odd question flew into Kathryn's mind. She asked it.

"Were the baby's parents married?"

"Yes, they were. It's not usually the case, you know."

"That's all you can tell me, sister?"

"I believe so, Kathryn."

"Thank you, sister." Kathryn strove for composure. She shoved the crumpled tissues into her bag. She favored the elderly nun with a smile and reached across the desk to take her hand.

"Thank you again, sister."

Kathryn walked to the office door, pivoted and hesitated. The nun's dark eyes stared at her. The young blonde felt more nervous than in her entire life. But she had to ask.

"The baby girl's father, sister. Was his name Kevin?"

The pause lasted a hundred years.

Kathryn rushed into the hall with a clear mental picture of the silent positive nodding of the elderly nun's head.

Two conversations with Abel Frohn.

"I've completed Suzanne Murray's assignment," Kathryn announced in the first call.

"I'll get back to you," Frohn said.

He called back the next day.

"Kathryn? Abel Frohn. Please enclose your report in an envelope addressed to Suzanne Murray. Seal it. Have it delivered to me. I will forward it to her. At the same time I will send you the promised draft for $40,000. I expect Suzanne's reply within two weeks. I'll contact you when it arrives."

"Kathryn deposited the $40,000 draft, and wrote herself a note to leave it untouched until Suzanne Murray contacted her.

Nine days later, a messenger delivered to Kathryn the envelope promised her by Abel Frohn. She was unsurprised by a Paris postmark, but appreciative of the colorful airmail stamps. She locked the office door, turned on Jimmy Buffet and sat down at her desk before opening the envelope. She looked at the quiet man in the family picture on her desk, and opened the envelope.

Paris, France
Dear Kathryn,
   My mother was a talented, wealthy, gifted Catholic girl who wanted to sample everything and have her own

way...always. If you check the history of New York's 'Irish Mafia' you'll find lots of Murrays.

She had but one doubt. She wanted to be a nun, and her family fought her on it. Her single doubt was whether they were right or she was.

She moved to a small apartment in Greenwich Village. She lived on a tiny budget while working at the Chase Bank. At night she drifted in and out of the coffeehouses.

She met your father at the Bank. At the time, he also occupied an apartment in the Village.

Your father's family wanted him to become a priest, and he fought them. It seems inevitable your father and my mother would meet.

Your father attracts wonderful women. It's something in his personality, I think. Your description of your mom parallels my mother.

Your father and my mother fought each other while trying to help. He encouraged her to become a nun. She tried to get him to become a priest. The battles raged and their mutual attraction became a roaring flame. She arranged their marriage, a private rite shared with neither family. Three months later she engineered her own disappearance. Your father's expensive annulment was quietly handled through the church courts by another branch of the Murray's.

Your father was right and my mother was wrong. He was not cut out to be a priest. After I was born, my mother went to Europe and did become a nun. She rose to head her order. I was fortunate enough to meet and talk with her 8 years ago, before she died.

Richard and Sheila were distant cousins, childless, willing to adopt me and wonderful parents. Eight years ago I met Adam Elliott. We are well suited.

Personally, I've always wanted to be my father's favorite daughter. Our conversation thrilled me because I know now I'll always be his favorite -- as you are.

I knew you would find me, Kathryn, as soon as I saw the bright colors in your office. Men don't think in color.

*One final mention: Odd as it may seem, your father
did not know his wife was pregnant when she disappeared.
He does not know he has a daughter named Suzanne, and I
can't tell him. I've tried to figure out a way and I just can't
do it. Perhaps I'm not the woman my mother was.*

*That's the $40,000, Kathryn, for telling him if you can.
I must admit, though, there's more to life than money. It's
your decision.*

*Grateful in every sense, your sister -- signing herself
for the first time ever with her full name.*

Suzanne Delaney Murray Elliott.

Kathryn put down the fine scripted letter and looked at the photo
in front of her. She tried picturing her father in the coffeehouses of
Greenwich Village or married to a wealthy Irish heiress. Instead, her
mind produced images of the quiet man she knew, supporting a noisy
Queens family on a limited income.

A half hour later she realized Jimmy Buffet had finished. Outside,
the sun slid lower in the west and afternoon shadows lengthened.

Kathryn thought about calling Amy for spaghetti while she
dwelled on the letter before her.

"Decision, decisions," she said. "Well, there's no time like the
present."

"Amy first."

"How about spaghetti at Enzo's tonight, Amy? On me."

"Fine, Kath. 6:30 okay?"

"I'll be there."

The svelte woman in the American embassy in Paris retired to
her room to read the letter from America. She recognized the return
address in the upper left corner of the outside envelope.

Mineola, Long Island, N.Y.

Dear Suzanne,

I enjoyed and appreciated your letter about our father.
I'm most pleased you are happy with the results of my

investigation. You may be certain I wish you all the personal happiness in the world, in every way possible.

After considerable thought, I have decided there is no reason for me or you or anyone to inform my father of your history. It would disrupt my own family and serve little purpose.

If you would like occasional notes as to dad's activities, I'll be happy to forward them to you at the embassy.

In the meantime, I've sent the $40,000 to The New York Foundling Home. They did a fine job for you. Others will benefit because of you.

Sincerely,
Kathryn

The blonde attorney sealed the envelope, checked her manicure and locked the office door. Her red Nissan awaited. She looked forward to another laughing night with her funny sister, Amy.

As she drove across Long Island, Kathryn's mind generated a surprising project which immediately grasped her attention.

"My resume'" she said. "It's time I updated it. One never knows..."

22

Anna Boylan

Gary Rogers stepped from the small elevator car and turned to the right. Like most corridors in the nursing home, the one on the fifth floor was antiseptically clean. He walked a few steps and stopped. His path was blocked. A very old woman had bumped her wheelchair into the wall. Her head was below the level of her arms and her fingers were locked on the top of the wheels.

He watched her twist and realized she could not talk. He reached for the hand grips behind her and moved her chair gently into the corridor. She nodded as he pushed her in the direction he was walking.

An aide appeared from inside the room to Gary's right.

"She belongs on the other side of the building," the aide said, pleasantly. She walked past Gary.

He turned the chair around and wheeled the woman back along the corridor. When he passed the elevator he saw a row of wheelchairs along both sides of the wall. Each chair contained an old woman. All faced the elevator.

"Put her there," a woman said, pointing. After she spoke to Gary she avoided eye contact. He rolled his passenger into line, walked a few steps without her, and stopped.

He surveyed the rows of elderly women. He had come to expect them on his courtesy visits to his aunt. Almost all had deteriorated physically. Twisted mouths marked many as stroke victims. All seemed bent and frail, staring ahead with expressionless faces.

Gary admired the determination he saw as they coped with their odd world. Despite handicaps of all sorts, they wheeled themselves onto the elevators, and most could get unaided to the pleasant, first-floor dining room. Managed, cared-for and at times manipulated by the aides,the women instinctively supported each other's needs as best they might.

He glanced at the wall near the elevator. The number 4 was a surprise and he knew he was on the wrong floor. He pushed the elevator button, and as he waited his eyes drifted across the faces turned toward him. Most avoided his glance, but one woman's expression changed as his eyes met hers. Her smile was a light, unexpectedly turned on. She sat erect in the wheelchair, without turning her head. Her hair was wavy and plentiful and grey.

"How are you today?" Gary said. To his right, a woman grunted. He turned.

The bent woman beside him pointed to her own ear. "Unnnh," the woman mumbled, trying to speak while pointing, first to her ear and then to the woman Gary had addressed. She shook her head.

Gary understood. She was telling him the wavy-haired woman could not hear. Still, that sudden smile had been a winner. He saw the name on the chair. Anna Boylan.

A noise behind him signaled the arrival of the elevator. He was on and off, and soon with his aunt. He was no longer certain she recognized him, or even knew he was there.

Awhile later, Gary was on the sidewalk, facing Van Cortlandt Park. Located in the northern reaches of the Bronx, it remained one of the few green spots within New York City's northern county. At least the nursing home people could look out and see trees and grass.

He walked the few blocks to his car. On the drive home he thought about the lives of the old women. He knew that none of them could manage alone, but not for the first time he found himself wondering what they were like when they were younger. He wondered about the message in the eyes of the woman with the lovely smile. Was it intelligence?"

"I'll probably never know," he thought.

A night later Gary sat reading a book about early American movies.

"Yes," the author wrote, "there is now general agreement that one of the greatest but least celebrated of the early movie stars was Louise Brooks. It's nice that through the movies seen on VCR's people have begun to recognize this talented lady. But for my money, the greatest of them all was Anna Boylan. I've often wondered what happened to her."

At first, Gary didn't relate to the name. The famous director's comments continued.

"Anna Boylan showed up one day looking for a job as a secretary. Actually, she was a superb typist. But what caught my attention and why we hired her was the combination of thick, wavy red hair with an absolutely flawless complexion.

"That was the beginning. She had a mobile face, a beautiful smile and though slender, a lovely figure. Best of all though, she had an incredible sense of humor. Anna Boylan wasn't her real name, either. She chose it because it reminded her of Anne Boleyn, who had her head cut off by Henry the Eighth."

"Someday, Max," she said to me, "we'll do a picture about Henry the Eighth. This time, though, Anne cuts off Henry's head. I've already bought the knife. Want to see it?" She laughed and made a move to open her bag.

"Great, Anna," I told her. "I've already got a list of actors we could cast in Henry's part."

"Forget it, Max," she said. "Alan Daily plays Henry." Then, would you believe it, two weeks later she and Alan Daily disappeared. Just like that. I thought maybe the studio had arranged something, but we never came across either of them again. As an actress though, Anna Boylan put Louise Brooks to shame. I've a full-length comedy that I filmed with Anna in the lead part. We're negotiating now, and if it's ever released, the world will be a better place -- and funnier."

Gary Rogers closed the book. The name Anna Boylan seemed to reach him. When he made the connection he shook his head.

"It can't be," he thought, "but it's worth a try, anyway."

After the next visit to his aunt, Gary went to the 4th floor nursing station. The seated nurse in her starched white uniform turned and faced him pleasantly.

"I'd like to ask a question or two about one of your guests, if you don't mind," Gary said.

"I'll answer if I can."

"What can you tell me about Anna Boylan?"

"Strange, interesting and different," was the prompt reply.

"What does that mean?"

"It means I've taken the trouble to read her folder. I like her, and I think she's playing games with us. And I like that, too," she added.

"Games? Here?"

"Anna Boylan has been here almost six months. For a woman in her mid-eighties, she's in excellent health. Most of our other women are in poor physical shape and have endured heart attacks or strokes or both. Yet, like them, Anna never talks. She's totally deaf. She was sent here from somewhere out West, accompanied by a sizable donation -- a very sizable donation."

"From whom?"

"I don't know, but I do know she spends a lot of time watching TV, which is unusual here. Sometimes she watches with the sound turned off, and sometimes with the sound turned on even though she can't hear it, and the nice thing is, every so often something makes her smile. Her smile, Mr. Rogers, is absolutely stunning and I love it." She laughed.

Gary faced the entry to the small office. A chair wheeled past the door. It was Anna Boylan, sitting erect and staring ahead as she soundlessly passed the door.

"What's so strange, then?" Gary asked.

"Several things. We've all seen that wonderful smile, as I told you. Most of the time it occurs when the TV is on and the sound is also on. I watched once, and when she smiled I asked a question to see if she would give the game away."

"And?"

"Nothing. Not a sign. Not a word, either. Somehow, Anna Boylan is either totally deaf, as the folder says, or far better at playing games than any of us, me included."

"That's all?"

"When I took her folder from the office, I noticed it was quite thin. I wondered if there might be another folder that I wasn't given. More surprising was that we usually document a family physician, a person to be called in case of problems, and a next of kin. Her document was most unusual."

"In what way?"

"She has no family physician. Other than deafness she has no physical complaint. She takes no medications. In case of problems -- hear this: if the problem is minor, call her attorneys. If the problem is major, use our own judgment."

"A bit of a switch," Gary said.

"Mr. Rogers," the woman said, "her attorneys are in Seattle, Washington, and this is New York. With high phone costs, we do no calling. I believe someone thought it all out, just as they did with her next of kin, where the listing is handwritten and almost impossible to decipher."

"So?"

"I made a copy. I'm a curious woman, and I like Anna Boylan," the nurse said.

"I enlarged it. According to her folder here, Mr. Rogers, Anna Boylan's next of kin is Henry the Eighth."

Gary laughed. He didn't know the details but he felt the situation reflected a lot of fun.

"Thank you so much for your interest," he said, adding "nurse Millman," as he read her name tag. "I can only tell you now that I think Anna Boylan probably hears as well as we do. I'm with you on this, and I'll do a bit of further checking."

Gary went across the hall and pressed the elevator button. He turned, and found the file of wheelchairs readied for lunch. In the third chair, squarely facing him, sat Anna Boylan. Her eyes focused, or seemed to focus, on Gary's face. He smiled. No reaction. He thought that, if anything, her eyes suddenly dulled, as if she had fallen asleep. He turned around and departed.

During the next three weeks Gary wrote to all the studios, asking for information concerning Anna Boylan. He wrote the publisher of the book with Anna's name, asking for any further details. He also enclosed a separate letter for the author and former director, Max Rathman, and asked that it be forwarded.

He visited his aunt twice. Both times he stopped on the nearby floor and chatted with nurse Millman. He tried to establish some sort of eye contact with Anna Boylan, but she seemed unaware of his presence. It was as if he didn't exist.

Frustrated, Gary reviewed the skimpy background data about the elderly woman. The facts told him nothing.

"We must be missing something obvious," he thought, "but I don't seem able to see it." It was then he came up with a new idea. "See it," he said aloud. "What if the problem isn't her hearing at all, but her eyes?"

Over the following few days he worked on his new theory He talked with the nurse and told her, too. Then he developed a plan. It would require cooperation from the home's management. Gary obtained the needed approval and put the plan into action.

Alongside them sat Anna Boylan in her wheelchair, and close by was a second wheelchair. This one was notably different.

"Hello, Anna," Gary said. "My hobby is old movies. I was reading about you recently. Your old friend Max Rathman says you were the greatest actress of your time. He's still alive, you know."

Anna looked straight ahead. Her expression remained the same, but Gary thought he noticed a slight change in her breathing, so slight he would have missed it if he weren't watching carefully. He was certain the woman had both heard and understood.

The nurse looked at Gary. He spoke to Anna again.

"I'm a fan of yours, Anna. I'm also interested in what you might want to say to us. So I've fixed up a new wheelchair. We'll put you in it now, Anna." The nurse waved him aside and efficiently moved the old woman into the new chair. Anna was arranged gently and with obvious care.

"If you put your hands out, Anna," Gary continued, "you'll find a rest for them. But if you reach further there's a keyboard. It's like a typewriter but it's really a word processor. The touch is light. Anything you might choose to write will be seen only by nurse Millman or myself. It's up to you, Anna. Can you hear us, Anna? Would you like to type?"

The threesome sat motionless. The nurse watched Anna, then Gary. He concentrated on Anna, who gave no sign she heard. All three sat in silence. The large hand on the electric wall clock made five complete sweeps.

Gary stood, turned towards the nurse and shook his head. As he did, a slight movement caught his eye. Anna's hands began to edge forward. She sat erect, as usual, but she moved her hands to the keyboard. The nurse turned a switch and the processor's monitor lit up.

Words began to appear on the screen, slowly at first and then slightly faster.

"i can type and hear. how do i make this thing go to the next line and where is the upper case key. i cannot see what i am doing my eyesight comes and goes and Max was right. i'm an actress and the best. i heard you both talk about me. memory is still good, too. my name is not anna boylan i've just used that for a long time it's a good joke. i am more tired than i would like but will write again. thanks for your brains, mr. rogers. sincerely, mary clare donovan, whose father always told her she was too smart for her own good and her big eyes would get her in trouble and he was right."

She stopped. It was obvious she was finished. The nurse looked at Gary and told him to wait. She moved "Anna Boylan" back into the regular wheelchair, rolled it out of the office and in a short while returned, alone.

"Well, Mr.Rogers, I compliment you," she said. "Your guess was accurate. Now, I've got to see the director and learn what we do next. I'm sure we'll be encouraged to let Anna or Mary Clare, if that's her name, do some typing. At her age an hour or so a day will be about what she can handle. Stop by in a few days and I'll bring you up to date."

"Be pleased to," he said. "By the way, your suspicions about her hearing also proved out. Please share the compliments."

He left the office and moved to the elevator. Aides were bringing women from their rooms and readying them for lunch. He saw Mary Clare Donovan. He walked over to her. "Have a nice day, Mary Clare Donovan," he said. There was absolutely no sign of recognition and she seemed to stare right through him.

He heard the elevator door begin opening behind him. At that moment Mary Clare Donovan smiled. Her smile was warm and friendly, but it lasted for only a flash, to be replaced by the same stare as before. Gary shook his head as he stepped onto the waiting elevator, wondering if they would ever solve the riddle of this strange woman and her unfolding past.

As luck would have it, for the next month Gary had little time to speculate about Mary Clare Donovan or Anna Boylan or his aunt or anyone else outside his work circle. A trip to Chicago was followed by another to Detroit. When he returned it was to find he received no response from the studios, and a brief, noncommittal reply from Max Rathman.

Gary's interest was piqued. Next day, he drove to Van Cortlandt Park. He locked his car and went directly to the Home's 4th floor station, where he met with nurse Millman. As soon as she saw Gary she reached for a stack of papers on the side of her desk and handed it to him.

"You'll find this interesting reading, Mr. Rogers," she said. "I know I did. I still marvel at the quantity, too. Anna Boylan has been typing every day, with little sign of fatigue."

"And the act?" was Gary's reply. "Does she still pretend she can't hear?"

"Read what she says," the nurse said, watching Gary sit down before she left the room, when he began reading.

"This is the life story of Mary Clare Donovan. It cannot be checked or proven or disproven. It is all true. When I am gone this belongs to nurse Millman and Gary Rogers. But then they won't need it, which is a joke. Which is my life story, too. Which is why Max Rathman knows I was the greatest actress.

That is true, too.

I was born in the Bronx, not far from here. My mother died when I was born. My father was a vaudeville comedian named Dandy Don Donovan. I had a sister a year older whose name was Celia. We both had red hair. My father was away more often than he was home, and we were assigned to his sister, Molly.

My father and mother and Molly are all in Woodlawn Cemetery, which is close by. It's where I will go when it's time, but not yet. Celia is still alive but she doesn't know I am.

I don't know exactly what happened when I was born but the results were spectacular. Also odd. I have hearing that is far beyond any person I have ever met. I can remember every word of everything I have ever seen in print or heard, and I taught myself to read before I was two years old. Why? I don't know why, or even how. I thought it was normal. Just as I thought I was normal, too.

Aunt Molly's husband had been wealthy, prosperous and well-educated. He died quite young, leaving Molly a well-fixed widow. His library was packed with just about everything, from the classics to economics, even to old joke books. Aunt Molly would go out to the store and I would take a book. By the time she returned I had flipped all the pages and entered them in my head. I put the book back, went off by myself, and tried to understand what I had absorbed.

Celia was quiet, and we didn't talk much. Aunt Molly thought little girls should be seen and not heard, so neither of them had any idea of what I was doing.

The one who caught me at it was my father. Whenever he did return home it was all noise and laughter and joke after joke after joke. He would manage to get Celia and Aunt Molly laughing, which wasn't easy. Then he would start on me. The two of us just traded laughs for hours.

But my father was wise in his own way. He would take Celia out one day with him. The next day was my turn. This way, we would each have him to ourself for the whole day.

My father and I were walking near Times Square on one of our trips. I was only about five. He happened to comment about a building we were passing.

"That's a fine-looking building," he said. "I wonder who built it."

"Louis Sullivan was the architect, daddy," I said, "but he didn't build it. Stone and Ford built it, in 1903."

"How do you know that?"

"It's on page 162 in Aunt Molly's encyclopedia."

"Oh," he said. "And I guess you know what's on all the other pages, too?"

"Yes, daddy," I answered. "Now, why did the chicken cross the road?"

"It was T street and he didn't want his tees uncrossed," my father said. Then he added "All the pages in the encyclopedia, Mary Clare? Is that all?"

"No daddy, that's not all. All the pages in all the books in Aunt Molly's library. That's all."

"And what do you intend to do when you grow up, knowing all the pages?" he asked.

"I don't know, daddy. I have to go to school first, don't I?"

"Let's you and me have some ice cream, Mary Clare," was what he said next, and we did. But for some reason he never let on he knew, and I didn't tell anyone. I didn't tell him about how good I could hear, either, because I knew he didn't like boasting.

So he thought we shared a big secret and we did, but he didn't ask me about anything else, so I didn't tell him about my eyes. I would be sitting and thinking about something I had read when suddenly it was as if someone pulled a shade down over my eyes. I didn't know when it would happen, and it was only once in a while, maybe once a month, It would last a few seconds or as long as five minutes. Then the shade would go up and I could see again.

This went on for years. No one knew, and there was no one to tell. It never happened when I walked, only when I was sitting. So I taught myself to sit straight. That way, by keeping my eyes ahead, no one but me knew that the shade was down.

Celia and I completed grade school and high school. She worked hard and did well. I was totally bored and by faking wrong answers was able to do as well as Celia but no better. Fortunately, I always had a handwriting that was very hard to read. In those days you could lose a lot of points for that.

We both went to a business school. I loved typing, and could type for hours without looking at the paper. Every once in a while the shade would come down while I typed, but no one knew. In my spare time I went to the libraries. Celia loved cooking, which I didn't. Not even a little bit. We were seldom together. When I had read through one library, I could always find another. I owe a lot to New York libraries.

Celia decided to become a cooking teacher. She went her way and I went mine. She later married and moved to Stamford, Connecticut. She still lives in Stamford.

My father lived until I was almost 17. Each time he came home we would spend a day together, sometimes several days.

I found out that when he took Celia out, he would suggest a place to go and she would agree. They went to movies, to restaurants and on train rides. They both really liked train rides.

For me, though, it was different. I would be asked where in the entire city of New York I would like to go. Daddy made it clear he wanted to take me where I wanted to go, where no one but him would take me.

We often went in the morning to the Columbia University Library. I would read all sorts of books and he would just sit and read a newspaper. Next we would have a nice lunch. Then we would walk all through Van Cortlandt Park which we both loved to do. He would ask me the names of the trees and shrubs and I would tell him. He would laugh at some of the Latin names and say "You don't say," or "really?" I would nod and make up a rhyme, like "deciduous and good for us." Then we would laugh some more.

When I was older, we went to plays and the opera and some of the city's rowdiest night clubs. We both liked the comedians and I just never seemed to get tired with him. Strange place for a young girl,

I guess, but I was different and he knew it. Once or twice the shade came down while we were sitting in an audience, but I don't think he knew it. He thought I had great posture.

Daddy died in a train crash in Colorado. Later, I worked as a secretary in the Brill Building in Manhattan, where many of the theatrical agents had offices. I was able to change jobs and work for one of them when I showed how fast I could type. Three years later the agent moved to California, and I was able to go, too. Aunt Molly thought the agent paid the expenses, but he didn't. I had saved up for two years. I wanted to go West in the worst way.

Prices were very high. After I paid my rent I had little left for food or anything else. I heard the studios paid better, even though they were still small. I went over for a job as a typist and instead was hired as a writer's assistant. I think it was because I was from New York, as most of the others had all come from the East.

They were all lonely. There wasn't much to do except work and drink. They did a lot of both. My writer was good and taught me how to write a script. Soon, he was drinking days as well as nights. When he was too drunk to write, I was writing for him. Then I helped with the office work and everything else. I didn't drink because it made me sick. I didn't like the taste much, anyway.

I had never liked my red hair. It was different from everyone else's and it was thick and hard to comb. I had a fair complexion and had to stay out of the sun. Lucky for me, I didn't have freckles. I really never paid much attention to my looks, until one morning I looked carefully in the mirror and realized I was very good looking as well as very different. It didn't make much difference then, because I spent all my spare time reading.

Max Rathman moved his team into our offices and I was helping with the work. Once or twice Max joked with me, and I responded with some of daddy's old jokes. We laughed a lot, and Max made two or three pictures which were well thought of. He never yelled, which was unusual with the directors.

One day Alan Daily came into the office. He was the handsomest man I had ever seen. He is still the handsomest man I have ever seen. He had been a leading man for a few years and was talking to Max about a picture. Nothing came of it. It was about the time Max decided on me for a part in the next picture he would direct.

I did two more pictures with Max, and my parts were bigger. Then the leading lady's drinking spree ruined her and she couldn't work at all. Max was convinced I should play the lead in his next comedy. We had a lot of fun and when Max saw the rushes he was really pleased.

Alan Daily stopped on the set towards the end of the picture and asked if he could take me to dinner that night. I was surprised. He could have asked just about anyone. We drove in Alan's new Duesenberg to a place miles away. It was my first ride in a convertible.

He had bought the car that same afternoon, but I didn't know that. When we reached the dining room, he asked the headwaiter's opinion of his 'newest acquisition.' The headwaiter smiled at me, then told Alan he thought her really nice and really built for speed. The dinner was one long silence.

When we got outside I asked Alan to please take me home. There was no conversation. When he stopped, I got out and slammed the door.

"I'm not your newest acquisition and I'm not built for speed, you filthy rat," I screamed. Then I ran inside. I hated Alan Daily.

Of course, Max picked up on my mood. He had also known of my date with Alan Daily, who soon became the butt of our jokes. Gradually, I sort of forgot the incident, although I wasn't upset when I heard rumors Alan Daily had lost a major role at his studio.

My picture was completed and I had a few days off. A well-known producer had invited me to a party at his house one evening, and I accepted. When I arrived and he led me inside he excused himself. I heard a door slam. From another room, Alan Daily appeared.

"Mary Clare, I am about to apologize and explain," he said. "You may as well listen because we are the party and all the doors are locked." He sat himself down on a sofa near me. I was angry. I was also scared enough to be quiet.

"I have thought about our previous meeting," he began. "I suspect the problem is what the headwaiter said. He was thinking about my new car. It is built for speed. I am terribly sorry."

He seemed sincere. I relaxed.

"I will open the doors," Alan said. "You are free to leave if you like, and you can take my car if you want. The keys are in it, but I hope you would do me the honor of staying."

He was absolutely charming. I was unsuspecting. A few hours later I agreed to elope with him. We went to Seattle, Washington. He thought it a great joke that no one would know where we were. So did I. I have always liked jokes.

He opened a joint account for us with $25,000 in cash. Three weeks later, I was pregnant and Alan Daily was dead. In those days, drug overdoses in Seattle were rare. It was no joke.

I thought I would put things together without help. I was wrong. I would sit down in the morning, and suddenly the shade would come down. I knew where I was, but I couldn't see. It began happening in the afternoons, too. I could not consider a job. I could not consider learning to drive. Temporarily, I had enough money, but I knew I would have to do something. I had been taught to write scripts.

I wrote scripts and sent them to Max Rathman. The author's name was Celia Clare and she was from Seattle. He bought, not knowing the source. The pay was top notch. Celia Clare knew what Max Rathman needed, and what he would pay.

My baby was christened Don Donovan Daily. He was a big baby with red hair. I cared for him until he was old enough to go away to school. He had a good memory and I taught him every comedy routine I ever knew. We had a lot of laughs. When he was small I called him Three-D. He didn't like that, at all.

As soon as he could, he dropped the middle initial. Most people think he doesn't have one. Once or twice I took him to the cemetery where his father was buried. I told him his father had been an artist, a good one. I told him nothing else, and when he pushed me I refused to say more. Soon, he stopped asking.

I was selling lots of scripts. I knew in a short time Max or someone would find me. I didn't want that. I found a lawyer who was smart and honest. He changed my routine.

I would send him the scripts, he would send them to a New York agent, and then they went to the studios. Celia Clare became a big name. When the agent checked, the lawyer refused to talk. It was a big joke but it worked. I became rich and I made him rich, too. He invested my money and much of his in real estate, and in ten years we owned half of Seattle.

My son went to West Point. He was a top student and a fine athlete. One year he came home and brought his girl friend to the house. The girl asked if I would mind if she smoked. It was pot. I sent berserk. I threw them both out and told them never to come back. He never did. He was 20 years old. He sent me a note saying he didn't want to see me again. I sold the bungalow. I moved, first to Arizona and then a lot of other places.

Each year on his birthday I have written him a card. I have the lawyer send it to him. It is addressed to Three-D and says "Happy Birthday." A check for a large amount goes with it. The check has always been sent back to the law firm. I've donated the money to the Actor's Fund.

You may think I'm bitter or something, but I'm not. It's a big joke and the joke's on me. The lawyer kept track of my son, and often volunteered to tell me about him. I wouldn't let him, until last year.

My son became an outstanding soldier. He was decorated for valor in two wars. He became a general. He married and has three children. The children are all girls and they all have red hair. Isn't that something? I have never seen any of them. My son is retired now. He lives not far from here. I guess that's a joke, too.

This is all true. There's more, too. I married the lawyer. He had a great sense of humor. We were a fun couple. He died last year. That's why I let him tell me about my son. Last year I let him do anything he wanted. He was sure I wouldn't let him tell me. After he was asleep I went downstairs and cried for two hours.

When he died, the shade was down almost all the time. I decided to wrap my life up and choose the role I would play next. I decided on a deaf mute. It wasn't difficult, because Max was right. I've loved every minute of it. Unfortunately, I seem to have suffered a small stroke recently. I'm not sure I could talk at all now even if I want to. I don't, really.

Daddy was right. My big eyes really got me into a lot of trouble.

Nurse Millman is right. Every so often I do hear a TV joke and laugh. But it's only when the shade is up. Usually, the writer has stolen from one of my scripts. Good joke.

My son's birthday is soon. I need your help. Please get me a card and help me sign. The law firm will send it to him, with a check for $100,000. As usual. Thanks for your help. Can you believe I forgot about this?"

The old woman with the thick, wavy grey hair sat erect in her special wheelchair, hands extended onto the keyboard before her. The old fingers typed with surprising speed, and the message on the monitor before her read "Dear Three-D. Happy Birthday. Love, Mother."

Nurse Millman watched carefully as the typing stopped. The hands edged back into Mary Clare Donovan's lap. She sat erect in her chair, still playing her part, still the greatest comic actress of her time.

Beside her, the tall man with the soldier's bearing stood absolutely still. Tears ran down his face unashamedly as he read the message over the frail shoulders.

"Thank you, mother," he whispered softly, as he placed his hands over hers.

There was silence in the nursing station. The large hand on the wall clock made four complete sweeps. Nurse Millman watched. Gary Rogers remembered reading great actresses cry only on cue.

Slowly, Mary Clare's hands moved to the keyboard before her. Once again, the elderly fingers moved.
On the monitor, below the birthday message, more words appeared.
"I guess," she wrote," this time the joke's on me." When the curtain suddenly went up, her marvelous smile appeared.